Selena's Journal
Walnut Creek, California
Spring, 1 AZ (After Zombies)

Daddy said I could have paper and pencil to write if I shut up. No. He isn't daddy anymore. He said I have to call him Juan. Juan says my father is dead and he is stuck with me. I think mommy is dead too. She was lying on the ground and not moving when we left even though I yelled and yelled for her. I tried to ask about her but Juan hit me so hard I fell to the ground. I won't ask again.

Other books by Jill James

The Lake Willowbee Series
Divorce, Interrupted
Dare To Trust
Defend My Love
The Reluctant Bride
Waking Up For Christmas
Baby Steps and Snowflakes

Shifters of San Laura Series
Dangerous Shift

Time of Zombies Series
Love in the Time of Zombies
The Zombie Hunter's Wife
A Time to Kill Zombies

Short Stories
The Christmas Con
Rogue Vantage

A TIME TO KILL ZOMBIES

JILL JAMES

 Gray Sweater Press

A Time to Kill Zombies
Time of Zombies, Book 3
All Rights Reserved.
Copyright 2016 Jill James
ISBN# 978-0692746868
Cover Art © Elaina Lee at For The Muse Designs
All rights reserved – Used with permission

Gray Sweater Press
www.graysweaterpress.com

DEDICATION:

This book is dedicated to my family who lets me play with the imaginary creatures in my head.

To the men and women of CrimeSceneWriter Yahoo Group who will answer any question no matter how strange.

To my readers who have gone along for the ride in the zombie apocalypse. Thank you for liking ooey-gooey zombies as much as I do.

CHAPTER ONE

Jack and Lila

Outside the RV Yard
Oakley, California
Spring, 1 AZ (After Zombies)

A warm breeze blew the lone tumbleweed down the middle of the road. Lila Sterling Morales gathered her tattered rags with hands that shook like it was the middle of winter. Her vision swam in and out of focus, gray fog hovering on the edges. It hurt to think.

Had she eaten today? Or had it been yesterday. The days clumped together in a montage of starvation and abuse. Relentless. Day after day after day.

She shuddered and dragged her mind away from her husband, Juan. That way led to madness and despair. A cough built in her throat. She covered her mouth as the moans of the undead echoed just beyond the dark, empty road in the backyards of what had once been suburbia. Her body shook as the cough wracked her too-thin body. Her other hand clutched at her ribs, praying they were bruised and not broken. She had no time to waste being injured. The thought of her daughter at the mercy of the evil and darkness in the world kept her going. She stumbled as a sharp rock tore open her bleeding foot. She slipped as her blood poured to the asphalt.

Only have to get to the red line.

The red line is safety.

The line is my goal.

The line divided safety and danger.

Finally-dead zombie bodies littered the pavement where a red-painted line had been sprayed across the street. She'd made it. A deep breath and she grabbed her ribs on a groan. She glanced up at the walls of the RV yard and her steps quickened into a stumbling jog at the sound of human voices and a welcoming firelight seen through the gate. There was life. There were people.

Her fingers tightened around the cold metal bars. She inhaled deeply and opened her mouth to scream. Nothing but a slight whistle of air passed her lips. She tried again.

"Jack." A whimpering whisper spilled from her tortured, dry throat. Her arms trembled as she shook the gate in feeble little movements. Not even enough to make them clang and get noticed.

She had to find Jack. Her desperation aided to push strength into her voice. She could do this. She had to—for her daughter, for Selena.

"Jack." Her scream echoed across the yard and brought the welcome sound of pounding footsteps along with the unwelcome moans of the skinbags in the fields beyond her.

"Jack," she whispered, her hands locked on the gate the only thing keeping her standing. The commander rushed to the other side and gave the signal to Paul, his second-in-command. An eternity passed as the gate slowly rumbled open enough for her to stumble inside.

All she saw was his face, his so familiar face as she fell into his arms. Her weight, slight as it was, carried them both to the asphalt.

"Lila," Jack whispered. "What happened?"

"He took her," she mumbled through the stinging pain of her split lips. "Juan took her."

"Juan took who?"

She shook as Jack's fingers cradled her head, his fingers brushing back what was left of her chopped off hair. His glance swept over her rags and the tears of anger spilled from her eyes. She didn't need his pity, she needed his help. They were wasting time.

"He took Selena. He ran away and took her. You have to get her back," she yelled, grabbing handfuls of his shirt. She had to make him understand.

"Lila, I've told you. I'm not the law. He's her father."

"He took her to be his whore."

Jack's face whitened and he squeezed her to his chest. "Even so, I can't do anything. It isn't my place. I have to take care of my people here."

"She's your responsibility, Jack. She's your daughter, mine and yours, not Juan's."

Everyone started talking at once, but she tuned them all out. Her focus was solely on Jack, who looked like a lightning bolt had hit him. His grip tightened and her sore ribs ground together.

"You're hurting me," she hissed out, tired of pain at the hands of men.

He yanked his hands away as if she were a fire burning his skin. She would have fallen if they weren't already on the ground. She deserved his look of disgust. She deserved all that and more. Whatever mental punishment he dealt out, she would take. Just as long as they went after her daughter.

Their daughter.

* * *

Jack's hands clenched into fists as he looked down at the woman he thought he knew. Like a bucket of icy water drenched over his head, the anger and disgust disappeared as his gaze took in Lila's too-thin body and the rags too torn to hide the bruises on her ribs and around her neck. His heart ached even when he didn't want it to. He wanted to stay angry. He wanted to let the anger consume him and burn away any feelings he'd ever had for Lila Sterling.

Hiding the fact he was Selena's father for nine

years was unforgivable, but no one deserved the fate life had dealt the woman he'd loved long ago. He'd wished misfortune on Lila many times over the years, but never this. Payback for being dumped wasn't abuse and neglect. The thought of such a man having a little girl like Selena made his stomach roil and spasm.

"I meant to tell you a thousand times after you found us," she whispered, her words just above the sound of the soft breeze.

"But you didn't," he said, his jaw locked and tight. He pulled himself up, taking Lila with him. His hands dropped away as a million thoughts and plans pulled him in separate directions. Shoving his hands over his buzz cut, he turned to his second-in-command.

"We're going through with our plans. This place is useless now with the tainted well and the psychos down the road."

"The church is gone," Lila spoke up. "The men left, taking their families with them. That's when Juan left with Selena. He choked me, left me for dead." Her voice faded away as a shaking hand touched her throat.

Jack grasped her hands. "I have responsibilities here."

"Family comes first," Paul butted in. The man moved closer and whispered. "You have to go after the girl. I can get the others to Ryde. I'll have Suz and Josh with me," mentioning his wife and her brother.

His gaze took in the diminished group huddled around them. He sighed. The RV yard had been bustling with activity and people just a few short days ago. The sudden illness had taken a large group and taking down the turned had caused a few more deaths. In a day, half of them were dead or missing. He needed to hold the shattered group together. Order. Discipline. It kept their world together. It kept him together.

Paul's hand rested on his shoulder. "I know what you are thinking, Jack. We can get them to the next location. You need to find your daughter. We'll be waiting for you down the river."

Like a load off his chest, he took a deep breath. The others would be safe with Paul as their leader, but he had another duty. He'd never shirked his duty in the army or the zombie apocalypse and he wasn't about to start now.

He held his hands up and faced the crowd. "Paul will lead the group to Ryde. You always have a choice. You can go elsewhere, but that is where Paul, Suz, and Josh are going. Safety lies in numbers. As you heard, the Fruitful Harvest Church is no more, but staying here is not an option. With the well gone, life is not sustainable here."

He looked over his shoulder to Lila. "I have my own mission, but God willing, I will see all of you in Ryde before summer's end."

Seth Ripley walked up to them as the crowd scattered to gather their belongings. The man's hands were slammed into his pockets.

"Emily won't go without Michelle. I've promised her I'll wait 'til daybreak, but we can't leave with the rest of you."

Jack shook his hand, hardly noticing the ever-present glove hiding the man's missing fingers. "I wish you well. Hopefully we will all meet again down the road."

Seth's gaze swept over Lila in her tattered clothing. "Emily has some stuff she can't wear right now. You're welcome to it."

Lila looked up at Jack. "Go; get some clothes and a good pair of boots. As soon as I tell Paul what he needs to take and get my own stuff, we are out of here. The man already has a lead on us."

She wrapped her arms around Jack and squeezed. "Thank you."

He stood still, his hands at his sides. Holding his tongue before he said something he couldn't take back, he stared as she walked with Seth.

Thank you? Did she think this was a favor? This was his daughter they were talking about. He would die to get her back. Didn't Lila know that?

Okay, he'd been adamant before about not stepping on Juan's fatherly rights, but the moment Lila had said she was his, his heart raced and pounded in his chest. Nothing would stop him from getting Selena and letting her know she was his.

CHAPTER TWO

Selena

Selena's Journal
Walnut Creek, California
Spring, 1 AZ

Daddy said I could have paper and pencil to write if I shut up. No. He isn't daddy anymore. He said I have to call him Juan. Juan says my father is dead and he is stuck with me. I think mommy is dead too. She was lying on the ground and not moving when we left even though I yelled and yelled for her. I tried to ask about her but Juan hit me so hard I fell to the ground. I won't ask again.

She folded the paper into a tiny square and stuck it in the pocket of her knapsack. Her fingers shook as she tucked the pencil in the pocket and zipped it shut. Juan didn't say he would read what she wrote, but it didn't matter since she'd only written the truth. The worse he could do was kill her, and then she would be wherever her mom and unknown dad had gone. She wasn't sure she believed in Heaven anymore.

Sitting on a couch with an old lady who said she could call her Auntie, she looked around the room. Boards covered all the windows in the large apartment and the only light came from candles on all the flat surfaces. Big, dark-skinned men filled the room. The only sound was their mean laughter and the clicks of their guns as they loaded and unloaded them. Even with lots of ladies moving from kitchen to dining room. None of the women said anything, just brought food and drink to the men. Her nose wrinkled. This place was as bad as the church had been. The long hair and clothing that showed the boobs on the women seemed the only changes.

She looked up to find Juan staring at her. He smiled a smile that didn't seem like one at all. Not like the ones when she did her dance recitals or learned to ride without her training wheels on her bike.

"How much do you think I can get for her?" he said to the older, gray-haired man at the table.

The man looked her up and down in a way that made her skin crawl. His words to Juan were confusing and at the same time, not. As if she could almost understand what they were talking about if she was a little older.

"Is she a virgin?"

"Of course. She's only nine. I kept a good eye on her. She's still a little girl."

She whimpered and snuggled closer to the comfort of the one called Auntie.

"Hush, chica. Don't listen to the man-talk," she whispered. "Most times it amounts to nothing."

A deep breath and her whimpers ceased. How well she knew that. How many times had the man she'd known as daddy told her they would go to Disneyland or some other exciting place and it never happened? How many nights had she heard her mother crying herself to sleep when Juan wasn't home, even when the big Grandfather clock bonged twelve times in the middle of the night? That had been before the zombies came. Before the scariest night of her life, in their broken down car on the freeway. When Commander Jack and the other men saved them.

She settled back against Auntie and bit her fingernails. Prayers hadn't helped when Juan took them to the church people and she didn't know whether they would help now, but she had to try.

Shutting her eyes, Selena prayed with all her heart. *Please God, save me. Let Commander Jack and the RV men find me. I won't ask for anything ever again. Well, maybe for my mommy to be alive. Amen.*

As if a big weight had lifted off her shoulders, she inhaled deeply and opened her eyes. Juan squatted in front of her. She squealed and pressed herself back into the couch. The man moved in closer and grabbed her arm and pulled.

"What were you doing?"

"Praying. Just praying," she stammered out.

He smiled that not-a-smile again and she shivered. "Prayers didn't help before the Z virus and they sure as hell don't help now."

She stumbled as Juan yanked her across the room to stand in front of the old man sitting at the table. Juan stood behind her and held her arms down at her sides. The man grabbed her chin and turned her head from side to side.

"Humph, she's pretty enough. Some like blonde hair like hers," he said, letting go of her face.

His glare and bad breath had Selena looking at the dirty carpet and holding her breath. Juan's hands loosened their tight grip and he shoved her back toward the couch. She rushed to sit back down and accept Auntie's warm hug.

"I'll have Miguel send some messages over the radio. She'll be off your hands in a couple of days. Not like we need another mouth to feed anyway," the old man said as he pushed himself out of the chair with a huff and walked toward the back of the apartment.

Juan stomped over to the couch and crossed his arms on his chest, glaring down at her. "Your puta of a mother deserved all she got and more. I just wish she could be here to see you sold to the highest bidder."

"Do not talk to the niña that way," Auntie said, a quiver in her voice. "You should not disrespect the dead."

Juan raised his hand and Selena ducked. She'd never feared the man before. He'd never hit her before the Z virus. Before the church. Now, it was as if he wanted to make up for all the years of doing nothing mean. Auntie glared at him and the man stomped away, muttering under his breath. An arm wrapped around her and pulled her in close. "This is a terrible world, Selena. I will say a prayer for you and pray God gives you strength to survive."

She stared in the direction Juan had stomped off. Hot, angry tears flooded her eyes and rolled down her cheeks.

Oh, she would survive. She would survive until she was old enough and strong enough to choke the life out of Juan Morales just like he'd done to her mother. When she was done with him, she'd take care of the rest of the men too.

CHAPTER THREE

Paul, Suz, and Josh

Paul Luther's Log
Temporary Command of RV group
On the road to new base
Spring, 1 AZ (After Zombies)

The RV yard is no longer inhabitable. Not my first choice of options, but still the right thing to do, our group has been splintered. Commander Canida and former member Lila Morales have gone in search of the child, Selena. We were forced to leave Seth Ripley and his wife, Emily at the compound. The woman was deep in her pregnancy and refused to leave without her friend, Michelle, Teddy, and the others still missing in action.

Given temporary command of what is left of our group, we are headed to the Antioch Bridge and the waterways beyond. Final destination: Ryde, a small community on the river.

Paul stood on the roof of a car, binoculars glued to his eyes. He swept the area. Wrecks sat on the bridge itself, but no sign of life or the undead. "Not yet," he muttered under his breath. The bastards seemed to appear out of nowhere, as if they could sense fresh meat and hear the humans breathing.

The cars appeared haphazard at first glance. But no pattern arose as he stared longer. No discernible obstacle course to use as a gauntlet for an ambush. It was what it was—the futile last attempt of people to get out of the city—and failing.

"Are we going to push the cars over the bridge?" the boys of Rogue Vantage asked.

He smiled as he lowered the binoculars and saw the young boys at the side of the car. Laughing at their gleeful expressions, he wished he could just push the cars over the side of the cement barriers, if only to hear them cheer and act like the little boys they were.

"Sorry, boys," he explained. "We might be able to push some already headed that way, but I think we need to scout for new transportation, hopefully at the other end of the bridge."

He jumped down from the car and stood in front of them. "Aidan and Bryant," he said, pointing to the two oldest. "You are with me to scout the bridge and see if we can find some transport, maybe a truck or two.

"Connor and Dylan, you go and help Suz and Josh get food organized. I want everyone to eat something and drink at least a bottle of water. Can you do that?"

The boys puffed out their chests, just like he'd planned when he set each pair to a necessary task. He kept an eye on the smaller boys until they reached Suz's side and she gave him a wave.

"Okay, boys." He turned to Aidan and Bryant. Each had grown in the past few months and was now only a head or so shorter than him. He made the mental decision and handed them each a gun from his pack.

"You're been shown how to be careful with these, but I want to remind you that an accident with a gun can't be undone."

"Yes, sir," they intoned.

The intense and calm look on their faces reassured him. He winced at the thought of boys becoming men before their time.

"Keep them pointed down unless I say shoot. Walk in front of me, one to each side. Keep your eyes moving at all times. Look under cars and in them. There are no supplies we need bad enough to try to get in a vehicle with an undead. Understood?"

"Yes, Mister Paul."

Satisfied they had at least listened to him, they moved out.

He watched with pride as the boys held the guns down at their sides with their fingers beside the trigger, not on it, just like they had been taught. Each boy's head whipped from side to side. Aidan ran up to a car, squatting to check underneath. He jumped up and peered in the windows. He looked back at Paul and shook his head. He moved on up the incline of the bridge.

Bryant walked up to a raised pickup truck, bending over to look beneath. The boy stretched on tiptoe to check the bed of the vehicle. He turned with a smile. "Boxes of stuff," he spoke in a low tone.

Paul walked up and checked the cab. No zombs. He pulled a piece of chalk out of his pocket and put a giant X on the door. Grabbing his walkie-talkie, he keyed it on. "Suz, we found some supplies, maybe. Blue raised pickup. X on door. Safe to this point."

"Will they come get them?" Bryant asked.

"Maybe. But it will be easier to get them on the way to the other side of the bridge."

The young boy's eyes brightened like a lesson learned. His heart clenched at the thought of all the lessons they would have to learn to survive when the older people were gone. It reminded him of ancient times when elders had to make sure to pass their knowledge on to the next generation or it was lost. The Internet had ruined people by letting them think knowledge was just a few keystrokes away.

His mind was snapped back at Aidan's cry and the pop of weight on a car roof. Paul whipped around and spotted the boy a few cars away, standing atop an SUV. Three undead surrounded the vehicle. They were moving in slow-motion, their legs seeming to not have enough flesh to hold them upright. He watched with pride as Aiden stood still with his gun still pointed downward, knowing shots would call more skinbags to his location.

"Bryant," he whispered. "You have my six." He pulled his knife from the sheath and put his gun in the holster on his hip.

"Yes, sir."

The boy turned and backed up to him. Paul moved slowly toward the zombs. He had two dispatched before the third realized he was there. The female turned with outstretched arms that he batted away before plunging his knife into her skull. The skinbag fell to the ground.

Aidan looked ready to jump down until Paul put his hand up. He squatted and looked under the SUV. Clear.

"I know it doesn't look far, but never risk twisting an ankle or breaking a bone unless it's an emergency and you can't help it. Even a non-serious injury could mean your death."

"Yes, sir," Aidan intoned as he slid down the windshield and then down the hood to the ground.

"Bryant," Paul instructed. "Check the car over there. Aidan, you check the brown truck and then we can move on."

The boys quickly squatted and checked and strode back over to him.

"Dead dead people in the car," Bryant reported.

"Nobody in the truck," Aidan said. "No supplies either."

Paul ran his fingers over his short hair. "Dead dead? Are you sure?"

"Come see for yourself," Bryant said, running back to the car. Paul and Aidan joined him. They stared through the window at the man and woman seat-belted in the vehicle. Their bodies were deteriorated like corpses in a grave but it didn't appear they had attacked each other or if one had attacked the other.

Paul located the answer in the piles of pill bottles in their laps and strewn across the seats and floor. Just like the parents of Rogue Vantage, the people in the car probably died too quickly and thoroughly to reanimate into zombies.

The back seat was covered in suitcases, but nothing looked important enough to violate the couple's last resting place. He wasn't digging pill bottles out of the couple's laps for a few drugs.

He stood straight. "Let's move on, boys."

At the apex of the bridge, Paul stopped and looked back to the toll booths where they'd left the rest of the group. Other than a small flock of blackbirds, nothing moved on the bridge. The whistle of the wind the only sound. The other side of the bridge had fewer cars since no one was trying to get into the cities and towns when catastrophe hit, but still too many to move with their small group.

Looking forward, the cars and trucks were widely spread out as if the bottleneck had happened in the middle of the bridge on their side. The hairs on the back of his neck stood up. He didn't like it. There should be more than three undead to cause the mess on the bridge.

"Boys," he whispered. "Step careful. Be extra alert. Check and double-check each vehicle. I believe this is where the mess started."

Aidan and Bryant stepped in front of him and Paul divided his attention between the cars and the boys. Seeing nothing, he was about to let his guard down when Aidan stepped around a large van and called out as loudly as you can whisper and still yell.

"Mister Paul. Over here."

He whipped around the corner of the van and stopped. Bryant came around the other end of the vehicle.

A pile of undead greeted them. Thankfully, they were dead dead. The camo uniforms and bullet-ridden corpses told a tale of the army trying to stop a flood of refugees from the surrounding cities. The k-rail barrier was skewed and several shot up cars filled the fields and marshlands beyond the bridge.

He smiled. Three Humvee sat just beyond the k-rails. If they worked, they would be more than enough for their people to get through. His thoughts scattered at a moan from the pile of zombie soldiers.

A bony hand groped from the mound. Bodies fell as one undead pulled itself from the group. Before Paul could reach him, the hand latched onto Bryant's ankle and tugged until the boy fell to the ground.

He rushed over, but before he could do anything, Bryant rolled over, placed the gun against the zomb's skull, and pulled the trigger. He shook his leg until the bony hand fell off. The boy jumped up and shook his body.

"Gross. I'm sorry, Mr. Paul but you said in an emergency we could shoot."

He put his hand on Bryant's back. "Yes, I did. Good job."

The walkie-talkie squawked on his belt. He pulled it up and to his ear.

"Are you okay?"

"Yes, we are fine. A skinbag grabbed Bryant but he took care of it."

"As long as everyone is okay."

"Suz, we found some vehicles. Can you send Josh our way? The bridge should be clear but tell him to keep a look out anyway."

"Will do. Over and out."

He put the walkie-talkie back on his belt. "Let's have a look at the Humvee, guys."

"Yeah," they whispered in a cheer.

Zombie apocalypse or not, boys would be boys.

CHAPTER FOUR

Jack and Lila

Commander's Log
Highway 4, Antioch, California
Spring, 1 AZ

Left RV yard at 0400 hours. Encountered a few zombs and zero civilian population. Lila believes Juan will try to make it to Walnut Creek where he had family before Z virus. Holdouts missed by the general's zombie army in the last autumn. Before the virus and the skinbags, the trip would have taken under an hour. With the wreckage on the freeway, I am hopeful we will make it within the week.

On a personal note, Lila shows all the signs of an abused wife. She jumps at every sound and has developed a nervous twitch of pulling on her ear and hunching her shoulders if I raise a hand or my voice. Have tried to take over most tasks on the trip to show her she is not a slave. Have made it as far as what would have been a BART station in Antioch. Was hopeful for more but clearing the road is not a one-man job and Lila is in no shape to help push or drive. The sun is setting and we will camp overnight at the remains of a never finished building.

Jack put the pencil and notebook back into the knapsack. He viewed Lila out of the corner of his eye. She hadn't said a word since they started after she mentioned Walnut Creek as Juan's probable destination, where a Morales family conclave still existed. Her thin arms wrapped around her body as if she were cold, even though Emily had provided her with warm enough clothing. The jeans fit well enough, but the long-sleeved T-shirt swam on her body.

"Are you okay with a cold dinner? I'd rather not risk a fire while we're just off the freeway."

Her curt nod was all he got. She added a short yes or no to each of his other questions about bread, jam, and peanut butter. He handed her a finished sandwich and watched as she took a bite and stared off into the darkening twilight. "Enjoy the bread. That's the last of it until the group gets to somewhere with an oven again."

"We're safe here," he added, wondering if she were still worried about the assholes that'd left the church recently.

She finally looked up, her hazel eyes awash in tears. "I know you'll keep us safe. But what about my baby?"

He rubbed the back of his neck. "I don't have an answer to that, Lila. I have to just hope and pray that Juan will remember she was his daughter for nine years. Was he a good dad?"

"He was okay," she stammered out. "He wasn't really mean until Reverend Bennett arrived. He could yell and stuff, but he never hit me until then. He never laid a hand on Selena, even when he realized she wasn't his."

Jack's head shot up. "He only recently found out she wasn't his? How could he not know?"

"He never asked and I never told him," she whispered. "He's always thought she was his child until he saw you and Selena together."

Reaching over, he gently grasped her chin and raised her face. "Are you positive she isn't his?"

She moved backward, out of his reach. "She's yours. I knew I was pregnant when I broke up with you."

His jaw dropped open and stayed that way. No words came that weren't vicious and cutting, and that wouldn't help either of them right now. Lila must have her reasons for the deceit, but he didn't want to hear them—ever. He turned his back on her and faced the freeway, even though it was invisible in the fallen dark. Rustlings of nocturnal animals caught his attention. A coyote howled nearby and Lila moved to a wall and huddled there.

He should comfort her, but he found himself unable to do so, if only because she was someone else's wife. All his training and instincts that had kept the Streets of Brentwood group safe and together for so long fell into a muddle of scattered thoughts. Memories of making love with Lila. Of their time together. Of that last day. He pushed his thoughts to a safer place.

A daughter.

He had a daughter.

His mind was a rambling stream of every laugh, of every remembered vision of the little girl who'd run around the RV yard with the boys of Rogue Vantage. Selena had been the instigator of practical jokes that kept the morale up of the entire community.

"I'm sorry," she stuttered out.

Jack leapt across the space dividing them and slapped his hand on her mouth. Her hazel eyes widened and tears slid over the lids to wet his fingers. He brought his other hand up and put a finger on his lips in the sign of silence.

She nodded and he moved his hand away from her mouth. Her small inhalation was loud in the silence. He moved closer and whispered in her ear.

"I hear someone. Take the knapsack and move quietly to the far corner."

He listened, noting she moved with stealth in the dark. He clenched his jaw at yet another sign of a battered woman. *Walk on eggshells, don't make waves.* He'd seen enough of them in the military to last a lifetime.

Crawling through broken cement blocks, he pulled his night-vision goggles down. The darkness exploded in green undertones. Five, no make that six, men moved down the freeway in a loose formation. Their yells split the quiet night as they spotted the intact pickup truck. Weighing their options, Jack decided to let them have the truck. All their gear was in here with them and he might take out two or three men, but if he missed even one, Lila would be at their dubious mercy and they'd never find Selena.

He didn't know all the church members by sight, but their attitude and mountain-man appearance laid good odds that was who they were. One of the men put a hand on the hood of the truck but the warm night air guaranteed he wouldn't know the difference between warmth from driving and normal temperature from the night. Sure enough, he nodded to the rest and they piled in the cab and the bed of the truck. A couple of minutes and the vehicle roared to life and sped off down the concrete road.

He sighed. They would be on foot until or if, they found another car. The zombie apocalypse never got easier. Patrol in Afghanistan had been easier than now getting from point A to point B in the Bay Area.

Jack made his way to Lila's hiding spot. "They're gone."

"But, they took the truck. What do we do now?" He could hear the fright and worry in her shaking voice.

"We'll find something to drive in the morning," he replied, pulling a sleeping bag from the knapsack and spreading it on the ground. "Why don't you try to rest? I'll keep watch."

"Don't you need sleep, too?" Her worry was undercut by a yawn she tried to hide behind her hand.

"I'm used to going on little sleep. The army is great at training you for that." He laughed. "Actually, the army was great training for the apocalypse."

Lila lay down, her head resting on her folded arm. "You sound like you enjoyed it."

"Well, it helped me through a rough time." His good mood died. "Get some sleep," he barked, as he grabbed his gun and went to stand by the broken wall, gazing out at nothing.

* * *

Lila bit her lip as she closed her eyes. Hot tears spilled down her face and pooled in her ear. They'd been so close to a real conversation. Like a light switch, he'd turned off his emotions. Before, his anger would have raged, he would have thrown things. This new, calm Jack was a stranger, a man she didn't know. Sleep pulled at her. A thousand worries fought her fatigue. Sleep won.

The limousine pulled away from the Canida family mountain house. She turned in her seat until a curve in the road hid it from sight. Still, she stared out the window.

Tears flooded her vision as her father's hand clamped onto her shoulder. "You did the right thing, my dear." He laughed. The laugh she hated with a passion. The one which said he won, just like he always did. A business transaction or dealing with his daughter; they were the same thing in his mind. A negotiation to win.

"It's not like you gave me a choice," she cried out.

He moved, his hand falling away. "We always have choices. We have to make the right ones for the family." He adjusted his cuffs on his dress shirt. "You had the choice of leaving the man alive or staying with him and seeing him dead."

"Daddy, how could you? What did Jack ever do to you?"

"He was an obstacle. One I have eliminated. Now nothing stands in the way of your marriage to Juan Morales. Our families will be connected. We will own Sacramento. I wasn't letting some measly army peon stand in my way. Nothing will stop us now."

Lila gulped down her rising bile and put a protective hand on her abdomen. She would marry Juan to save Jack and to protect their unborn child.

She awoke with a start and Selena's name on her gasping breath. Her gaze shot to the opening to find Jack still standing sentry as if he hadn't moved all night. A lightening to gray outside hinted at a rising sun down the road and over the hills.

That tenaciousness was going to help them find their daughter. She could almost pity Juan when they found him. But if Jack didn't kill him, she would. His cruel words and threats still rang in her ears. He hadn't taken Selena to keep her; he'd taken her to sell, to use, to abuse. Her arms trembled as she wrapped them around her shaking body.

The sky lit up to a clear blue through the openings in the roof. She scrambled to get up, roll the sleeping bag, and stuff it in the knapsack. The longer Juan had her, the more risk that Selena would be lost to them.

She let the tears come. This was the last time she'd allow herself the luxury. She would find Selena, or die trying. A million pictures flashed through her mind. Selena learning to walk with determination on a face that so looked like Jack's it'd taken her breath away. Her daughter saying her first words. The little girl saying 'dada' to Juan, bringing tears to Lila's eyes at all Jack was missing. To that last moment, with the little girl's screams echoing in her head as she fought unconsciousness trying to reach her.

Jack's voice brought her back to the present. "Have a protein bar," he said, handing her one as he chewed on his own. "We can eat as we go."

The man's eagerness to get started matched her own, so she said nothing as he hefted the pack to his shoulders and strode out the opening, jumping with ease over the fallen cinderblocks. Random strands of hair got in her eyes as she tried to imitate his easy movements over the obstacles. A breeze blew a lock in her face. She swiped it back and cursed under her breath. Her lost long hair another strike against the man she'd called husband. Before he'd chopped it all off she had been able to put it in a ponytail or braid to get it out of the way. The hair was finally growing back, but the strands seemed to come back in odd spots and textures, with some long, some still short, and some curly when she'd had no curls before.

Jack stopped and pulled a bandana out of a pocket of the backpack. He whipped it into a band and tied it across her forehead. His fingers ran over the short hair at her neck, raising goose bumps on her arms. Other than when she'd stumbled into the camp, he hadn't touched her in nine long years. Not even when he found them in the abandoned car on the freeway months ago.

Her breath caught as his fingers trailed down her cheek. His brown eyes warmed as he gazed at her. Warmth filled her chest and face as he pulled her in close to his chest.

"I'm so sorry he hurt you."

She pushed him away. "I don't need your pity, Jack. In the old world I would have left him for the bastard he was. But in this world I knew I couldn't take care of Selena and myself. It is what it is." She shrugged and moved away, walking toward the concrete freeway.

She called back over her shoulder. "I'm going to get my daughter. Are you coming, or not?"

CHAPTER FIVE

Paul, Suz, and Josh

Suz's Notes
Antioch Bridge
Spring, 1 AZ

Just a quick note while we wait for Paul to check in at the far end of the bridge. Wish we could just drive on but too many cars to deal with, especially with our depleted numbers. After the surprise outbreak of the mysterious virus at the RV Park, we were left with no choice but to leave. Fingers crossed for Emily and baby and those we left behind.

She shoved the pencil and paper into her backpack as the echo of a gunshot came from the end of the bridge. The end of the bridge where Paul and the boys were. Only silence followed the dissipating sound, the echoes disappearing in diminishing waves. Grabbing the walkie-talkie off her belt she smashed the SEND button.

"Are you okay?"

"Yes, we are fine. A skinbag grabbed Bryant but he took care of it."

Suz took a long, even breath and slowly exhaled.

"As long as everyone is okay."

Paul's voice came through again. "Suz, we found some vehicles. Can you send Josh our way? The bridge should be clear but tell him to keep a look out anyway."

She looked over at her brother to make sure he caught their husband's words. "Will do. Over and out."

She put the walkie-talkie back on her belt as Josh strolled over. Josh grabbed a couple of waters from a truck and put them in his small pack. As he hefted it onto his back, Suz ran her hand over his hair. "He said it should be safe, but be careful anyway. Give him a kiss for me."

"Suz," he whined. "The boys are there."

She laughed as she hadn't been able to laugh in a long time. "The boys know about me, you, and Paul."

Even with sunburn, she spotted her brother's telltale blush. She cut him some slack and let him go without another word.

Their relationship was still new to Josh; the first serious relationship in his life. It should have been awkward to share a man with her brother, but Paul made it work. She sighed. She'd thought she was so independent before Paul came into her life. She could kick ass and take names with the best of them. And if she couldn't, her brother had her back. It had been enough after the influenza epidemic and the Z virus to at least have her brother left of all their big family. Until Paul showed her there was more than just survival in the zombie apocalypse.

Showed her and Josh that life went on in new and amazing ways. She brought her head out of the clouds as Doctor Shannon walked up to her and pulled her to the side of the bridge. Suz looked over the woman's shoulder to see her husband Jim slumped in a chair, his large hands hiding his face, his shoulders shaking.

Her heart sank and then broke as Shannon's words confirmed it. "I used the long-range walkie-talkie to see if the RV yard knew anything yet." Her voice trembled and her grip on Suz's shoulder tightened. "Beth and Jed didn't make it."

"What about the RV yard group we left?"

Shannon gave her a shaky smile. "Emily had twins. Michelle, Teddy, Miranda, and Cody made it back."

"Twins?" She shook her head. "They have a rough journey ahead."

Shannon hugged her. "Don't we all?"

Suz stood stock-still as Shannon went back to comfort her husband. The quietly-spoken words took the breath from her lungs. She turned to stare after her brother as he crested the peak of the bridge and disappeared over the other side. Everyone she loved was hidden from sight.

* * *

The upsetting blush still heated Josh's face. He and his sister might look a lot alike with their blonde hair and blue eyes, a gift from their Nordic ancestors, but inside they were as different as the undead and the living. He let his actions speak for him. Making the undead finally dead and pulling his own weight with the group. Those were the things he knew how to do. Talking about his feelings or showing them for all to see was not his thing. Suz could share her deepest, darkest secrets and then laugh it off.

He smiled to himself. He'd been as surprised as anyone in the RV group to not only fall for Paul, but to have his feelings returned. In the beginning he'd been stupid about it, fighting with Suz and avoiding Paul, until his sister and her lover pointed out what he'd been too blind to see; he and Suz both loved Paul and he loved them.

Any awkwardness left was all on him. To Suz and Paul and the rest of the group, they were a romantic unit. He sighed. Maybe those fundamental Mormons out in Utah had it right all along. Maybe multiple husbands and wives was the way to go. Maybe jealousy was a relic of the past, just like frozen food, television, and professional sports.

He left the deep thoughts behind as he reached the first of the crashed and crushed cars and trucks. Quickly reaching a blue truck with a chalked X on the door, he leaned over and spotted the cases of water and boxes of supplies. He smiled. They could use all the food and water they found. Thirst and hunger killed as easily as the zombs.

Spotting the Humvee and the boys of Rogue Vantage at the bottom of the bridge, he rushed forward. Determined to get his awkwardness behind him, he hugged Paul quickly and stepped back. Paul's smile said he appreciated the effort. Just as Suz said, the young boys were more interested in the turret gun on the Humvee than anything he and Paul did or said.

Paul turned at the creak of the gun. "Aidan, point it north. Remember?"

"Yes, sir," the boy replied. "Away from the civilians."

Josh laughed. "You're a great teacher. I don't remember my dad and uncle having such an easy time teaching Suz and I to follow the rules."

Paul looked up at him. "Rules are important, but they seem a little more important now, don't they?"

He stared at the young boys who should be playing on swing sets and riding bikes instead of learning to operate turret guns and kill zombies. Thinking back on his childhood, he wished these kids could have that again but in his heart he knew it wasn't going to happen. Even if they did fight back the tide of undead and the living taking advantage of the utter chaos, it wouldn't happen for years, maybe generations. Their best hope was for the children of the children of the kids in front of him.

"Bryant, Aidan," he called over. "I've brought water." As he squatted down to open his pack, Aidan slid down from view and reappeared at the vehicle's door. Bryant's dark head popped up beside him. The two rushed over and gulped down a bottle each in seconds.

"You should have seen it, Josh," Aidan said as he put the empty bottle into his own backpack. "The zomb' had Bryant's foot and he just flipped over and POW." The boy mimed a gun with his finger and thumb. "Right in the head."

Josh put his hand on Bryant's head, noting the boy had grown a few inches recently. "Glad you're all right."

"Sure thing, bro." The boy grinned. "Mister Paul wouldn't let anything happen to us."

He was going to laugh, but the boy was right. Paul wouldn't let anything happen to them. At least, not if he could help it, but every day was a struggle against hunger, thirst, disease, and the skinbags, and Paul wasn't GI Joe, he was just a man.

CHAPTER SIX

Jack and Lila

Commander's Log
Dow Chemical Plant/The Wetlands
Antioch, California
Spring, 1 AZ

The wetlands in front of the chemical factory exploded with wildlife. The absence of humans let the mammals and birds and reptiles and insects take back their natural habitats. More than a year after civilization fell; nature was taking her world back. They'd left the highway by the burned down County East Mall, a victim of the early days of the Z virus outbreak. Jack meant to take them to a back road, but passing by the forgotten Auto Mall dealerships had been an unexpected bonus.

With only three undead in sight, he'd taken the time to let Lila hone her killing skills. By the third skinbag, her swing had strengthened and it only took one swing to decapitate the last zomb'.

A kit fox mama and babies trotted across the road as he pulled into the facility with their new SUV. He wrapped a chain around the gate. It wouldn't keep out a car or a horde of the undead, but it would rattle enough to warn them. The wetlands stretched out in front of them in untouched splendor. If not for the gray building at the end of the road, the land looked like it had more than a hundred years ago.

Jack held his breath. No moans or sounds other than the noisy cries of blue jays. He breathed deeply. No smells except for the pungent scent of marshes. This kind of place could lull you into false security. He stayed alert as Lila hopped out of the vehicle and shut her door with an almost silence nudge.

He smiled. She was learning. Slamming the door at the dealership and seeing a small group of zombs running for their SUV could do that to you. His smile died. He would have to give Lila some survival skills if they were going to rescue Selena. The woman had been too protected for someone living in the ZA. Protected behind cement walls in the RV yard and then the oppressive confines of the church had left her totally unprepared for killing the undead and staying away from them in the first place, not to mention the dangers of the living.

"Lila," he called to her in a low tone.

She came to his side. "Why don't you whisper? Something might hear us."

"Lesson one," he intoned in the same low voice. "It is better to talk in a low tone than to whisper. Whispering causes your s endings in words to slur and carry."

"Was that an army lesson?"

"Yes it was. One of many."

"Was it hard? The army," she asked. "You never said much about it."

"It kept me sane when the world turned upside down."

"I'm sorry about that."

His jaw tightened. "Thanks for that. But I meant the zombie apocalypse. The end of the world as we know it."

"Oh," she whispered and stopped. "Oh," she intoned in a deep low voice to match his.

A smile broke out on his face. "Good job."

"Why did we stop here? Shouldn't we keep going down the road?"

He pointed to the large chemical complex down the road. "This place was abandoned early on after the Z virus. It has potential to be a fallback location. Look at all the land for crops. The fence encloses the whole facility."

Lila crossed her arms on her chest and glared at him. "How does that get Selena back with us? Anything could be happening to her, and we are scouting future homes."

He stepped up and put his hands on her shoulders. "We'll get her back, but we have to always look to the future. Overlooked food locations, friendly compounds, and especially ones that are not. We were almost wiped out by General Peters and we had to leave a perfectly good place because of the Reverend. I won't have that happen again. We will always have two, three, or more locations to retreat to if we must."

Lila stepped back and his hands fell off her shoulders. She straightened her spine and took a deep breath. "Okay, so show me how to scout a location and how to see what is right and what is wrong. I have a lot of catching up to do and I don't have nine weeks for boot camp."

He smiled. "Okay, first lesson. What do you hear? What do you smell? What do you see?"

Lila turned slowly, taking in their surroundings. "I hear the birds and probably small creatures in the tall grass and weeds. Not loud enough for zombies. I smell green things growing and dirt, nothing yucky like dead people."

She stared at the building down the road. "I don't see any cars so people probably left during the pandemic, or they didn't come to work at all. There is fire damage on the wall to the left, but ivy is growing over it, so it was probably long ago, not recently."

His smile grew. "We'll make a soldier of you yet. Put your rifle on the SUV hood and get out your knife."

"But," she started to say, as he put his hand on her shoulder and pointed to the zomb' crawling out of the marshy field. Its body was covered with mud and missing an arm and a leg. Jack strode over and planted his foot on its back. The skinbag hissed and moaned, its fingers digging into the dirt, trying to pull forward. His chomping teeth rattled and broke.

Lila came over, a grimace marring her face. "Why don't they just fall apart and die already?"

"The brain doesn't send the message to the body that life is over. The virus killed the finer functions of the brain, the things that make us human. All that was left was the basics of search for food and eat. So they continue on."

He pointed to the other side of the creature. Lila moved to the spot. "You have to finish the death of their brains. You don't want to know how many guys I saw die in the beginning because they kept shooting in the chest and guts until they ran out of bullets. Decapitation is the best. Swift and clean and allows you some distance. But you won't always have a machete or a sword. Sometimes they will sneak up on you and all you have is your hands, your feet, and a knife.

"The ones who have been around a while have grown soft, so you can usually pierce the skull. But you can't guarantee that, and there is nothing worse than fighting for your life and breaking the knife blade on a hard head."

He stepped back and loosened the zombie. "Go for the spine at the base of the skull. Sever the brain from the body."

She stabbed it several times, jumping back as she missed and the undead snapped its jaw full of rancid teeth at her.

"Hold the head still, stab, and move on," he instructed. "Be aware of your surroundings at all times. Don't let anything sneak up on you."

With a grunt, Lila pressed down on the creature's head, stabbed between the vertebrae with a resounding crunch, and jumped back, turning with the knife at the ready in front of her.

Jack walked up to her and gave her a soft, silent high five. He took the knife and wiped it off on the zomb's threadbare shirt and handed it back to her. "Always take care of your weapons and they will take care of you. Only put the knife back in the sheath dirty if you are on the run. One small cut pulling it out and you have infected yourself."

"But I thought we were all infected," she asked. "Didn't Miranda save Seth when he got bit?"

He nodded. "She did. But I wouldn't want to have to cut off some body part of yours to save you."

"I wouldn't want that either," she spoke in a low tone, staring at him.

"But we would do it if we had to, understand?"

She nodded, tears forming in her eyes. "I hate this. Why did the world have to get so ugly?"

"Maybe because we thought we could play God and He said no."

* * *

Lila sobered at that thought. The man was right. They'd played havoc with the world around them and the world had said, 'enough.' The president deciding to vaccinate the entire country in one fell swoop was just the last in a long list of mistakes humankind had made and now the bill had come due as her father would have said. Rest his filthy soul.

Thinking of family brought her full circle back to Selena. A sob caught in her throat at the thought of her little girl in the clutches of Juan. *When had the man she'd married changed so much? When had he let his machismo overrule his common sense? When had he turned into a monster who forgot Selena called him daddy?*

She pulled herself together. The sooner she learned survival skills, the sooner they could rescue her baby. Refusing to face the option of not finding her, Lila turned to her former lover and absorbed all he knew of how to get along in this scary new world.

They grabbed the rifles and walked up the road to the deserted building. Jack taught as they moved to the doorway. "Stay away from windows, just in case. We have two ways to enter a building; stealth mode or hot and fast. Pick one and commit. No half-measures. That gets you killed. By zombies or the living."

"But, it's deserted," she complained.

"Is it?" he asked with a quirk of his eyebrow. "Can you know one-hundred percent?"

Swallowing any further words, she followed Jack as he turned the doorknob slowly and pulled the door open. He stuck his head inside and looked right and left. He pulled the door wider and she caught hold as he moved inside.

The door gave a little squeak as she let it shut slowly behind her. Her feet shuffled over the grime-covered floor. A broken window to her left had let dust and debris pile up on the floor in wind-driven drifts.

Jack moved down the hallway, beckoning with his finger for her to follow. She pointed the rifle to the ceiling and kept an eye on his back. Every few seconds she turned to make sure nothing snuck up behind them.

An eerie silence filled the cavernous building. The silence of nothingness. No footsteps. No moans. No life; dead or otherwise. Jack silently opened doors and shone a flashlight beam inside before moving on.

A door at the end of the hall led to an enormous open space. Marks on the ground and the greasy outlines of circles and squares showed where large equipment had been bolted to the floor. A flutter of wings drew her gaze upward as birds flew from the catwalks to the rusty beams in the ceiling. Large skylights showed wispy white clouds traveling across the sky.

"No supplies here, but easily defensible and large enough for a group bigger than we are now," Jack said, his gaze traveling the room.

"You could even build sleeping quarters on the catwalks for somewhere to retreat if needed," she added.

He reached over and put an arm around her shoulders and squeezed tight. His body's warmth surrounded her. "That's my girl. Thinking ahead."

Her face warmed at his unexpected praise. All day it had seemed as if he only told her what she was doing wrong and how inept she was at survival.

"I wonder what Selena would have been like with you as her dad?" she mused. And just like that, his arm dropped away, he moved from her side, and his stoic soldier face returned. The one she'd seen at their rescue when he realized she was with her husband and child. The one she'd seen the whole time they'd been at the RV yard. The one shutting everyone out and making him a leader of people.

"Selena is tougher than you think," he muttered, moving away.

I pray that you are right. Lila kept the wish in her head, holding it like a talisman.

CHAPTER SEVEN

Selena

Selena's Diary
Apartment Complex
Walnut Creek, California
Spring, 1 AZ

The old man said it would be a few days, but when I woke up there was a loud noise outside. Not the moaning of the skinbags, but man voices. Loud man voices. And hammering. I want my mommy.

She found a crack in one of the boards on the window and pressed her face to the wood. Bright colors filled the parking lot of the apartments. Men moved all around. Some were talking in groups and some were laughing. A few women and girls stood with some of the men, but their hands were tied with rope. The same rope was around their necks and held by the men like dogs on a leash. A chill went up her spine.

Spotting Juan and the old man, she watched as they hammered on a platform like the ones for her dance recitals. She racked her brain. She'd seen a scene like this before. On television. A movie she wasn't supposed to watch. For adult audiences it had said.

A slave auction.

Selling men, women, and children.

Her teeth started chattering. She was old enough and had seen enough since the Z virus started to know things weren't the same as they used to be. No more playing outside. No more going to visit friends' houses. No more junk food. No more lots of things.

Mommy told her the rules had changed. She hadn't understood then when her mother told her men were in charge now. It hadn't been that way at the RV yard. The women there helped with all the chores, even zombie patrol. She glared at the platform.

She understood now. Those with power ruled. Like the bullies at the playground.

Auntie came up behind her and put her shaking hands on Selena's shoulders. "They want you cleaned up and outside now."

"I could run away," she spat. "Run far away."

Auntie hugged her. "You are old enough to know that is not true. The undead are out there past the barriers. A little girl would never survive. Your time will come, my strong one. But not today."

Her shoulders slumped. She had no way out except to be sold like a car or a horse or a basket of fruit. She tried to imagine she would be bought by someone nicer than Juan had been, but she shuddered as she remembered the looks the men in the apartment had been giving her.

At the bathroom, Auntie gave her clothes and a washcloth. "There is a bucket of water inside. Wash all over and get dressed. Please, Niña. Don't make them wait."

She nodded her head, at a loss for any words that mattered. Shutting the door, she put the clothes on the toilet seat lid and started pulling off her T-shirt and shorts. The water was ice-cold and set her teeth to chattering again. She washed quickly and put the washcloth in the sink.

Picking up the shirt, she stared at the shape of her hand through the material. The shirt would be see-thru when she put it on. Her teeth ground as she clenched her jaw.

"Hurry up, girl. Juan is coming."

She blanked her mind and pulled on the flimsy top and short skirt. Clean underwear was missing. She started to grab her old pair, but she realized they were left out on purpose. She was meant to only wear the shirt and skirt. She cried. Glad her mom was dead and not able to see her now. She took the washcloth and ran it over her tear-stained cheeks.

Picking up her old clothes, she bundled them into a pile and clasped them to her chest and opened the door. Auntie handed her the knapsack and she tucked the clothes inside as Juan strode up with his smile that wasn't a nice smile.

"Stand up, turn around," he ordered. "Excellent. Let's go."

He grabbed her arm and yanked her down the hallway and out the door. She blinked at the sudden light after the time in the dim rooms. The noise of the crowd was deafening. A couple of girls already stood on the platform with their clothes in a pile at their feet. The men hollered and whistled as the sun shone down on the women's pale skin and bowed heads.

Her heart pounded in her chest and the blood left her brain. She tried to pray but no words came to mind other than no. She looked up at Juan.

Don't you remember being my daddy? Going to my dance recitals. Calling me your sweetie. Teaching me to ride my big girl bike. Why can't you remember all those times?

When they reached the platform, he put a hand on the back of her neck and held her there as the two girls above cried, led away with a rope on the neck and a man yanking them down the stairs.

"Go," he ordered, shoving her to the steps.

Selena stared at the splintered wood, taking the steps one at a time. A big hand grabbed her arm as she reached the top. He placed her in the middle of the platform and moved to the front, directly above the crowd.

"This is Selena," he yelled. "The girl is nine years old and a virgin. Her father will guarantee that in writing. She isn't a woman quite yet, if you know what I mean. So no babies for a while."

Several men laughed in the audience and she cringed. Her hands shook as she rubbed them up and down her arms. A breeze wafted over her and goose bumps broke out on her exposed skin.

"I'll give you a cow for her. A milk cow," a voice rang out.

Selena looked up and spotted the old man in the crowd with his hand raised. He smiled at her and his dark eyes lit up with his smile. A woman stood beside him with a hand on his arm and no ropes or ties she could see.

"I'll give you three hens and a rooster," another voice called.

Her gaze traveled until she spotted the man with the mean voice. His looks matched his voice. A scar traveled down his face, a bright white in his dark skin.

Don't let him get me. She prayed with all her heart, although God didn't seem to be listening lately to any of her prayers. Or else, why was she here?

Several other voices yelled out with calls of goods to offer for her. She stared straight ahead and let her mind wander. No one touched her. No one demanded her clothes be taken off. Maybe there was a God after all.

Soon, the voices dwindled down to the old man and the mean man. Her head shot up as the mean man bid a car and twenty gallons of gasoline. The old man stood silence and dropped his head to stare at the ground. His woman grasped his arm and pleaded, but the man shook his head.

Through a haze of tears, Selena watched as the mean man and Juan shook hands. The other man slapped Juan on the back and almost knocked him over. Her legs shook and her breath caught. He would kill her. She was going to die. Every lesson she'd been told about going with strangers flooded her brain.

Juan signed the two papers and handed one to the man. The man's head came up and his dark eyes glared at her. His smile revealed missing teeth and the ones remaining were yellow and disgusting. She stood still as the man she'd thought her father ran up the stairs and grabbed a handful of hair to yank her off the platform.

"I hope your mother does show up here. I can tell her all about Toby Hill who now owns you," he hissed at her.

"Daddy, please. Don't do this to me. I'll be good. I promise," she cried, stumbling in her bare feet.

"I'm not your daddy," Juan whispered in her ear. "I never was."

He shoved her into the man she now belonged to. What had Juan said his name was? Her brain was scattered. No thoughts stayed in the forefront for long enough to catch and hold.

His large hands settled on her shoulders and squeezed painfully. "You can call me Mister Toby. Do you understand?"

She nodded.

He squeezed tighter. "Say it."

"Mister Toby," she squeaked out.

"You got shoes, girl?"

"Yes, Mister Toby. In my backpack."

He smiled that evil smile again. "You're a fast learner. That should make it easier for you. Get 'em and put 'em on. We got some traveling to do to get back to my camp."

Selena sat on the ground and dug through the knapsack, finding her shoes and putting them on as quickly as possible. Toby hadn't hit her yet and she was not going to give him a reason to do it now, in front of Juan.

As soon as she slipped on her shoes, he yanked her to her feet. "Get your pack. We are outta here. You try to run and the undead will get you. Follow along and you'll be fine. Understand?"

"Yes, Mister Toby."

She left Juan behind without a backward glance. The man had sold her as a slave. She would wipe all her happy childhood memories away. Standing tall, her spine straight, she wiped her childhood away, as well as her tears.

Toby grabbed her arm and dragged her along toward a monster truck sitting on the road outside the apartment complex. The moans of the undead echoed in the woods to her left. She shook as they stood in the open with nowhere to run.

The man grasped her around the waist and tossed her into the bed of a truck. He pointed to a box full of weapons.

"Hand me a gun."

She grabbed a big one that looked like the ones soldiers used in the movies. Toby took it and started firing at a few skinbags headed their way. The moans grew in volume as more and more undead shambled out of the trees, some headed toward the truck, but the majority headed to the complex where the loud voices turned to screams and gunfire.

"Sit down, girl," he ordered as he jumped into the truck's driver seat. "We are outta here."

Selena sat on a mattress in the truck bed. Over the side, she hung, watching as a horde of skinbags shambled, stumbled, and jogged into the apartment complex they'd just left. Sporadic gunfire still filled the air and smoke rose from several fires. An explosion rang out as they turned the corner and the buildings disappeared from sight.

CHAPTER EIGHT

Jack and Lila

Lila stood with her back to Jack as he spray painted a large R-1 on the chemical plant's front gate. The padlock and chain rattled as a breeze set it to swinging and hitting the metallic post. A large crow sat on the front and called to them in a rusty caw. She shuddered. The large birds had always seemed like harbingers of doom, like a scene from a horror movie. Sitting on fences. Their beady black eyes following you as you drove by.

She thought back to Jack's words inside the plant. *Selena is tougher than you think.* Prayers flooded her mind. Prayers to a silent God she'd given up on believing in. But old habits die hard as she whispered and crossed herself with a silent 'amen.'

The hissing of the paint can stopped and Jack walked up beside her. "Ready to move on?"

"More than ready," she replied back in a low tone.

His hand settled on her shoulder and squeezed before falling away. "We'll find her."

Her body warmed at his confident voice and the reassurance in his eyes. His eyes that had twinkled in the old way for just a second and passed. Almost too fast for her to notice, but she did. She also noticed the flush to his face and the look of forbidden thoughts.

She shook her head at her random romantic thoughts in the middle of survival. Jack was her past. She'd blown it and married Juan. No matter what the man had done, he was her lawfully married husband. That she'd be a widow as soon as she got Selena back didn't make a difference. Even if she were willing to forget her wedding vows, Jack wasn't ever going to let her forget what she had done. He wasn't the kind of man to come between a man and his wife, even if it was the apocalypse and vows of any kind didn't matter anymore. They'd always matter to Jack Canida. He hadn't needed military service to drill it into him. His values ran core deep.

After a few hours of stopping to investigate a wasteland of deserted encampments looking for news, Lila was ready to believe there were no live people left in the world except for her and Jack. A woman's shrill scream broke the unnatural silence, heard over the rumble of the car's motor. The hairs on the back of her neck stood on end at the desperation in the cries.

They pulled over to the side of the road and jumped out, weapons ready. Jack held up a hand

and stopped them beside a tree. The bark rubbed her arm as she pressed against it, wanting to be one with the tree and invisible. The sobs rose and fell along with the harsh laughter of men. Underlying it all was the growl of an undead.

"Hold on to my belt and don't let go until I tell you to," he whispered in her ear.

Her fingers wrapped around the webbed fabric as Jack moved forward in a hunched squat. The mean laughter grew louder as they reached a scrub bush in front of a clearing. Two men shoved an undead child between them while an older woman grabbed their arms, begging them to stop. Her pleas fell on deaf ears as they flung the young girl between them and cut her with their knives whenever she stumbled nearby.

Lila gagged and swallowed the bile down. Hot acid burned her throat. She recognized the two men from her time at the Fruitful Harvest Church. Zeke and Grant had been among the worse of the men, raping young girls and tormenting the skinbags for their enjoyment.

Tension swarmed up Jack's back where her fingers grazed above his belt. He turned to her.

"On three, grab the old woman. I'll take care of the men," he hissed.

"What about the girl?" She looked into eyes of the darkest, coldest brown.

"We'll put her down once the woman is safe."

She nodded and loosened her hold on his belt. At the count of three she was off like a frightened deer, bounding around the bush and at the woman's side in seconds. She ignored the sounds of the scuffle, pulling the woman to her feet and dragging her away from the clearing.

"Please. Kelly." The woman stretched out her arm toward the undead child.

Lila rubbed the woman's hand. "We'll take care of her."

The woman sagged in relief or exhaustion, she wasn't sure of which, and crumpled to the ground at her feet.

The silence from the clearing had her on her tiptoes to glance over the bush. Jack stood alone, wiping his knife and slamming it back into the sheath on his belt. The bright pink of the girl's shirt glared from the ground a few feet away.

She squatted beside the woman. "It's over. The child is at peace."

"Thank you," the woman whispered. "Now she is in Heaven with her mother."

"You're the grandmother?"

The woman smiled and looked even younger than Lila had thought at first.

"Kelly is my only grandchild." Her smile fell. "Was my only grandchild."

"I'm sorry for what Zeke and Grant did," Lila started to speak.

The woman scuttled back until she was up against a tree. Her body shook and her eyes darted as if looking for an escape route. "You're with those monsters?"

Lila shook her head. "No. I just knew them when I was trapped with them and a bunch of men just like them."

Even without looking, she felt Jack's presence at her back. He strode around her and squatted by the woman. By degrees, the woman relaxed and took his hand. He stood and pulled her to her feet.

"You're safe now," Jack said. He squeezed her shoulder and his hand fell away.

"Thank you," she whispered.

"I'm Jack and this is Lila," he said, pointing to her over his shoulder. "We are looking for a young girl. Blonde hair. Green eyes. Nine years old and traveling with a shorter Hispanic man."

"I'm Mary," she said, looking up at Jack and shaking her head. "Kelly and I haven't seen anyone in a week except for those two. We heard some cars on the freeway, but they were too far away to see the people inside."

"Damn," Jack muttered, striking his fist into his palm. "We need to get to Juan's relatives. Walnut Creek might as well be the far side of the Moon for how hard it is to get there anymore."

Mary started crying. "Don't leave me alone. Please."

Jack gathered the woman in his arms and smiled down at her. Lila felt her heart race in her chest. Yet again she was reminded of why she had loved this man, and wondered for the millionth time why she'd let her father bully her into giving him up. Death threat or not, she should have believed in them. In him.

"Of course, we wouldn't leave you alone. You're coming with us," Jack murmured softly. "If you have somewhere to go along the way we will take you, or you can just stay with us. Eventually we'll be heading to Ryde, down the river."

"Can we bury Kelly first?" Her voice quivered.

"Of course."

He got the foldable shovels out of the SUV. He and Lila dug a shallow grave for the little girl. Her eyes watered and her vision wavered as Mary cleaned her granddaughter the best she could with the limited water available. The woman wrapped the little girl in her Disney sleeping bag and Lila lost it. A few years ago, Selena had one just like it with princesses on the bright-colored fabric. Hot tears rolled down her face as Jack lifted the feather-light bundle and gently placed her in the ground. Her breath caught and hitched in her throat. That would not be Selena. They would find their little girl and she would be safe. She had to be. Lila wouldn't survive any other outcome.

* * *

As if he could read her mind, Jack turned to Lila after placing the finally dead girl into the grave. He wanted to reach across the clearing and gather her in his arms and guarantee they would find Selena, but he couldn't for so many reasons, the least of that he was a realist and knew their journey might not have a happy ending. The most important reason: she wasn't his to hold. His hands clenched into fists at his side as his wants and desires warred with his honor. A deep breath and his hands relaxed at his sides. Honor and integrity was all he had left in the chaos of their new world. Too easy to squander, impossible to get back.

He brought his mind back to the present as Mary's whispered words petered off and died as she huddled on the ground at the foot of the grave. The woman stood up, rubbed the tears from her face, and stiffened her spine.

"I'm done," she said, looking off into the far distance.

Jack dug into the hard dirt and shoveled it back into the hole. Once it was level, he folded the shovel and set it aside. He turned to the women. "Find some good-sized rocks to cover this up. We'll protect it the best we can."

Lila found a pile of busted up concrete and they had the grave rocked up in no time. He looked up to find the sun on its downward trajectory. He couldn't ask Mary to stay here with the grave and the dead tormentors. They would have to get down the road as far as they could manage before total darkness.

He grabbed the shovels and watched as Lila helped the woman gather her few belongings. Mary strode to the far side of the clearing and returned with two backpacks. Lila helped as the woman pulled some things out of the smaller one and added them to hers. The small pack she placed on the grave, Kelly in bright pink letters shining on the front flap.

"I'm ready to go," she announced.

"If we keep going and don't hit any roadblocks, I think we can make it to the BART station on the freeway," he told them as they started walking out of the brush and back along the side of the broken asphalt road to the SUV.

Just before the sun would set over the nearby hills, they arrived at the transportation station. They got out of the vehicle and Jack squatted down in the weeds beside the freeway. The building appeared deserted but he had learned in the zombie apocalypse that appearances can be deceiving.

He stayed down in the tall brush, motioning to the two women to join him. "I'm going to scout ahead. Give me ten, fifteen minutes and I'll whistle if it's safe for you to join me. If you don't hear from me continue on to Walnut Creek, your duty is to find Selena."

The familiar stubborn look on her face let Jack know she wasn't listening to a word he said. He'd seen that look too many times before in the past, but she had to listen now.

He put his hands on her shoulders and squeezed, forcing her to look at him. "You will leave me behind. There could come a time when you have to make it on your own. You can't worry about me; you can only worry about finding Selena."

The small nod was almost lost in the growing darkness but it was there. He would take what he could get. Standing, he settled his backpack on his shoulders and ran down the embankment. Once on the broken asphalt of the freeway, he turned and looked over his shoulder. The tall weeds hid any view of the women he had left on the hillside.

A quick glance right and left showed no one on the road, dead or undead. Jack took a deep breath and held it. The only sound in the desolation was the calls of the birds returning to their roosts for the night.

A few moments at a steady jog and Jack crossed the median through a ripped fence and the other lanes of the freeway. The empty parking lot contained mostly weeds and a few abandoned cars. The tires had flattened long ago and glittering shards of glass pebbled the pavement from smashed windows and parking lot lights.

The hairs on the back of his neck stood on end. The location was too deserted. No sentries stood on patrol at what was a very defensible spot. Jack stepped through where once turnstiles had stood. The faint sound of voices filtered down from the cement stairs in front of him. A baby's soft cries were quickly hushed with a mother's lullaby. The scent of a wood fire wafted down to him.

Jack strode up the stairs with his hands held out in front of him to show his lack of weapons. He knew it was a gamble but, with the lack of male voices, one he was willing to take. He stepped out onto the platform, his eyes sweeping back and forth quickly to assess the situation. No one to the left. To the right several women sat by a barely smoldering fire, the wisp of smoke lost before reaching the open roof. A young boy who barely reached Jack's chest rushed forward, his shaking hands gripping an AR15.

"Jacob, put that down before you hurt yourself," a voice called from the dark corner. A tall figure stood and shuffled toward Jack. A man with long gray hair, a long gray beard, and gray tinged skin reached out a hand and pushed the gun toward the ground.

With an angry look on his face, the young boy stomped off to the fireside circle. The man nodded his head and Jack placed his hands down at his side.

"Mighty dangerous coming to a camp this late in the evening," he said.

"Didn't have much of a choice," Jack supplied. "Rescued a woman earlier. Had to bury her granddaughter. This was the first place I could think of with defense capabilities. We only need a place for the night. We're headed to Walnut Creek in the morning."

"Well, not too sure about the defense capabilities, but you're more than welcome to share the spot until morning. I'm Mitchell by the way and you already met Jacob."

"I'll let the others know that it's safe to come. We have some food to share and I'm willing to trade for some information."

"Information we got; food not so much."

Jack let the man know he would be right back with his companions only to be greeted by Jacob and his gun at the bottom of the stairs. Trying to be a man as a preteen was hard enough in normal times, let alone in the zombie apocalypse. He looked him straight in the eye and talked to him man-to-man.

"I have two females with me. That's it. We'll be gone by morning," Jack told him. "We just need a place to rest for the night."

"I'll be watching you," Jacob piped up in a cracking voice.

"I'm sure you will. It's an important job you do for your group."

The boy stood taller and almost cracked a smile. Jack stepped out to the weed-filled embankment and whistled long and clear. In seconds he spotted Lila and Mary making their way down their side and across the freeway. He was pleased to note that Lila checked out both sides of the road before they crossed. A leftover habit of a dead civilization, but just as useful to look for roaming gangs of zombies before you put yourself in the open.

He met them at the edge of the parking lot and introduced them to Jacob. The sullen teen found a smile for Lila, he noticed. As a group, they made their way up the stairs where the elderly man greeted them. Mary began to cry and rushed into the man's arms.

"Mitchell," she sobbed between gasps of air.

The man's arms tightened around her and his gray eyes watered before he shut them.

Lila and Jack stepped back to give the couple some privacy. Jacob shrugged his shoulders like he didn't understand grown-ups and strode back to the group by the fire.

Mary and Mitchell stepped apart, although the man kept an arm around her shoulders. The woman smiled through her tears. "You found my brother. My twin brother."

Jack blinked. *Twin? The man looked as if he had twenty years or more on Mary. Desperation would do that to a person. The group reeked of it. They'd given up on life and were just waiting to die. Seen it before in groups too small to survive.*

He turned to Lila. "I told Mitchell we had *some* food to share." He tried to put an emphasis on the word 'some' but he didn't want to be obvious.

Lila caught his thoughts as if they'd been spoken out loud as she dug into her pack and pulled out four cans of soup. A more than generous offering. Not enough to make it appear they had a bottomless supply, but not stingy enough to appear rude. When she squatted to dig inside again he wondered what she was adding to the pot, until he spotted the smashed box of animal crackers. She'd noticed the group of small children as well. He smiled to himself when he realized she wasn't willing to share her chocolate bar as well. She'd always had a wicked sweet tooth.

Jack was pulled away from his dangerous thoughts of what had been at Mitchell's soul-wrenching sobs. Mary must have told him of the young girl they had buried. Yet again, he was reminded of all the loss in the ZA. Time and time again, families were ripped to shreds.

His hands clenched into fists. He closed his eyes and all he could see was Selena's sweet smile and her bright-green eyes. He would put his family together.

CHAPTER NINE

Paul, Suz, and Josh

Paul Luther's Log
Brannan Island State Park
State Route 160
Spring, 1 AZ

The Humvee were a great find although we were not able to use them until the next day. We have lost Jim Evans. The news of his daughter's death hit him hard and his already weakened heart was unable to take it. Doctor Shannon was forced to put him down but we will take him with us to bury in a safe place.

Paul stood at the edge of a grassy field with his back to the river. Suz and Josh stood to his right and Doctor Shannon stood to his left. Her heartfelt sobs carried over the silent gathering. The young boys of Rogue Vantage stood ready with their shovels to bury Jim. The idea of the little boys as a burial detail broke his heart but they had begged to be allowed to help.

Shannon's shoulders were hunched as she huddled next to him. Her usual tidy bun was missing as strands of pale blonde hair blew in the wind. He bowed his head and felt as Suz took his hand, her strong fingers wrapped around his. She was warmth at his side.

His thoughts wandered to all the times he had been here at Brannan Island, camping with friends and boating on the river. Fun times that seemed a million miles away. Another time. Another life.

Wildlife was already claiming the deserted campground. Had probably been a never-ending battle with nature before the apocalypse. If you had to believe things happened for a reason, then Jim's death brought them here to spot a small herd of deer that would feed the group for the rest of the journey ahead. A small thing, but nowadays that seemed all they got, small things to be thankful for.

"Say something," Shannon whispered at his side.

He cleared his throat. "I'd like to believe Jim is now in Heaven, watching over us with Jed and Beth at his side. Their travails and pain are gone. The rest of us must continue on without them."

"Amen," the group intoned quietly, Shannon's a bare whisper at his side.

She pulled away and ran to the grave. Her knees gave out and she fell to the ground. "Why?" she cried.

Paul didn't have an answer. None of them did. The past year had been harsh and harder than any of them were used to. They were living outside, or pretty darn close to it. Food and water was in constant short supply. Things like vitamins and medicine were becoming scarcer by the day. Paul shuddered to think what they would look like in ten or twenty years. Probably like the pictures his mother had of her great-grandparents, worn out by the time they were forty.

He started to move, but Josh beat him to it, as he knelt beside Shannon and pulled her gently to her feet. He didn't catch what he said, but Shannon moved toward the vehicles with Josh cradling her in his arms. Suz came to his side.

"We'll get through this. We always do," she said, her arm around his waist. She nodded in the boys' direction as they started shoveling the dirt over Jim's wrapped body. "We have to protect the next generation."

"What about Beth and Jed? They were the next generation too."

She pulled him in tight, her face against his. "We can't save them all."

He shook his head. Suz knew him so well. He wanted—no; he needed—to save them all. To save the group. To save California. To save the world.

Like a sheepdog with a herd, Paul noted where each member of the group was at all times. The boys of Rogue Vantage finished up their duties and ran to the vehicles, pushing and shoving each other. He knew they were arguing who got to ride with the turret gun on the lead Humvee. He saw as Sarah and Stephanie, the tow-haired twin orphans ran and slammed into Shannon until she pulled them into a hug. He breathed deep. One less worry, two if you counted the doctor herself. He smiled as Josh peeled off and Joseph Jones came up to the doctor's side and shared the twins' hugs. Another family unit forming before his eyes. They would all help each other heal, the orphans and the left behind.

His mind was ripped away from his thoughts at the low hum of a horde on the move. Whipping around, he could do nothing but stare as the undead walked out of the shallow water by his feet. Vegetation hung from gray flesh. Their water-soaked clothing fell into pieces with a splash into the water. The moans rose as they scented fresh prey. The stench of rotting flesh reached him before the first skinbag cleared the river and shambled across the grass.

He grabbed Suz by the hand and set off in a run to the Humvee. "Get a move on. We are out of here."

Counting heads as doors slammed, he let himself breathe as he and Suz jumped into the lead vehicle and slammed the doors with Josh's foot already pushing the gas pedal to the floor. Rubber burned as they peeled out of the campground that had become the land of the undead.

He couldn't wrap his head around the thoughts swirling inside. Had they walked across the bottom of the river? He rejected that thought almost before it was fully formed. Had they sat in the shallows and waited for food? As scary as that thought was, he was sure that was pretty close to exactly what had happened out there. He turned his face to the window and stared as they just kept coming from the river, row after row of skinbags, no end in sight.

Suz leaned against him, her body shivering. "It will never be over, will it? If even one survives somewhere until a human comes along, it would start all over again. They can hide and wait—forever."

* * *

She didn't really expect an answer from Paul, but she thought he would at least comfort her. But he was lost in his own thoughts. Thoughts probably just as dark as hers. Suz leaned back against the seat and closed her eyes. Paul's hand grabbed onto hers, his fingers wrapping around tight. She smiled and allowed herself to fall asleep.

The nightmares rose up and claimed her. They were the same every time she let herself sleep without help. The pills in her knapsack were getting low and the doctor hadn't found anymore yet. She didn't even know what she was taking, but they worked. They let her sleep with no dreams at all. One moment she was falling asleep and the next it was morning.

She usually was fine on the nights she slept with Paul and could cuddle afterward, only allowing herself to take a pill when it was Josh's night with their husband. She'd tried cutting the pills into smaller pieces to make them last, but it wasn't enough. The further they traveled beyond the cities and towns, the harder drugs would be to come by.

The hordes rose up and chased her. Her athletic fleetness, her hunting and killing skills were gone. She barely kept a few steps ahead of the shambling skinbags. Their stench overwhelmed her until she couldn't breathe. Their skeletal hands grasped her, the bones scratching her skin. Black ooze coated her body and fell into her mouth.

Fingers tangled in her hair and pulled her to the ground. Her eyes stared into a pale-blue sky but all she saw were bloody mouths and gleaming teeth preparing to feast on her.

She awoke with a scream bursting from her throat. The vehicle swerved as Josh fought to get it back under control. Paul wrapped his arms around her and she pushed him away, the terror clinging to her even as she awoke fully and realized what she'd done.

"Jeez, Suz," Josh yelled, his hand clenched on the steering wheel. "Are you trying to kill us?"

"That's enough," Paul said in that tone of voice that everyone in the group recognized as his angry voice.

"Sorry," her brother gritted out.

"It's nothing," she stuttered. "Just a bad dream."

"I'd say it's more than a bad dream," Paul muttered.

She took a good look at him and cringed. Bloody furrows ran down his cheek, the blood dripping onto his shirt. Her sore fingertips told her she had done it. Her stomach heaved and only a lack of food kept her from vomiting in the car.

"I'm so sorry," she whispered, her fingers touching his cheek.

He flinched but didn't turn away. Her hand cradled his jaw. Paul was the last person in the world she wanted to hurt. But hurt him she had and he would be even more hurt when he found out she'd said nothing about the pills. Lies by omission were still lies.

Her fingertips trailed down his neck to his shoulder. Wide shoulders that carried the weight of the whole camp on them. A weight he seemed to carry without effort. Only she and Josh knew the man he became when he let his guard down and worried about everything from a lack of schooling for the kids to the dangers of dehydration for the entire group. They saw the other side of Paul Luther.

He sighed. "I'll be glad when Jack is back with us."

"You know he might not make it back. You may be forced to be the leader permanently."

His eyes turned dark and hard. "He will make it to Ryde."

She nodded. How could she have forgotten that Jack wasn't just their leader, he was Paul's best friend? She leaned back and tried to move to her own seat, but his strong hand pulled her back.

"We'll get through this," he said.

"Is that your favorite saying, or what?" Josh called from the driver's seat.

The three of them laughed and broke the tension in the Humvee until Josh slammed on the brakes and Paul caught her before her head could slam into the back of the seat.

Peeking out the windshield she spotted what made her brother stop. A raised pickup truck with enormous Monster truck tires stood across the road. A pair of men stood in front of it, their AK47s pointed at the Humvee.

Paul reached to the front and flipped the switch for the vehicle's PA system. Josh handed him the microphone. He pressed the button.

"Clear the road. This is your one and only warning."

The reply came fast and deadly. The men opened fire and their shots pebbled the vehicle. The pings echoed inside like hail on a tin roof.

Before the last echo died, Paul was over the seat and in the turret. The roar of the gun filled the interior. Suz slammed her hands over her ears. Shell casings clinked to the floor and her eyes couldn't unsee what was in front of her.

Blood spatter coated the side of the white truck and two torn bodies sprawled on the cracked asphalt. Paul slid down from the turret. His face white, the gashes she had put there standing out red and deep.

"Josh, leave the motor running. Suz, you get in front to drive. We'll move the bodies, which is more than they deserve, but I'm not running over people. Once we're clear, you can push the truck off the road."

Suz and her brother moved swiftly. She didn't know about Josh, but she wanted to be out of here as soon as possible. The men moved out in front of the Humvee, back to back as they checked the road, the ditch on the side, and the bridge to the left.

In a moment, they had the bodies out of the road and placed in the ditch with more care than she would have given them. She stepped off the brake and put her foot on the gas and all hell broke loose.

The road rocked and swayed and the Humvee joined it. Suz held on to the steering wheel with both hands as an explosion hit to the left and metal twisted and squealed as the bridge fell to the water in a cloud of dust and smoke.

Cheers carried from the other side. The explosion had been planned and executed on purpose. The people in the town on the other side of the river sent a clear message—leave us alone.

Suz shrugged her shoulders and put the Humvee into gear to push the truck off the road to join the pile of metal from the bridge. She stomped on the brakes and traded places with her brother and slid in the back seat. An empty back seat as Paul took the passenger seat up front.

Her throat convulsed as she tried to swallow past the dryness and the lump. She stared out the window at the river and trees going by, wishing she were alone and could take a pill.

CHAPTER TEN

Jack and Lila

Lila's Notes
On the road again
Pittsburg/Concord
Spring, 1 AZ

As I suspected, Mary decided to stay with her brother. They tried to have us take the young boy, Jacob with us, but he refused and hid until we left. Selena always asked for a brother, but that young man is not it. When I see how this new world has scarred him, I wonder how Selena will be when we find her. My greatest fear is finding her and having her not want us or need us anymore.

The rising sun was at their backs and made long shadows from the stranded cars on the road. Her eyes played tricks with the light and saw imagined zombies under every vehicle or waiting around the side of the trucks and vans. The whistling wind became the moans of the undead in her overactive imagination.

She cocked her head and listened, trying to figure out how Jack moved carefully and quickly at the same time. His boots made a soft thud, while hers stomped and made an echo down the canyon of cracked asphalt. Constant glances to the left and right just leftover childhood lessons of not playing on a busy street.

Lila exhaled a breath she didn't know she was holding as they reached the parked SUV still sitting on the side of the street where they'd left it the night before. She would march over hot coals to find her daughter, but a drive would be nicer and faster.

After a few miles, the cars came closer and closer together. Sometimes it seemed as if they'd been caught in a flood and stranded in a metal tangle beneath the overcrossings. The idea of a swift drive to Walnut Creek died in her mind. As if to prove her point, the SUV clipped a small sports car, sending it rolling across the pavement in a squeal of tortured metal.

Soon, it was as if the SUV wasn't going any faster than they could walk. Her fingernails dug into her jean-covered thighs. *They had to get there. They had to stop whatever Juan was planning.*

As if God heard her silent prayer, the way up ahead cleared. The higher they drove up the hill, the fewer cars there were on the road. She started to smile until they reached the peak just before Willow Pass Road.

Jack slammed on the brakes and the vehicle fishtailed before jerking to a stop.

Her hands fisted on her lap and tears blurred her vision. *It's not fair.*

As far as she could see, it was a parking lot of cars, trucks, and buses. There wasn't room between them for a bicycle, let alone a vehicle as big as the SUV. Even before Jack spoke, she was grabbing her backpack from the floor and yanking the door open.

"We're walking."

She rolled her eyes at him. "You think?"

"Don't be childish," he said.

"Childish. Is it childish to think fate or karma or the gods might just give us a fucking break once in a while?"

"We got to drive this far, didn't we?" He didn't allow her time to answer. "We may find a car once we get down the road some. If we don't, we can walk. We *will* get there."

Her breath huffed out and she swiped her wet eyes. "Fine. We walk."

"Lila," he said.

She turned toward him. "We have to take what each day hands us. We had a safe place to sleep last night. We reunited a family. You gave cookies to a group of kids who hadn't seen any in months."

She smiled at the thought of the young faces at the battered box of stale animal crackers. You would have thought they were truffles or those outrageously expensive chocolates with the fancy name, not broken and crumbling lions, tigers, and bears.

"That's it," Jack's deep voice reached past her thoughts. "Enjoy every moment. It is all we have. All we ever had, we were just too stupid to realize it."

She nodded and started walking down the cracked asphalt at his side. Her hand rested on the knife strapped to her belt and her eyes darted from car to car. A deep sniff brought nothing to her nostrils but the scent of oil and long-gone gas fumes. The cry of a hawk drew her eyes to the deep-blue sky. The raptor dropped like a bullet and came back up with a squirming rodent in its talons. A reminder of survival of the fittest constantly at play.

A canine growl had the hairs on the back of her neck rising. Her gaze darted to her right. What looked like a German shepherd cowered beneath a car. His teeth gleamed in the semi-darkness where he huddled. Where she huddled, Lila corrected herself as a ball of fur rolled over and became a puppy at the dog's side. Keeping her eyes on the dog, Lila stepped back until the hackles lowered on the dog's back and she returned to giving her attention to her baby and not to the human interlopers.

That's all they were, she mused. Interlopers on this planet. They were just one species among millions. Not even the top species anymore. The undead had taken that spot. The living were just biding their time until it passed and none of them were left. No one left to remember music or art or technology. No one left to remember they had walked on the Moon. They had split the atom. They had created life.

She shook herself out of her dismal thoughts. They still had survival and love and life. Where there was life, there was hope. She didn't know who first uttered the saying, but it was becoming her new mantra.

"Do you think we'll get there today?" she asked Jack in a low voice.

"We may if we step up the pace and don't stop except for water and food. We're both in decent shape, so I don't see why not."

She started to laugh out loud, but caught herself in time before making enough noise to wake the dead. And wasn't that a not-so-funny saying now? Her gaze swept over Jack. He'd been a jock before, but his years in the army and now daily survival had honed the man into a lean, mean, fighting machine. She, on the other hand, had been thin to start with. With the lack of food at the church and Juan's withholding of food as punishment most days, she felt like a good wind would blow her over.

She shook her head but Jack spoke up.

"Do you remember those stories we heard as kids? How a mom pulled a car off their child with her bare hands?"

She nodded, wondering where he was going with this train of thought.

"That's you. You could be on your last leg, but you would drag yourself to save Selena. That's what mothers do. What good mothers do. No matter what, I've seen what a good mother you are."

Wasn't that a backhanded compliment? That 'no matter what'. No matter you left me. No matter you dumped my ass. No matter you didn't tell me I had a child. She felt each of those thoughts as if they were knife wounds to her heart. And she deserved every one of them.

* * *

Jack opened his mouth to take the words back, but they were already out there, hanging in the tense air between them. He shrugged. Maybe it was better this way. If he kept Lila angry he could fight the feelings struggling to escape. That he had to remind himself hourly she was a married woman warred with the memories of the past. Better to think about Selena and finding the girl before too much time passed. His teeth clenched and his jaw ached with the thought of what the delicate little girl could be going through. He'd seen too many small undead to think everyone got a happy ever after ending in the ZA.

His mind whipped back to the current situation as a dull thump sounded up ahead. Off to the right he spotted the familiar silhouette of a school bus. Blood smeared windows painted an ugly picture. The gory handprints too small to be from adult hands. He pulled the knife from the sheath and squatted to peer under the large vehicle. The thumps grew in sound and speed as he drew near.

He started to walk ahead when Lila grabbed his arm. "You can't leave them there."

Tears pooled in her eyes and rolled down her cheeks. He cursed under his breath. "Probably twenty to thirty kids in there. We can't risk going in that bus."

"We have to do something. What if Selena was in there? Wouldn't you want someone to put her out of her misery? Those are someone's children."

Her hand dropped away and he started pacing. Going in that bus was not an option. It would be a slaughterhouse, with him the slaughtered. Getting the kids out was impossible as well. They wouldn't be able to get them all and if they got overwhelmed there would be nowhere to run. That left option C as his drill sergeant would say. Not a great plan, but at least a good plan, a doable plan.

Shrugging out of his backpack, he set it on the road and opened the flap. He reached to the bottom and pulled out the crowbar and a lighter. Lila moved to his side.

Her eyebrow arched. "What's the plan?"

"See the logo on the side of the bus?"

"The flame one?"

"The bus runs on propane. Just a giant propane tank on wheels. How about we make the bus a giant Molotov cocktail?" he replied, pointing to the side of the road. "Grab that T-shirt and tear it into strips."

Jack pried open the fill valve. A whiff of gas took him back a step. "We're in luck. It's probably full," he said as Lila returned to his side with the strips of cotton fabric.

The pounding on the windows reached a frantic tempo as they huddled by the side. Jack moved as fast as he could as Lila's shoulders tensed and he heard the grinding of her teeth. "Just a little bit longer. Get your backpack on and get ready to run straight up the road between those two cars," he said and pointed.

"Tie the shirt into a long rope," he instructed her. Once the material was a long cotton rope, it took it and shoved one end into the fuel tank.

She hefted her backpack onto her shoulders and set his by his feet.

"Ready?"

She nodded and Jack flicked his lighter and set the dry cotton ablaze. The flame caught as Jack grabbed his pack in one hand and Lila's hand with the other. The only sound was the pounding of their boots until with a whoosh the bus exploded.

He pushed them to the side of a car and huddled over Lila. Metal fragments rained down amid other parts of things he didn't want to identify. A wave of heat passed overhead and then he rose.

The once-colorful bus was a mass of burned, twisted metal, flames shooting out the sides. He focused on spotting any zombs who'd escaped the inferno, but the only sound was the crackling of the fire consuming flesh and metal and the only smell was fuel and burning flesh. He'd smelled enough of it in Iraq to never forget the stench.

"Thank you," he heard Lila whisper just before her lips found his.

He allowed himself two seconds of pleasure before duty and honor reached up and slapped him upside his head. His hands gripped her upper arms as he pushed her away. His hold tightened and he stared at her wince. He didn't know who he wanted to punish more; Lila or himself.

CHAPTER ELEVEN

Cody, Miranda, and April

Ran's Journal
RV Yard
3 days after breakup of camp
Spring, 1 AZ (After Zombies)

I'm so never having a baby. We have sat here with barely any food, not enough water, and crying babies. Jed and Carla are so cute. When they aren't crying. They cry for food. They cry for going poop in their diapers. They cry for no reason I can see, but what do I know, I'm not a mom and never going to be. Ever.

She looked up from her writing to find April yet again draped all over Cody. Technically he was Ran's boyfriend or mate or something, but in the ZA nothing was permanent, not even relationships. Cody could move on if he wanted to. Her heart twisted in her chest. When she'd found him in the library in Concord it had been like fate. The feelings she'd had for Seth Ripley had been revealed as the crush it was. But Cody had been different. He accepted her; her history meaning nothing to him. Cody lived for today and that's what he had with her. Today. But tomorrow was no guarantee, for life or love.

Pulling her knife out of the sheath, she sat sharpening it as Cody and April approached her. The redhead had the grace to blush in a color as bright as her chopped off hair. Ran winced. Not so long ago she'd been where April was, a victim of abuse and rape. She slammed the knife back into its holder and stood up.

"Ran," Cody said, putting the basket of clean clothes on the picnic table. "I thought we could clear out the area so there are fewer skinbags when Seth and Teddy are ready to leave."

A smile broke out of her face with a matching grin on Cody's. "Let me get a machete and I'll meet you at the gate."

April's whine carried as Ran hurried to the weapons shed. Running back, she caught the tail-end of Cody's speech.

"You can't go with us, April. We need to know the other has our back. You'll get loads of training on the journey, and then you can be a fighting team with Ran and me."

Ran smiled wider. Since the girl couldn't even fight with a knife yet, it would be a long time before she had to worry about the newbie edging into her zombie hunting time with Cody.

Cody tied a bandana around his head to hold back his bleached blonde hair. Along with his tie-dyed shirt, he looked like a surfer minus the board. He knocked on Teddy's trailer door and the large black man filled the opening.

"We need you to do the gate, bro," Cody said.

"No problem, kids. What are you up to today?" He walked over and stood by the large button for the gate.

"I told Seth we would clear out the area a little so it will be easier to leave in the morning."

Ran laughed. "You didn't say we were finally going tomorrow."

"I wanted it to be a surprise. I know you've been antsy and I thought a little zomb' stomping would help."

She ran up and hugged him, kissing his neck and face. "Thank you, thank you, thank you," she whispered.

"Yo, you don't have to thank me. I'll do anything for you, babe. You are my one and only."

"Okay, you two. Break it up. Keep your head in the game out there. I only spotted a few from the walls this morning, but that doesn't mean you can't be surprised by a cluster or a surprise ambush. We don't have the repel sound anymore since the others took the ham radio and the recording," Teddy lectured as the gate glided open.

"We won't be gone long, man. An hour or two tops. Heading toward the bridge to clear the way for tomorrow," Cody said as they stepped through and the gate glided back closed.

Ran heard nothing but the wind rustling in the blooming trees. White petals coated the street like a layer of snow, the slightest gust sending them swirling across the pavement. She sighed. The world was still a beautiful place. Or it would be, minus the zombies and the renegades and the madmen. She sighed again. Okay, maybe not anytime soon, but it used to be.

She breathed deeply and sneezed. Nothing but pollen and everything coming to life after a long winter. No rot. No zombs. No nothing.

"I miss the sounds," she whispered to Cody. "Planes flying overhead, cars whooshing by on the freeway, kids playing in the street, all that noisy, wonderful stuff."

"Me, too." He put his back to hers as they surveyed the area, walking slowly to the north. "But mostly the food. Ice cream, a thick, juicy steak, French fries, and junk food other than Twinkies. Although we may miss the Twinkies too, I think Dylan took the last of them with him."

She glanced at him. Cody smiled and her world brightened. She hated to burst the Ran/Cody bubble but the moan of the skinbags at the end of the street popped her happy thoughts. Pulling her knife from the sheath on her belt, she gripped a weapon in each fist and nudged him with her shoulder.

"Three of them, due north."

Cody's ax blade glinted in the sunlight as he raised it. "This should be a piece of cake; they look like they are on their last legs—literally."

He pointed to one undead missing most of his leg below the knee, threads of flesh holding it together. She grimaced and rushed to finish the job of separating its foot from its body. The skinbag fell over with a clatter of bones and the sound of a ripe melon hitting the pavement as the zomb' finished the job of making him dead dead by cracking his skull open and letting his brains spill out in a black, stinky mess.

Ran looked up to find Cody on the ground, fighting off four zombies who'd come out of nowhere. A shambling group appeared from the gas station on the corner. Her head whipped around. They would be surrounded if she didn't think fast. She dropped her knife and picked up Cody's fallen ax. Yelling like a wild woman, she swung her weapon back and forth and prayed he didn't get any contaminated blood in his mouth or eyes.

The last body fell on his chest as the head rolled across the asphalt. Ran grabbed his hand and yanked him up. His blood-soaked clothes didn't bring any comfort. She couldn't tell if it was the zombs or his. A sob caught in her throat and she swallowed it back down. They didn't have time to worry about it; a group cut off their retreat back to the RV yard and another smaller group stood between them and the gas station. Handing the ax back to him, she pointed to the station and started running.

They'd have to go by the numbers and push through to the gas station. Ran took the two on her left and Cody finished up with the three on the right. Someone had tried to shore up the building in the past, as evidenced by the welded metal plates where the door used to be, the ones for the window having fell off and sat on the concrete. Cody hit the door first and pulled it open. Ran was a step behind him. She turned to help him get the heavy door shut and a bar placed across it.

They slammed the bar home as a pounding started on the other side. Metal clangs echoed in the small room, but it looked designed to hold out the horde. They hadn't discovered the glass windows yet, but they would. She pulled a flashlight off her belt and switched it on in the murky room. A dark entryway stood to her right. She sniffed at the doorway. Musty and dusty scents filled her nose. Blocking out the pounding to her back, she listened for any sounds at all. Zombies weren't the only dangers in the ZA.

She swept the dark car repair bay with the light, her machete held at the ready. Emptiness greeted her. No cars filled the space. A few chairs sat against the far wall beside a wooden ladder leading to the roof. A hole in the roof let light fall down the rungs, pooling on the concrete floor.

"Anything?" Cody whispered at her back.

"No one is here. But I think they stayed on the roof like the Streets of Brentwood people. We should check it out. Maybe they left something useful."

He wrapped an arm around her shoulders and her whole body warmed. "Maybe they left a bed."

Her face flushed and she was glad he couldn't see it. Having fun and joking about sex was still so new. After everything with General Peters she'd thought she'd never have anything to do with men, but Cody was different. He made her feel young and innocent again. Like the girl she could have been, without Peters happening to her. He'd made her see sex was different when there was love involved.

"You know I love you, Cody, don't you?"

"Of course you do. I'm so lovable."

"Don't kid. I'm being serious. I want you to know what you mean to me." She turned so she was looking him in the eye. "What you've done for me. I was broken and you fixed me."

He reached out and wiped a tear off her cheek she hadn't even noticed she'd cried. "You were not broken. That is giving power to that monster. He couldn't break you. You are too strong for that. He stole something from you. He was a thief. Nothing but a stupid thief."

"Wow," she said on an inhale. "That is so deep for a surfer boy."

He smiled. "I love you, Miranda Stevens. For always and forever."

* * *

Cody took a deep breath and held it until his chest ached. He let the air out slowly as his gaze tracked Ran's progress around the dark, empty room. The odors of gas, oil, and sweat lingered in the deserted gas station. When his girlfriend started up the ladder to the roof, he strode over and followed her up the rungs to sunlight.

He went to the edge of the roof and stared southward. The solar panels of the RV yard glittered in the bright sunshine. Just another reminder that help and safety could be so close but so far away in the ZA. Pulling the walkie-talkie off his belt, he pushed the button and tried to get someone to hear him.

"RV yard. Teddy. Seth. Anyone there?"

"This is Teddy. Are you kids okay?"

"Yeah, man. We ran into a cluster at the intersection, so Miranda and I are on the gas station roof, but we're fine. I'll call back if we need you."

"Don't wait too long, Cody. We can be there in minutes."

No way, Jose," he said. "Stay there with the babies. I'll let you know if we can't escape."

"Okay, over and out."

"Over and out," he finished up and turned off the walkie-talkie and attached it to his belt.

He spun around when he didn't hear Ran's breathing at his side. Their gazes locked when he spotted her sprawled in a hammock with a canopy. One leg draped over the side, pushing the hammock slowly, back and forth. Every inch of her sun-kissed skin was bared to him. He swallowed deeply and started whipping off his own clothing and leaving a cloth trail to her side with one stop to shut the trapdoor on the roof and slam the bolt locked. The zombs couldn't climb the ladder, but the undead were only half of their worries.

Ran licked her lips and smiled at him. His heart pounded in his chest. His boots stuck like glue to his feet as his fingers tangled in the laces. With a groan, he ripped them off and flung them behind him as he reached Ran and the hammock.

Perspiration glistened on her long arms and legs. In another time, before the influenza, before the Z virus, she would have been a school athlete. Cross-country runner or track and field member. His erection swelled at the thought of those long legs running across a field or wrapped around his hips.

A lump formed in this throat whenever he thought of what had turned Miranda into the woman she was today. When they talked of the past, she told him of a young schoolgirl, afraid of the zombies, afraid of men, afraid of life. He shook his head. That was not his Ran. The ZA made you live for today, and who they were today was what he wanted to focus on. Not the tormented and abused Miranda and not the spoiled college-boy Cody whining about not finding his mother.

He slid in beside Ran and shut his mind to the scared, man-child he'd been after the Z virus hit and the dead rose. All he'd wanted to do was get home to his mom. Instead, he'd been holed up in a library for months, fighting for every scrap of food he could find and hiding at any sound he heard outside. He'd been ready to end it all when Ran and Seth showed up. One look at Miranda and Cody knew he had a reason to live for.

She snuggled in next to him, her fingers trailing over his naked body. He laughed and he stared at her as her eyebrow rose in question.

"I was just thinking about when we met and it was like a lightning bolt hit my head. Wham! She's the one."

She swatted his arm. "Oh, you. I looked awful back then. Skinny as a little kid and no hair on my head."

"Don't forget your Seth crush." His fingers slid over her soft, brown hair, the strands tangling and twining.

She blushed as she turned and straddled his hips. "That was just a crush. This is more."

"More," he moaned as she slid down on him and her muscles clenched tightly.

"Much more," she groaned as her lips found his and her hips found a rhythm he matched.

She wrapped herself tight around him and it wouldn't have mattered in that moment if the entire zombie population burst through the locked hatch, he wasn't letting go.

CHAPTER TWELVE

Jack and Lila

Commander's Log
Highway 680, Walnut Creek
Short of Objective
Spring, 1 AZ

We are forced to camp for the night mere blocks from destination. Heavy smoke is rising from vicinity of apartment complex where Lila is sure we will find Selena. Will find safe location for the night and hit the complex at dawn.

SHARON, WENT TO GRANDMA'S. LOVE MOM AND DAD.

The words covered the garage door in faded blue letters, the dripping paint long dried out and flaking. Jack stared at them wondering if Sharon found her parents or if the parents made it to grandma's. If they did go, they didn't go in the motor home in the driveway that he and Lila were using for the night.

The front door to the house had stood wide open when they'd slid down the embankment off the freeway. A quick recon with Lila glued to his back showed the house was empty and had been for months, if not longer. No squatters and no zombs.

She'd wanted to use the house until he'd explained it would be the first place renegades would check. Once in the motor home, they'd closed all the shades and settled in. The vehicle smelled neglected and musty, but it would do for the night.

The scent of tomato soup soon pushed the unused smell away. Lila moved slowly around the tiny kitchen, making as little sound as possible. He smiled. Survival skills were easy to learn when real survival was the incentive. He'd seen it enough times in Afghanistan when young soldiers realized what all those drills and endless repetition had been for back in boot camp.

They sat and sipped the soup out of mugs as the day drained away and shadows filled the RV. Lila jumped as an owl hooted nearby. He put his hand on hers and squeezed. When she squeezed back, he yanked his hand away and stood.

"I'll do another check while you get settled. We'll leave at dawn."

"Jack, wait," she said, stopping him with a look in her eyes. "It was just a kiss. It doesn't have to mean anything if you don't want it to."

He fell to his knees in front of her and grasped her arms, pulling her down to the floor with him. "What if I do want it to mean something? What does that make me? You are married to another man. I don't have the right to want anything from you." His voice cracked and his heart stuttered to a stop as her hand rested on his chest and she gazed at him as she had all those years ago.

"Oh, Jack," she whispered, her hand warm on his chest. "You were too good back then and you are definitely too good for this world now."

He reached and pulled her hand away from over his heart. It felt too damned right resting there. "If I was so good. If we were so good. Why did you leave me?"

"You said you didn't want to know why. That it didn't matter." Her eyes swelled with tears and they rolled down her face.

"It does matter," he said, taking his thumb and wiping her tears. "Everything about you and Selena matters now. I was stupid to think otherwise."

She sat back against the couch and stared off into space. "I wanted to be with you."

"But," he interrupted.

"No buts. Let me get this out while you're still willing to listen," she said. "I wanted to be with you. I wanted to tell you we were going to have a baby. But my father did what he always did. He arranged things the way he wanted them."

"You could have come to me," Jack said. "We could have stood up to the old man."

"He threatened to kill you if I didn't let you go,"

she whispered as if her father could still hear what she said and hadn't been dead since the influenza pandemic.

He laughed and then stopped at the look on her face. "You're serious. He threatened to kill me? Did he think he was the mafia or something? Was he going to get a hit man?"

She said nothing. That sobered him like no outpouring of words could have. The man had pulled all their strings like a puppet master and denied him the life he was supposed to have. His fists balled on his thighs. A good thing the man was already dead.

Her pale face and watery eyes hit him right in the gut. He wasn't the only one who'd lost out. "Tell me about Selena."

"You already know her. We were at the RV yard for months," she said.

"No," he said. "Start at the beginning."

He pulled her to his side and placed her head on his shoulder. "Start at the beginning."

"Okay," she said. "It was the easiest pregnancy known to woman, at least that's what my mother said. No morning sickness. The right amount of weight gain. Baby born right on time."

He smiled and rubbed her arm. "Did she do all the baby stuff right on time too?"

She laughed. "Of course she did. Walking, talking, reading, writing. Her first word was dada."

He tensed and Lila sat up with trembling lips and more tears. "I'm sorry."

Jack pulled her back to his side. "Don't be sorry. We'll make up for lost time. We will find her."

"You promise?"

"I promise."

Hours passed as Lila told him every moment of Selena's life so far. He was surprised to hear she was a dancer, since he had worse than two left feet. His drill sergeant had yelled at him enough times during training that he'd trip over his own landmine and get himself killed. He was thrilled to hear she loved sports and played them all. He ached inside for all he'd missed and yearned for all he wanted to experience in her life. He didn't stop Lila's flow of words, but it didn't escape him that her memories were peppered with 'Juan was away on business for that and Juan was gone for that.' The man had been given a gift that Jack would have killed for and he'd squandered it. They would fix that tomorrow.

Failure was not an option. They would find Selena and get her back.

* * *

Lila felt a smile stretch her face as she recalled every moment of her child's life. Selena had been such an easy baby and a bright and wonderful child. No, was a wonderful child, she corrected herself silently. Her daughter was out there, and with Jack's help, they would all be together soon.

"You should have seen her face when we took the training wheels off her bike," she continued for Jack. "Not a wobble at all. She laughed and sped down the bike path, her long hair flying, and her legs going like a machine. I had to yell and yell to get her to turn around and come back. I was afraid she would just keep on going forever until she was out of sight."

The tears came out of nowhere. The picture in her mind of Selena just going and going on her bike until she disappeared was too real. What if she didn't get her back? What if Juan had done something with her? What if he'd killed her in spite?

She yanked herself out of Jack's arms and started pawing through her backpack, throwing things right and left. His arms came around her and she shrugged them off.

"What are you looking for?" His hands held her arms gently.

"I have to find Selena's picture. I know I put it in here," she said, sobs making her voice break.

Finally, her fingers felt the edges of the tattered photo and she pulled it out of the backpack. Her hand trembled slightly as her fingertips slid over the surface of her daughter's last school picture. She'd given into Lila's begging and worn a dress for picture day. The muted peach color made her skin glow and her blonde hair had shined with streaks of summer-bleached lightness.

Jack pulled her gently back against him and she accepted the warmth and comfort. She tried to put her fears into words for him.

"What if he killed her?"

The words hung out there as Jack's face hardened along with his voice. "You are never to give up. You are her mother. You would know if she were dead. In here."

His fingers touched between her breasts. It should have startled her. It should have felt sexual. But it didn't. It felt comforting. Selena was in her heart and so was Jack.

Yes, she would know in her soul. A piece of her would die with Selena. The glow would flicker out and it hadn't. The glow of hope and love and knowing her child was alive somewhere was still there.

CHAPTER THIRTEEN

Paul, Suz, and Josh

Paul Luther's Log
On River Road (has a highway number, but River Road since I was a kid)
Spring, 1 AZ

The demolished bridge was the first of three such detonations. The river people have made their point crystal clear—leave us alone. All hopes are pinned on Ryde being more welcoming. We've had no news recently from the recon group sent on earlier, but we've had neither the time nor the skill to set up the ham radio on the move. The boys of Rogue Vantage have reassured us they've learned to use it and can do so when we reach our destination.

The brakes squealed as Josh stood on them. Paul's hand shot to the dashboard and pushed. The

Humvee jerked to a halt. The road was gone. Just gone. At least twenty feet of levee and asphalt was gone, with the river gushing into the fields on the other side.

He slapped the dash and slammed back into his seat. "If it isn't one damned thing, it's another. Is a little help too much to ask for?"

Paul turned to Josh. "I'll tell the others. Once I get them moved back, you follow. I want us at least fifty yards back. Then we'll see what we've got. I want everyone out of the vehicles. A car is replaceable, people aren't."

He opened the door and stepped out. Moving down the line of vehicles he let the others know what was going on and to get out of the Humvee. At the last one he was faced with a million questions from the boys of Rogue Vantage.

He held up his hand and they fell silent, even Dylan, which was a miracle all on its own. "I don't know if it was an accident or on purpose. I don't know if we can get across. I do know you boys are staying back here. If the levee starts to go, fall back. That's an order."

His heart swelled as they all saluted him with precision that would have made a drill sergeant proud. He ruffled Dylan's hair and strode back to the gap in the road. He and Josh moved forward as Suz pulled their backpacks out of the Humvee.

One glance painted an impossible picture. The flow had become a small river on its own, they were not crossing here; Humvee or not. A rumble built from the other side of the break. A flash of orange filtered through the trees at the curve of the road until a large tractor turned the corner. A large man drove the machine with a load of boulders in the front bucket. Boulders he poured down into the break with a boom and a crash. As the bucket dropped, the man spotted them and his eyes bulged in his head as if he hadn't seen live people in a while.

The man turned the machine off and jumped down to the pavement. He rushed to his side of the gap. The man was enormous. He might even have Teddy Ridgewood beat in the muscle department. A grin broke across his freckled face as he pulled off his hard hat and revealed a head full of bright-red curls.

"People. You're alive people. Not the bad ones," he yelled across the break.

Paul smiled back. "Yes, alive people. Not the zombies."

He held his hands out as if they were puppies or other small animals learning to sit. "Stay. Don't leave. I'll fix this real fast." His yells carried over the rushing water no problem at all.

The big man hopped back into the tractor and turned it around and disappeared around the corner. Paul looked at Josh and his husband just shook his head and started laughing. Josh's smile hadn't been seen enough lately. He grasped his arm and squeezed.

"Maybe our luck is changing," Paul said.

"Maybe someone is listening after all," Josh added, placing his hand over Paul's.

Paul turned and got back to business. The Humvee were moved back and the group had gathered near the back of them. He spotted Suz's bright-blonde hair among them. He slapped Josh's arm. "Let's get everyone updated."

They joined the group. The doctor and the twins stood in front of the rear Humvee, with the boys of Rogue Vantage sitting on the hood out of the way. The rest had formed a semicircle. Paul leaned against the vehicle and picked up one of the girls.

"There's a break in the levee road. But a man from the other side is already fixing it. Once he pours enough boulders into the gap, we should be able to cross and help him. We only saw the one man, but we all know to be cautious by now. I'll talk for the group and get Intel from him before we share any of our own. Hopefully he knows what happened to the recon group as well. They had to go through here and the break looks fresh."

* * *

Suz stretched and moaned as her back cracked in all the right places. What had seemed like a small repair had grown into eighteen hours of watching rocks pour into the water. For the first few hours, people had watched each batch of boulders drop and listened to the clatter of stone on stone. The young boys of Rogue Vantage stayed the longest, until even their young boy excitement for heavy machinery was done and over.

By the middle of the night, the rocks were almost even with the road and the last load had been gravel to even out the patch of the levee break. Paul walked toward her from the dark. His gait one she would know anywhere.

He leaned over and his lips found hers. He tasted of salty sweat and a flavor uniquely his own. The kiss deepened and his tongue slid along hers. A moan broke from her. This man could get her motor running with something as simple as a kiss or a touch.

"I'm going to go with Fisher to get a final load of tar to seal the road," he muttered once they broke for air. "Josh will stay here with you. I want to get a lay of the land before we all just drive down the road to God knows what."

"Fisher?"

"Brandon Fisher. That's what he says his name is." He smiled.

"What?"

"Nothing. It's just that he says his name repeatedly, like he might forget it if he doesn't keep saying it. He's either severely autistic or it's an act. After all this group's been through, I can't risk it if it's just a con game."

She bit her lip. "Can't you take Josh with you?"

He gasped her arms, his hands rubbing up and down them. "You and Josh need to protect the others. Especially the kids. I'll be fine."

Her heart pounded. She couldn't let those be their last words. Where had that rotten idea come from? She mentally pushed it away and locked it in the cellar of her thoughts.

"I love you," she whispered.

"I love you, too."

With a quick kiss, Paul turned and walked away. Her gaze followed as he strode over the pile of gravel and hopped up on the tractor with Fisher. She wrapped her arms across her chest. His smile seemed so sincere, but hadn't they all? The cult leaders. The serial killers. The sociopaths and psychopaths. They all had smiles that said 'trust me,' didn't they?

Trying to bury the thoughts, Suz grabbed her brother and they did rounds of the other vehicles and the groups sleeping in them. Joseph and Doctor Shannon had gathered the young boys and the small girl twins and put them in the middle Humvee. As Suz walked up to the vehicle, Joseph Jones walked around from the rear.

Suz caught a moment of sadness on the man's face before he wiped it away with a small smile. The loss of his partner, Robert had torn the man's heart out. Her breath caught at the thought of losing Paul. She would lose a part of herself if that happened.

"Repairs done yet?" Joseph asked.

She brought herself back to the present with a snap. "They went to get a load of tar for the repair. Don't know how long tar takes to harden, but I would think sometime tomorrow morning. Guess that would be this morning."

"They? You mean Paul and the ginger?"

She laughed. "Seems the big man's name is Brandon Fisher, or so Paul says."

"Do we trust him?" Joseph's smile disappeared and a grim look came into his eyes.

"Paul's not sure yet. He seems honest, but we can't tell anymore, you know."

Her thoughts traveled to the devastation of The Streets of Brentwood mall by General Peters and his zombie army, to the deviousness of Reverent Bennett and his twisted flock of followers. She sighed. *Couldn't they just find a safe haven? Couldn't anyone be good in this apocalyptic world? Evil wasn't supposed to win, was it?*

As if he read her thoughts, her brother wrapped an arm around her shoulders and pulled her in tight. "The man seems okay. Paul asked him about the recon group and he said the brown men came through here a while ago."

"Brown men?" Suz stared at Josh.

"Pretty sure he meant Charlie and his sons, Zach and Tyler. Brown hair, brown skin, and mostly brown clothes if I remember."

Suz nodded. Paul had said the man might be autistic. Maybe to him they were brown men. Her breath came out in a sigh. Did it mean the man was honest or was he just good enough to give them little tidbits to drag them along?

Her head came up at the rumble of the return of the tractor. She spotted Paul in the cab as the bucket came down and dumped a load of steaming black tar over the rocks and gravel. Her heartbeat returned to normal and her lungs filled as she took a long, much-needed breath.

Her hand grasped the strap on her rifle as she realized the dumping of the tar put Paul on one side and the rest of them on the other. She didn't take a deep breath or let go of the strap until Paul and Fisher placed boards over the hot mess and walked over.

Her husband could have a poker face when needed, but his smile seemed genuine while he talked to the redheaded man. She put a matching smile on her face and watched as Josh had one to match. She knew the next few minutes were a test of the other man's intentions.

Paul came up to her and took her hand to pull her toward Fisher. Josh took a step and moved behind her. She put her hand out as Paul introduced them.

"This is my wife, Suz."

Her smile grew as he swiped off his hard hat and wiped his hand on his dusty jeans. "Ma'am," he whispered, shaking her hand.

Paul placed his hand on her brother's shoulder. "And this is my husband, Josh."

The man lost his smile for a moment and a furrow cut across this brow as if he were doing some deep thinking.

Suz held her breath as the big man looked down at Paul. "Aren't you supposed to have just one of those? My mama said you get a husband or wife. She didn't say nothing about having both at the same time."

"We have a friend, Emily who says in this new world we get to be anything we want now and I wanted this to be my family," Paul explained as Suz waited to see what happened next, afraid that even with her, Josh, and Paul they might not be enough to take on this lumberjack of a man if he decided he were angry with their family setup.

A bigger smile broke out on the man's face, shoving all his freckles into a solid section of pinkish-red skin. He reached out and took Josh's hand and shook it. "Well, I'll be. Maybe that was what Billy and Grace and Tabitha were talking about."

"Who are they?" Paul asked.

"My friends from down river. They come and trade sometimes because I got goats and make cheese and they got chickens and have eggs."

Paul squeezed her hand and she squeezed back. Along with her husband's safe and quick return from a location down the road, out of sight, maybe things would be better for their group.

CHAPTER FOURTEEN

Jack and Lila

Commander's Log
Objective Reached
Apartment complex
Walnut Creek, California
Spring, 1 AZ

The sunlight burst through the thinly-leaved trees and coated the devastation in a bright light. Smoke still wafted to the blue sky in wisps of gray and white. Jack placed a hand above a smoldering pile of embers.

"A day or two at the most," he told Lila as they skirted the edge of the apartment complex.

He shook his head. Why would people choose to stay here? The complex offered no defenses other than the K-rails placed across the roadway that they'd hopped over once they reached the apartments where Lila was sure Selena was being held.

No moans filled the morning air, but their passage through the land of the living was clear. The corpses on the ground had chunks of them missing. The single bullet holes in the foreheads implied someone had been alive long enough to make the undead dead.

The unnatural silence continued as they hugged the building and made their way across the grounds. At one time it had been a beautiful setting, sitting on the edge of a creek. Tall trees shaded the area and cooled the air. A breeze rustling in the higher branches was the only sound other than their boot heels scraping against the pavement.

Their footsteps echoed across a metal bridge bringing them to the front of the buildings. The area was cleared of any cars, making the wooden stage stand out. The cluster of the dead was heaviest in this area as if an event had been going on when the skinbag horde attacked.

Bile rose in his throat, and Jack spit to the side to clear it. Naked women and young girls carpeted the stage, along with their blood and guts. He didn't need the hand-painted banner above to know this had been a slave auction. The bright blue lettering confirmed it.

The buzz of flies grew as they approached the stage. Lila gripped his hand and squeezed. The tremors in her body filtered through to him. He cataloged the death and destruction in his head and his heart sank. One little girl couldn't have survived this massacre.

Lila yanked her hand away and pounded up the stairs to the platform. Her eyes swept the area, her head swiveling back and forth, searching for one blonde-haired child. He watched as she stood up and inhaled deeply.

"She isn't here," she said.

"We'll search the whole place," he told her, taking her hand again after she came down the stairs.

"If she got bit and turned, we'll never know." Her voice shook and he could see the tears coming next. He had to get her to pull herself together.

"We'll check every body. If she's dead, we'll at least know."

She nodded and continued to look as they strode on across the pavement and scanned every overgrown garden. A moan sounded from the edge of the creek embankment.

Jack pulled his knife and Lila swiftly followed. He smiled at the determined look on her face. She may never be a zombie hunter, but she could protect herself if need be. That's all he could ask of her.

"Help me," a male voice whispered from among the overgrown weeds.

Jack held a hand up and moved forward. He stopped at a tattooed arm he'd recognize anywhere. They'd found Juan Morales. Or, at least, what was left of him.

***

She didn't know what she expected to feel, but this sadness swamping her wasn't on the list of emotions expected when they finally found the man who'd tried to kill her and stolen her child.

Lila searched the area around her husband, but no young girl, blonde or otherwise, lay nearby. She squatted by his side. Blood was everywhere. It coated the dirt he sprawled across and covered him from head to toe. Several fingers were missing on his hand and his ribs showed through his torn shirt where sections of flesh were gone.

For years she'd resented Juan. For taking her away from Jack. For not being Jack. Once she'd finally let Jack go in her heart, she and Juan had at least reached a comfortable understanding in their marriage. She'd hated him over the years, at no time more than the nightmare time at the toxic church with Reverend Bennett. But she'd never wished this torture on her husband. Soon to be her deceased husband. She had no doubts about that. The man had moments to live and if he'd ever felt anything for her, he would clear his conscience and tell her where Selena was.

"Juan," she whispered.

His head turned and he stared blankly at her, the beginning of the film that would cover his eyes starting to form. "You made it."

"Yes. I'm here. Where is Selena?"

He smiled. A cough rattled in his chest and exploded out of him with a gush of blood through his teeth and over his lips. He calmed and smiled at her again.

"Wouldn't you like to know?"

Heat filled her face and her chest. She grabbed a hold of his shirt and shook him, yelling into his bloody face. "Damn you, Juan Morales. Tell me where my child is."

His back arched, his eyes rolled back in his head and he seized. His body jerked and thumped on the ground.

Lila grabbed him until it passed. "Don't you dare die on me yet, Juan. Where is our child?"

The man stared up at Jack standing behind her. "She isn't *our* child, is she, Commander? Now, that little puta is no one's child. I sold her."

Lila fell back on her butt, her bloody hands held out in front of her. "You sold her?" she whispered. "Juan, how could you?"

"Easily. I got a car and twenty gallons of gas for her. You know what that is worth nowadays?"

She moved forward, grabbing Juan's hand where his missing fingers used to be. A scream tore from his throat. She ignored it, squeezing harder.

"Where is my child?"

He stared at her, tears of pain mixing in watery, bloody tracks down his face. "I'll never tell you, slut. You'll never know where she is, whether she is dead or alive. Payback's a bitch, bitch."

His voice trailed off, his eyes filmed over, and a moan built in his throat as the thing that had been Juan tried to sit up and reach for her.

"I should leave you like this," she cried as she

pushed the knife into the base of his skull and the thing collapsed to the ground.

She fell back and the tears poured down her face. A moan grew and she stopped when she realized it was coming from her own throat. Strong arms wrapped around her and pulled her up. His voice whispered in her ear. "He sold her. That means she isn't here, lying dead somewhere."

Hope blossomed in her heart at Jack's words. And died just as quickly. "But we don't know who he sold her to, or where they went."

"Search him. Maybe there is something in his pockets. With the dead on the platform and the crowds here, I'm thinking the auction was going on when the undead hit the place."

They dug through his pockets. Jack scooped up car keys and put them in his own pocket. The money was useless and Lila let it fall to the ground and blow away. Out of the corner of her eye she spotted a bloody scrap of white paper a few inches from Juan's hand. It could be garbage, but she snatched it up anyway.

Her cry of joy brought Jack to her side. "It's Juan's. I recognize his writing. It's a Bill of Sale."

"I can't believe he sold her," Jack added. "He wasn't a great guy but I never would have believed he'd stoop that low."

"He did it to hurt me," Lila said, her eyes scanning the rest of the page. "He sold her to Toby Hill of the land below Mount Diablo."

She shook her head. "The land below Mount Diablo. That could be a million places," she said, her mind traveling to the large mountain and all the land nearby spread out in all four compass directions. Hell, that covered at least three or four good-sized cities. The tears came and flooded her vision. They would never find Selena.

Jack's arms came around her and surrounded her with his strength. She sniffled and sucked up her tears. She was done with crying. It didn't solve anything and it didn't get anything done. Time to pull up her big-girl panties, as her friend, Karin used to say. She was probably out in the world somewhere. If anyone could survive the end of the world, it would be Karin.

"No. No, you bastardos. I will not be your breakfast."

Jack grabbed Lila's hand and they ran toward the flood of Spanglish coming from an apartment nearby. The moans of the undead and their pounding of fists on a door made them easy to find.

Lila watched his back as Jack waded through the group, his knife flashing in the sunlight. The only sound in the hallway his slightly heavy breathing and the thumps of the skinbags as they hit the floor in a graceless heap.

"Ma'am?" Jack spoke at the door. "They're all taken care of. Can you open the door?"

"How do I know you don't want to kill me or rape me? Angela Ramos is no one's fool."

"Let me," Lila said as she stepped over the dead and stood by the door. "Tia Angela, es Lila Morales. Can we come in, por favor?"

Jack raised an eyebrow as the multiple locks clicked open on the door and a small Hispanic woman filled the small crack. A smile brightened her face as she swept the door open to let them in. Lila felt Jack's hand on her back as they moved in quickly and Angela shut the door with no sound except for the turning of locks.

Lila looked around the darkened room. She jumped as Angela hugged her tight enough to take her breath away. The small woman started jabbering away in Spanish faster than Lila could keep up, although she did catch Juan's name and several colorful curses in there.

"Slow down, Tia. You know I only know a little Spanish."

The woman grabbed her hands and squeezed until the blood left them. "Where were you, mija? A mother is supposed to protect her baby?"

Lila gasped and would have fallen to the floor if Jack hadn't caught her and pulled her to the couch. She fell into the cushions and as if she'd fallen into a deep mine of darkness, all around her was black.

Angela sat beside her and rubbed her hands with her own. She had so many questions and she didn't know where to start. The most important question fell from her lips.

"Did you see Selena?"

"Yes, the niña was here. But that perro, Juan, sold her. The little one was so afraid."

Her heart broke. "Why didn't you stop him? Why didn't Tio do anything? Why didn't Abraham stop Juan?"

"Abraham? May Dios have mercy on his soul because I don't. My husband is the one who arranged all the auctions. He started selling our children into slavery months ago."

Her mouth dropped open. Abraham had always been the patriarch of the Morales family. He'd taken care of all of them well. He'd been a hard man, but not an evil one. What had all the devastation done to him to turn a good man bad?

The paper crinkled in her hand. She held it up to Angela. "Who is Toby Hill? Where can we find him? This paper says he has Selena. He has my baby." Her voice cracked and she coughed to clear it.

Angela shook her head and tears fell down her dark, wrinkled face. "Don't go there, mija. The little one is lost to you. Better that you never find her. The young ones don't last long when the men get a hold of them."

Lila stared at the woman. Her dark eyes were dead. They held memories of worse things than the undead roaming the Earth. She was getting a clearer picture of what this enclave had become than she wanted.

Her gaze swept to Jack standing by the coffee table. His face was stone-cold but his eyes held a fire she took strength from. "We will find Selena and get her back."

That was all Lila needed to hear. She turned back to Juan's aunt. "Tia, you have to help us. This man could be anywhere. How do we find him?"

Angela ran shaking hands through her gray-streaked hair, pulling it from the braid to fall around her face. "Toby Hill lives by Mountainside, a gated community they built in the shadow of Mount Diablo, on the edge of Concord. That is all I know. I've never been there."

"Is there anyone else here, ma'am?" Jack's deep voice rumbled in the room. "Are you all alone?"

Lila sighed. She knew she should care about the lonely old woman, but a dark side in her heart burned at the woman just letting the men sell not only Selena, but the other young women and girls they had in their care. She didn't know what Angela could have done against the male-dominated center of their group, but she could have tried something, anything.

Like you tried at the church. Her inner voice mocked her for taking Juan's abuse and not leaving there with Selena. She ripped her mind away from the past she couldn't change.

"Thank you for your concern," Angela answered in the quiet room. "But I don't have long to be alone." The woman pulled up the side of her dark blouse and exposed a deep bite mark to them.

It wasn't long, but she wasn't alone as Lila sat beside her and held her hand until her breathing stopped. Jack stepped forward and made sure she didn't turn.

He put his hand out to Lila. "Let's go get our child."

CHAPTER FIFTEEN

Cody, Miranda, and April

Ran's Journal
Returned to the RV yard
Spring, 1 AZ (Will be Autumn 1 before we ever leave!)

The zombs moved on after dark and Cody and I were able to get back to the others. This morning we were supposed to leave but one of the twins was fussy all night and we are letting Emily and babies rest today. Again. No babies. Ever.

The hairs on Ran's neck rose. She whipped her head around and found April leaning over her shoulder trying to read her writings. Reaching out, she slammed the notebook shut.

"Personal space, chickie."

The young woman giggled like a little girl. "Oops, my bad."

Really! Who talked like that anymore? Maybe it had been okay when your greatest fear was missing a test.

She sighed. And counted to ten in her head. If anyone should have sympathy for the woman's turmoil, it should be her. She might have more empathy for what she'd gone through if April hadn't tried to latch onto Cody and acted as if she was thirteen instead of almost twenty.

Ran snatched up the notebook and pencil and threw them into her go bag. She sniffed deep as she caught a whiff of pancakes and smiled.

April smiled back. "Came to get you. Michelle is making the last of the blueberry pancakes. If you don't hurry, that guy of yours will eat them all."

Her smile grew. April had acknowledged Cody was hers. She swung an arm around the woman's shoulders and pulled her in close.

"He better save some for me."

At the picnic table she took the spot next to Cody and watched with amazement as April seated herself on Ran's other side instead of snuggling up to her boyfriend. Maybe their time away from the group had clued the chickie into how things stood.

The bench on the other side groaned as Teddy took his seat. April giggled and Ran allowed herself a small smile. The man really was a mountain of muscles. That he had been a bodyguard pre-Z came as no surprise.

He scooted over a bit when Seth came to the table with plates and utensils. Michelle arrived seconds later with a platter of pancakes that the group made gone in short order.

"Did Emily get some?" Seth asked about his wife.

Michelle nodded and attacked her own short stack of pancakes. "I took hers to the trailer first. She needs to eat for three."

She swallowed. "Little Jed is sleeping well. His fever is gone. We should be able to leave in the morning, no problem at all."

Michelle tried to sweep her hair out of her eyes and grimaced at the out-of-control short ends she wasn't used to yet. Teddy handed her a bandana that she rolled and placed across her forehead, tying it in the back.

"Thank you," she whispered to the large man. A blush washed across his dark face.

"I'll get used to it," she said, looking across at April.

The woman shuddered beside her and looked down at her plate. Ran nudged her with a shoulder. "Just makes it easier to hunt zombies."

April shuddered harder against her side. "Why can't we just leave the monsters alone?"

Michelle spoke from the other side of the table. "Because the monsters won't leave us alone. It's us or them."

"But they're dead. Don't they have to fall apart someday?" April said, looking up.

"Not all monsters are undead," Michelle replied, gathering plates and utensils and getting up from the table.

April started crying and Ran looked around, left with nothing to do but put an arm across her shoulders and squeeze tight. The bench moved slightly as Cody got up and gathered the rest of the stuff on the table. A squeal issued from the other bench as Teddy and Seth beat a fast retreat.

She sighed. A few female tears and men became babies. Trying to change the subject, she racked her brain until she hit on the trip tomorrow.

"Are you excited to leave here?"

April stared at her with shock in her eyes. "How can I be excited? We have cement walls to protect us and instead we're going out there."

"We'll protect you."

The woman shook her head. "Don't make promises you can't keep. You and Cody went down the street yesterday and you could have been eaten and never returned."

Ran moved back and took April's hands in her own. "We will protect you. With our lives. You are one of us now."

April's smile grew as fresh tears ran down her face. She leaned forward and gave Ran a deep, warm kiss.

She jumped back. "Hey, I don't swing that way."

A deep chuckle emerged from April. "I don't either. But if I liked girls, I would love you."

Ran laughed and put her arms around the other woman. "Let's just be sisters. I've never had one."

"Me either," April whispered back.

* * *

Cody watched from a distance as Ran and April went through a gamut of emotions; tears, laughter, smiles, and a hot chick-on-chick kiss that pumped blood to his groin and led to the universal male vision of two girls and a guy.

The dream whisked out of sight at Seth's loud words in his ear.

"We have work to do, dude."

He blushed and turned away from the women at the picnic table and brought his mind back to the tasks at hand. They were to leave in the morning and there were still decisions to make of what they were taking and what they would be forced to leave.

"I think everyone should have several weapons. As many as they each can comfortably carry," Teddy stated as he piled their meager arsenal on a spread-out blanket.

He thought back to the two women. "What do we give April? She doesn't know how to use anything yet."

Seth went into the armory trailer and came back with aluminum poles. "We'll add some blades to these for her. For Emily as well. They won't have to do close fighting and they can push the skinbags away if nothing else."

Teddy grinned. "Miss Emily is gonna miss that crossbow of hers."

Seth smiled. "She can't use it and carry a baby too. We'll let Ran carry the crossbow. She's gotten good with it in the past few months."

He scratched his head. "Who is carrying the other little one?"

Seth pointed at Cody. "What? Why me?"

"You and Ran will protect the babies, Emily, and April. Teddy and I will be able to roam further and deal with skinbags and any other troubles before they even get to you."

He grimaced at the thought of carrying a wiggling, crying baby, but Seth's plan sounded like the right thing to do for the group. But, man. A baby?

Seth patted him on the back. "I'm trusting you with my child and his safety. It's not something I do lightly."

Standing taller, he smiled. "I'll guard him with my life."

"I know you will," Seth replied, his eyes watering as he turned toward the weapons pile.

The rest of the day passed in a whirlwind of activity. By the time the sun set Cody was more than ready for his bed, especially since there was no telling the next time they would have a bed and the privacy to use it.

He opened the door to their trailer and stepped up inside. Flickering candles sat on every flat surface. Turning in a circle, he spotted lights from the other trailers. So, the electricity was still working, just not in use in their trailer.

All thoughts of the outside world dimmed as the bedroom door opened and Miranda stepped out wearing a T-shirt and nothing else. Her soft, brown hair was slicked back and wet from a shower. Ran hadn't bothered to dry off at all, as the fabric of her shirt clung to her damp body.

Cody swallowed and swallowed again around the lump in his throat. His woman was beautiful. Inside and out. And she was all his. He whipped off his shirt and flung it to the floor, his pants following in seconds. His erection pulsated against the cloth of his underwear.

"Dude," he whispered.

Her eyebrow shot up and she grasped her breasts. "Really? Dude?"

"Dudette," he stammered back.

"Miranda," he choked out as she slithered toward him, dropped to her knees, and kissed him through his underwear. He went from hard to stone hard in a nanosecond.

Her fingers rubbed up and down his length and he grabbed her under her arms and yanked her up. "I would rather do this in bed. A nice, comfortable bed."

"We can do this here and in bed," she whispered, just before she whipped his erection out and knelt in front of him. Her hot lips slid over the flesh of his erection in a silky, sexy glide.

Between her lips and fingers sliding up and down he was unmanned in seconds. His yell echoed in the trailer.

He caught her up in his arms and her legs wrapped around his hips. He carried her to the bed and proceeded to prove her right. He proved her right several times.

CHAPTER SIXTEEN

Paul, Suz, and Josh

Paul Luther's Log
Fisher farm
River Road (New base still further down the road)
Spring, 1 AZ

"It's not as bad as it looks, Suz," Paul said with a smile. "We can help Brandon and his friends set up a compound and then we'll be on our way."

Suz spread out her arms as if to encompass the whole flat land surrounding them and huffed out a breath. "There's no way to protect this place. Only God in his kindness has protected the guy so far."

Paul looked around at the well-run farm and the hills of dirt the man had piled around his house. As a barricade it sucked. Why the clueless man hadn't been swarmed by a horde of zombies by now was anybody's guess.

Paul wrapped his arms around his wife. "We can help the man for a few days. Ryde is just down the road. If it hadn't been for Fisher, we wouldn't have gotten across the levee break."

His gaze swept past Fisher's farm to the flooded fields beyond. Everything out beyond the farm's stables under two to three feet of water. Brandon's farm was spared by the slight mound the house and outbuildings sat on.

He turned Suz around and took her hand as they walked from the house to the barn. Sweeping his arm out, he told her of taking the dirt and surrounding the house, the barn, and the stables to corral the area into a defensible position.

Josh walked up and gave them both a hug as Paul finished. "We'll make trenches in reverse, defending the area from above. Use the roofs as well. Some two-by-fours, along with plywood and we'll have guard towers."

Suz punched his arm. "What is this *we* you speak of?"

He smiled. "Sorry. Sometimes I get carried away with army stuff."

Josh laughed. "Our own GI Joe."

They were laughing together as Brandon trotted up to them with a scraggly cat draped over his arm like a damp rag. What fur they could see was matted and dirty, a little of the marmalade coloring peeking through.

"This is Tabby," Brandon announced, holding up the cat and presenting her to the group. "But don't tell Tabitha I named the cat after her. When she gets mad, she gets really mad."

Paul nodded. "That's one of your friends down the road, right? Will we get to meet them?"

The man looked at his watch and moved his lips as he talked to himself. "Today is Tuesday. They'll come with fresh eggs because it is Tuesday."

He racked his brain trying to come up with a not suspicious way to ask about numbers of unknowns when Suz spoke up.

"How many friends do you have down the river?" Her smile and friendly voice got the man talking. He really needed to work on his people skills. Not everything was us versus them.

The man's brow furrowed and he held up fingers. "There's Billy. He's my best friend. Then Grace, his wife. They have a baby with no name yet last time I saw them. And Tabitha."

He blushed as he said the last woman's name. Suz reached and patted him on the arm. "Is that all?"

"They did have more people at Billy's house but his mama died and bit his father and a couple of his brothers. After that, it was a mess until just my friends are left."

The man looked on the verge of tears. Paul steered the questions in a new direction. "Would they come live here if we helped you protect it from the skinbags?"

"Skinbags?"

Paul shook his head. "Sorry, zombies. Skinbags is just what our group usually calls them."

"You have a group? More than these people?"

The man's face brightened up.

"We hope we do," he explained. "The men you saw were headed to the Ryde Hotel to be our new home and we had some friends we had to leave back in Oakley that we hope make it by river to the hotel."

His thoughts caught at Jack and Lila searching for Selena. He held a small flicker of hope in his heart, but his brain said they would probably never know what happened to their former commander or the lost child.

Suz squeezed beside him, wrapping her arm around his waist. Between her on one side and Josh's warmth on the other he felt all the support he needed.

"If you leave, I won't have that repel sound you're using," Brandon spoke up, looking sad and dejected.

"Do you have a computer? Flash drives?"

Brandon scratched his head, and then smiled. "Tabitha has all that stuff. She was a computer geek at the computer store, you know, the ones with their own cars. I can call her and tell her to bring one when they come."

Paul's mouth dropped open and he was sure Suz's and Josh's did as well. "You have a phone? That works?"

The man nodded so hard Paul thought his head would fall off his shoulders. "Billy worked for the phone company before the flu came. He helped us have phones from here to Ryde and Locke. He explained it to me one time, but I've done forgot, something about the hub is at his house and Grace works it."

He caught onto the one important word in that rambling speech. "You have phones to Ryde? What about the hotel?"

Brandon nodded again and Paul's breath caught in his throat. "Old John lives there by himself. Used to be a Young John, but he died with the flu."

"Will Old John be upset that our men came to the hotel to use it?" Suz asked in a whisper, her fear for Charlie and his boys plain on her face.

The man nibbled on his lip and scratched his head again. "I don't think so, but let's ask him."

They followed Fisher into his house. It had clearly been the home of an older couple. Lace doilies covered the arms of the couches and the overstuffed, comfortable chairs. Knickknacks of porcelain farm animals covered every flat surface. Dust eddies followed in the big man's wake, but the rest of the house was neat and tidy. With the wind off the river, dust was probably an endless battle the guy had lost.

Brandon walked over to a phone on the wall and picked up the handset. Paul hadn't seen a phone like that in a long time. The man tapped the hang-up bar a few times and Paul had a memory of his grandmother talking about party lines and sharing a phone with neighbors.

"Grace, it's Brandon. Can you get me Old John at the Ryde Hotel?"

He turned to Paul with the phone held to his

ear. "It's ringing."

"John, it's Brandon Fisher, out here at the Fisher farm. Do you have some strangers there?" He looked over at Paul. "Names?"

"Charlie Muncy and his sons, Zach and Tyler."

Fisher relayed the names. For a moment, there was nothing but a bunch of monotone answers to obviously John's questions on the other end.

"Yes."

"Yes."

"No."

"Not infected. Good people."

"Because, I say so, that's why."

"Okay."

Brandon turned around. "He went to get your men. He had to untie them. But it's okay now, because I told him they were friends."

Paul stepped up and took the phone, wondering how many men it took to take on Muncy and his boys. He was greeted with silence on the line.

"I thought you said there was just Old John there?"

"Yep, just him. He don't need no one else, him being Special Forces and all."

He groaned as a voice came on the phone. *Great, they'd have to deal with Rambo.*

"Charlie, is that you?"

"No, this is Tyler. Dad and Zach are still tied up." The boy's voice held a tinge of disgust and frustration. "But the guy is untying them now. Here's Dad."

"Paul, you didn't tell me we needed Delta Force to take this hotel," Charlie mumbled.

"Sorry about that. Is it all cool now?"

"Seems to be. The old man says we're welcome now and make ourselves at home." He groaned. "That would have been nice a couple of days ago instead of sleeping tied up on concrete. I'm not as young as I used to be."

Paul smiled. Charlie might moan he was old, but he was as tough as they came. He couldn't wait to meet the one guy who took him on and won.

"Will we see you soon?"

"In a few days. We owe the guy here a favor and we're going to fortify his farm before we move on."

"See you then, Commander."

The man hung up before he could correct the guy. He wasn't the commander. That was Jack's job. He was just the temp and he didn't want anyone to forget that.

* * *

Josh stared as Paul hung up the phone. As amazed as he was with the idea of phones still working and communicating with others, he didn't miss his husband's grim face and his sad eyes. Paul thought he was so stoic, but he was only human like the rest of them.

He ran his fingers through his hair and grimaced at the grimy, greasy strands. He shook his head at the long strands. Pretty soon he'd need to tie it back. The thought of long hair and summer around the corner had him determined to find the nearest pair of scissors. He glanced at Paul's short buzz cut and smiled. He wasn't willing to lose that much hair.

A clap of hands brought him back to the present. He knew that look on Paul's face. The man was never happier than when he was doing army shit. He groaned. Heavy digging was in his future, he just knew it.

He'd been right. Although, most of the digging was done by Brandon and his tractor, with Paul doing the directing and Josh and Joseph doing the heavy work. By mid afternoon, they had a good start to earthworks surrounding part of the house and barn. It would take another good day to complete it around the stables as well. Fisher let the goats out once the heavy machinery was turned off.

Josh took a handkerchief out of his pocket and wiped his sweaty face as a truck pulled up the driveway and stopped. A young man and two young women stepped out, one carrying a bundled baby.

Fisher rushed over to greet his friends. He and Billy, he assumed, shook hands and slapped backs. The big man hugged the woman with the baby and then he just stood and stared at the other one. Even Josh found himself staring. The woman had long brown hair down past her waist and a body that must have stopped traffic when there was traffic to stop. She could give Suz a run for her money in the looks department.

Fisher leaned down and whispered something to her and she nodded with a blush. The guy picked her up and swung her around.

His yells of "she said yes," heard all around the yard.

After a quick conversation with the two other young people, Josh noted they all nodded and smiled and looked up at the big guy. His grin was brighter than the sun heating up the dirt-filled yard. They all hugged and kissed and moved up the rest of the driveway as a group.

Paul came over and draped an arm around his shoulders. "I'm sorry you didn't get to have me make it all official like that, like I did with Suz."

Josh shrugged. "I was such a jerk back then, I probably would have said no."

He leaned over and kissed Josh on the cheek. "I'd like to think I could have gotten you to say yes," his husband whispered, turning and walking away to greet the young people.

Josh followed with a much slower stride, musing that thought. Knowing Paul, he just might have said yes, if he'd been asked.

CHAPTER SEVENTEEN

Cody, Miranda, and April

Ran's Journal
RV Yard
Last Day (fingers crossed)
Spring, 1 AZ

Finally! We are leaving this place and moving on.
More later tonight.

Ran rushed to shove the notebook into her backpack. The rest of the group had gathered at the gate to start on their journey. They'd gone over the plan last night. She and Michelle would protect Emily and one twin and Cody and the other twin. Seth and Teddy would be outlaying scouts. All that left was April to learn to protect and kill along the way.

She scanned the area as she strode to the gate to make sure they were leaving nothing of survival value behind. A smile curved on her face at Cody with a baby slung to his chest, a protective hand cradling the little one's head.

"I expect you to have my and the little dude's back out there," he whispered to her.

She kissed his lips and peeked at Jed's sleeping face. "Looks like he is out for the count."

"I think Seth slipped them some medicine to make them sleep for a little while, but he doesn't want Emily to know."

Ran caught her breath on a gasp. Didn't most medicine say two years and above? Medicine at their early age had to be dangerous. But so was having the babies cry out in the open. Nothing about this journey was going to be easy. She stared back through the RV yard as the sun edged over the cement wall and bathed the area in a golden haze. The only thing missing was Michelle's cat, Hope. She'd called for the kitten all morning, but been forced to acknowledge they would have to leave without it. The woman cried a few tears, but Teddy's hugs brought a smile to her face. His whispers in her ears brought a red-hot blush to her face.

The big man gathered them into a circle. Teddy coughed and stammered. "I know we've had a little too much religion lately, but I wouldn't feel right going on a journey of this magnitude without a little prayer to the guy upstairs."

She grimaced. Reverend Bennett had destroyed their camp, their friends, and their lives. But one man was not all there was to God. General Peters had tried to destroy her and he was not all men either, she thought as she took and squeezed Cody's hand. He smiled down at her as Teddy's rich baritone wafted over them.

"We don't ask for much, Lord. Just help to make our difficulties doable, keep the little ones safe, and watch over us. Amen."

A soft echo of 'amen' filled the space, along with Nickie's bark, as they squeezed hands and moved back to let Seth and Teddy open the gate for one last time. They filed through and Ran's heart ached a little at the click of the closing gate as the men manhandled the gate into place with no one inside to push the button.

Seth took a can of spray paint and put a large X on the metal along with the words; Not Safe. She shuddered. *Would they ever be safe? What did that word even mean anymore?*

"Okay, gang. We head north to the river. My boat is tied up at the dock. At least it was the last time I saw it. The Emily awaits," Teddy informed them.

The consensus had been to walk to the pier, since a car would just draw the undead with them and make it impossible to get on the boat safely with the babies. Ran took her protection duties seriously and watched as Michelle did the same. She noted that the woman wasn't the same as she had been before she faced the Reverend and almost lost her life to save Teddy. There was a toughness about her that hadn't been there before. Along with the shorn hair, Michelle was now an official zombie hunter and kickass chick.

She ran a hand through her own short, curly hair and came away with a wet palm. The rising sun promised another hot day, definitely too hot for spring. Shoving her machete into the holder on her belt, she grabbed a bandana and tied it across her forehead.

A moan sounded from the gas station where she and Cody had been holed up a couple of days ago. A thunk reverberated through the still morning air as its bloody hands flung against the window. Two steps to the skinbag's right the window had shattered and lay in glassy pieces on the ground, but the brain-dead zomb' didn't know it and continued to pound on the intact window in front of it over and over again.

Ran shook her head in amusement and moved on. An unnatural silence slammed into her ringing ears. No birdcalls. No insect sounds. No voices; alive or undead. Like the calm before a storm. She snatched that thought back before it could be given voice in her head. Karma was a bitch she wasn't willing to tangle with.

They passed buildings so run-down they must have been abandoned before the influenza epidemic and the Z virus. Full-grown bushes grew from rain gutters and trees sprouted in the pavement to block doors and windows. No window frame was totally filled with glass; instead it lay in glittering piles on the pavement.

A flock of small, gray birds filled the skies to break the eerie silence with their chirps as they flew, landed, and flew again from the sagging telephone wires. A few telephone poles had fallen and lay across the roadway, the wires draped across the asphalt.

Teddy and Seth rushed to check both sides of the road. It might have been a storm. It might have been neglect. Or it might have been deliberate. Those were the options in the ZA and it was usually option number three.

A grunt and a groan sounded from the right side of the road as the bushes shook and Teddy came back to the group with a large hand on the back of the neck of a young boy. He looked fourteen or fifteen at the most, skinny as a starved zombie and shaking from head to toe.

She turned her head as Seth returned with a smaller version of the boy Teddy held. They looked at each other and started to cry, even louder at Nickie's growl. The border collie could look vicious when he bared his teeth and growled deep in his throat.

"We were just trying to get some food. We haven't eaten in days. We were staying at the hotel on the corner but the groaners broke in a couple of days ago and we had to leave."

The men shoved them together in the middle of the road and stepped back to the group. "What do we do?" Seth asked them. "We can't leave them at our back and I don't trust them to take them with us."

The problem was solved when the taller boy pulled a knife from his boot and rushed at Seth's back. The blade whooshed in the air as it caught the edge of his shirt and sliced open the fabric with a ripping sound. Seth turned in a whirl and his knife plunged into the boy's stomach. Blood coated his shirt and dripped to the ground as he fell with a moan. The smaller boy pulled his own knife, held it to his throat, and sliced across it. Blood shot into the air as he fell and the knife dropped from his lifeless hand.

Ran turned to survey their rear as she heard the groans of the newly undead. They were silenced in a moment with the sound of knives plunging into heads, a sound she would never forget as long as she lived. The eerie silence returned as even the birds fell quiet.

* * *

His fingers itched to join in the fight as his hand cradled little Jed's head. The soft fuzz on top tickled Cody's palm as the baby stirred slightly, popped a thumb in his mouth, and went back to sleep.

He rocked his hips back and forth as he'd watched Emily and Seth do when they held the babies. It seemed to work as Jed snuggled deeper into his chest. Cody let out a small breath as the little one's eyes stayed tightly shut.

Looking up, he saw the fight was over before it began. The two young men were dragged to the side of the road and rolled into the ditch. His heart pounded in his chest. The boys hadn't been much younger than he was. So young to have already turned renegade. Would he have done the same if he hadn't been found and had a place with the group?

He caught Ran's glance. Never. As long as he had Ran, he would do the right thing. They didn't have much left in this world, but they had their own set of values. Miranda needed a strong, honest man and he would do everything in his power to be that man.

The breeze freshened and the scent of the river reached him as they trekked across the gravel parking lot to the pier. Soon they would be on a boat and he could hand off the little one to his parents. His happy thoughts were shattered at the view beside the pier.

The Emily sat on the bottom of the river, small wavelets lapped against the sides and over the deck. Cracks and a large hole showed where the vessel had hit the pier during rough weather, probably the big storm they'd had in January. The one where he and Ran had snuggled beneath all the covers they owned and watched the lightning and counted and waited for the thunder that rocked the trailer and rattled the windows.

The big man cursed and kicked a pier post. The thud carried over the silent area. The groans of the undead came in waves from the weeds along the parking lot. He reached for a knife that wasn't there and turned to find Seth, Teddy, Michelle, and Ran taking the four points with the rest of them in the center.

He swallowed the lump in his throat. The river was in front of them and the zombs were coming out of the weeds to the left and the right. They couldn't go back the way they'd come. He didn't see an option until Teddy pointed back down the road they'd come and to the right and the left.

"There are boat harbors to either side of us. Our only chance is to find another boat. Most people didn't take to their vessels, so odds are we won't find many skinbags once we leave this group behind." Teddy explained as he moved up next to Ran and sent her back to his previous position.

Seth got them moving double time since stealth was no longer an option. The jostling woke Jed and Carla and their baby cries added to the loud moans of the undead thundering in his head. He held the baby as gently as possible but there wasn't a thing he could do for the crying.

Their boots pounded loudly on the asphalt as they turned down yet another side road and found acres of boats. A few still had their owners aboard—permanently undead. The big man passed the smaller boats until he found a likely one. The chipped and flaking paint job had been a bright blue at one time, but weather, time, and neglect had washed most of it away.

Cody turned at the shuffling of feet at his back. A cold sweat trickled down his back as Ran hacked and shoved the horde headed their way. Michelle rushed to her side and the two of them managed to dispatch most of them, until two of them lurched into Miranda and sent her flying into the water and followed her in.

His heart stopped as her head didn't break the surface. Bubbles burst thickly, thinned, and stopped. Still nothing. His feet wanted to carry him to the edge so he could dive in, but he couldn't. He still held the baby.

A streak ran past him and hit the water in a flying leap. All he saw was a flash of pale skin and bright auburn hair. The young woman dove into the harbor like an Olympic swimmer. Seconds that seemed like minutes, then hours, passed. With a gasp and coughing, Ran and April surfaced and swam to the pier where Michelle pulled them to the wooden deck.

He rushed to Ran's side. Her face was pale and her breathing was shallow. Michelle's hands ran over both girls' arms and legs. She sat back with a loud exhale.

"Nothing. No bites."

Cody let out his held breath with something between a sigh and a sob.

With a jerk, Ran turned to her side and vomited a mouthful of river water and took a deep gulp of air.

His arms ached to hold her. He longed to tell her how much he loved her. At the renewed shuffling, he cursed the fates that he couldn't do any of those things. As he looked around, lost in frustration at not fighting the undead, getting Ran to the boat, and wondering how they were all getting out of this, he jumped at Teddy's yell and the gunning of a boat's motor.

Michelle stayed as he grabbed one arm and April grabbed the other and they got Ran onto the boat. The three of them fell onto the rotted cushions and he gagged at the scent wafting up from the deteriorating fabric.

Ropes were flung onto the boat as Seth grabbed Michelle and flung her onto the boat. She found a seat beside them and Teddy pulled the boat out of its berth. The zombies kept coming. One after another, they fell into the water, arms outstretched, trying to reach the boat and missing. The distance grew and when Cody finally looked around again they were out of the harbor and onto the river.

CHAPTER EIGHTEEN

Selena

Selena's Diary
Mister Toby's Treehouse
Near Mount Diablo (he told me the name of the mountain)
Spring, 1 AZ

Mister Toby is nothing like I worried he would be. He works me hard, but he works just as hard—harder to protect his camp and his belongings. He found my diary and says I can keep it. His voice is still rough and his eyes still glare at me, but he is nothing like the man who bought me from Juan. In my nightmares I can still see the zombies attacking the apartment people. I hope they ate Juan.

She put the paper and pencil into her knapsack, along with the small knife Mister Toby gave her when he showed her how to sharpen the pencil. He'd said she could just call him Toby, but Mister Toby didn't sound so bad for the large man. The boys of Rogue Vantage had called the grown-ups Miss and Mister in the camp.

With a deep breath, she blew out the stub of a candle and cocooned herself in the pile of blankets she'd been given. Mister Toby's snores carried through the little hut from his side of the dwelling. She snuggled down into the warmth and fell quickly asleep. After a few sleepless nights worrying about the man attacking her, now only the nightmares disturbed her rest.

When they'd reached his camp in the shadows of Mount Diablo, Selena had stared in surprise at the treehouse the man had built in an enormous Live Oak tree. He'd sent her up first and quickly followed. He pulled the rope ladder after them and pointed to a far corner of the treehouse.

"That is where you sleep." He pointed to the other side. "That is where I sleep. We only sleep if all the work is done."

Her heart thumped in her chest. At least eight feet divided the piles of blankets. Her confusion must have shown in her eyes because the man threw his head back and laughed. At least she thought it was a laugh since his dark eyes still glared.

"I like my women to be all grown up. I do need a slave and I'll work you hard, but not in my bed. Do you understand?"

She nodded, tears filling her eyes. "Yes, Mister

Toby." She didn't know if she could dare hope yet or not. *Should she push her luck or not?*

Taking a deep breath, she went for it. "My mommy will find me. Juan said she was dead but I didn't see her die, so she might be alive."

He dropped to a knee. "Selena, if your mother finds us I will let you go. I promise."

Toby held out his hand and she shook it. Her tiny hand was swallowed in his giant palm.

She sighed as her thoughts drifted away and memories became dreams.

One day slid into the next as they worked from sunup to sundown. Mister Toby taught her to hunt rabbits, to clean them, and to cook them. She learned to walk through the tree-covered hills without making a sound.

Today was foraging. She walked silently behind the giant man as they skirted the edge of a neighborhood built in the shadow of the mountain. He talked softly as he scanned the nearest house through a pair of binoculars.

"See the gray house. Watch how the deer eat right by the back door. That house might be safe."

"Might be?" She squinted and stared at the mother deer with its baby. "If the deer think it's safe, isn't it? You said the animals know."

"It probably doesn't have any undead since the animals seem to sense them. But even in the before Z days, deer would go right up to the windows and doors of houses with people in them."

"And living people are just as dangerous as dead people," she repeated the lesson she'd learned at great cost. Her fingers played with the bandage on her arm. The cut itched as it healed but she wouldn't forget the lesson that just because a person was young it didn't mean they were safe. Her nightmares now included the small grave by the treehouse and the boy who wouldn't stop when Toby told him to.

He patted her on the head and Selena saw stars. She knew he meant well, but Mister Toby didn't know his own strength sometimes. The light flashes passed and she went back to checking out the house. Movement appeared behind the sliding glass door. A second later, metal appeared in the slight opening. A gunshot rang out and the larger deer fell to the ground. Another shot and the baby joined its mother.

A cry filled her throat, but she swallowed it down. A gun could shoot people as easily as it had shot the deer. Mister Toby gave her a nod and they faded back into the shadow of the trees. It wasn't until they'd passed five or six houses that the man returned to scouting.

Selena stood still as she'd been taught until Toby brought the binoculars down and nodded to her. She fell into step behind him as they moved toward the house. Weeds filled the backyard, with toys and a kiddy pool half-hidden in the abandoned grass, now dry and filled with dust and dirt. The large man easily hopped over the fence, and then reached back to lift her over as well.

"Why didn't we use the gate?" She pointed to one a few feet to her left.

"Gates squeak. Hasn't had oil in long time."

She nodded, feeling stupid inside. If she ever needed to survive alone, she needed to know this stuff. Use your head, Selena, she admonished herself silently.

Concentrating, she noted everything Toby did. He went up to the glass door and peered inside. Tapping gently on the glass with his gun, his body tensed as they waited. When nothing appeared at the glass, he finally slid the door open, an inch at a time.

He held a hand up as she tried to follow right on his footsteps. "Just a minute. Let me check this room."

In seconds, he was back. "Kitchen is clear."

Her breath caught as she stepped inside. They'd hit the mother lode, as her Grandfather Sterling used to say. Boxes and cans filled every countertop. Some had spoiled, as she spotted cans with split sides and goo oozing out onto the tile. But most of it looked great. She didn't see any bugs or a trail of ants.

She frowned. Why weren't there any bugs? Like the rest of nature, the insects were taking back their part of the planet, too. Her answer came swiftly with the telltale moan of the undead coming from beyond where she saw a dining-room table and overturned chairs.

Toby rushed forward and she followed right behind him, with the butcher knife she'd just grabbed off the counter. Selena slid in a blood pool as the large man ran forward and stabbed a skinbag in the skull. What had been a woman fell to a heap on the floor. Something grabbed her foot and she jumped, falling in the sticky pool. Her eyes widened at the sight under the table.

A small child crawled toward her, his mouth full of white, gleaming teeth and his eyes dead and hungry. She raised her knife as the boy got closer. The weapon shook as her hand and arm trembled. He was just a baby.

"It's not alive, Selena. Its mother would thank you if she could."

She pressed her lips together, closed her eyes, and plunged the knife down. The sound of metal against bone filled her head. She wanted to scream. She wanted to cry. She wanted to go back to being a little kid.

"Good job, Selena. Now it is dead dead."

She wanted to laugh at the big man using Rogue Vantage's favorite saying for killing the skinbags, one she'd told him yesterday. It bubbled up inside her until the laughter became sobs and her body shook with the force of her emotions.

His footsteps moved away as she pulled herself together. He still had rooms to check. She looked away from the mess under the table and busied herself with closing and locking the glass door and sorting through the food on the countertop.

Once she'd moved the spoiled food away and checked and found some insects in food after all, they'd still have a nice foraging day, with enough food that they would both have full knapsacks to carry back to the treehouse.

Her stomach grumbled as she eyed the box of chocolate chip cookies. Mister Toby didn't take much junk food from the houses they foraged. He said their bodies needed good stuff. Protein and such. She craned her neck and didn't spot the big man in the living room. Opening the box as quietly as she could, Selena stuffed a couple of the crunchy snacks into her mouth, chomping away before he could get back. She sighed. Even stale, the chocolate chips melted in her mouth.

A thud sounded from the glass door, making her jump and a small squeal escaping her. Looking over her shoulder, the undead man stood inches from her, only the glass separated them. She stood motionless. His head swung back and forth, his face sliding grossly across the clear barrier, blood and black gunk coating the sliding door.

"Don't move," Toby's deep voice boomed from the edge of the room.

"I'm not," she intoned back to him, as quietly as she could.

"I'll be right back."

His steps faded as Selena continued to stare into the lifeless depths of the zombie's eyes. She'd never been so close to one before without someone running forward to kill it. It raised its head, twisting and turning, as if to get her scent.

What was live? What was dead? Maybe they were all dead and they just didn't know it.

Out of the corner of her eye, she spotted the big man stalking up to the thing at the door. His knife shone in the bright sun as he raised it up and brought it down on the skinbag's head. The zombie fell to the ground like the bag of bones it was.

"Toby," she tried to yell as a bunch of people surrounded the big man. He tried to fight back, but the blows rained down on him from clubs and other weapons. Too many for the man to fight, no matter how big he was. He fell to the ground a last time and didn't get back up. His blood flowed onto the cracked dirt and splattered across the weeds.

"Toby," she yelled again. She was stopped as a hand clasped across her month and an arm grabbed around her and lifted her up.

She felt a stinging pinch in her neck and then she felt nothing else. Time passed in increments of light and dark and bouncing against a metal floor. Slowly, she opened her eyes a small slit and looked around her. The metal floor belonged to the bed of a pickup truck. The flashes of light and dark were the truck passing under streetlights. Her surprise had her forgetting she was supposed to be spying, not staring with her mouth open. She hadn't seen working streetlights in months as they failed one by one and left the streets in darkness.

"She's awake," a soft voice intoned in the surrounding darkness. A light passed by and Selena saw a woman about her mother's age. One with a smile and dark hair and eyes.

She sat up, noticing she wasn't tied up or gagged. "Where's Mister Toby?"

"You don't have to worry about the male. We took care of him, just like we take care of all the men"

Her head swiveled back and forth. The truck was full of females. Young. Old. Children as young as her and younger. They were all dressed like Commander Jack and Mister Paul back at the RV yard. Everyone dressed as if they were in the army.

The dark-haired woman moved toward her and placed a hand on Selena's head. "My name is Alaina. Welcome to the Sisterhood of the Earth. What man has destroyed, woman will rebuild."

CHAPTER NINETEEN

Jack and Lila

Lila's notes
Somewhere near Mount Diablo
Spring, 1 AZ

I don't know how Jack does it. Just when I think all hope is gone, he finds a person who knows a person who saw Toby Hill or Selena or at least a little blonde-haired girl. The only way I continue on is with the rumors that Toby is a nice man although scary looking. I hold on to hope he has not hurt my child or killed her.

"You take this road until it dead ends. Hop over the guard rail and there is a path, not much bigger than a deer trail. Follow that for about two miles and look for the largest Live Oak. Toby's treehouse is in the clearing," the man told them, then started walking back to his storage container home.

"Thank you," Jack called out.

"Good luck," the man replied.

"We're getting closer. I can feel it," she said as they started walking down the road. "This has to be it. The man knew who we were talking about. He even said he saw a little girl."

Jack took her hand for a moment and then dropped it like a hot stone. "I don't want to get your hopes too high. Just because these people think this Toby is nice doesn't mean he is when he is away from people. Even in the old world, pervs hid their true natures.

"Why else would he live all by himself? There is a reason we find groups of people. Even if they are small groups. There is safety in numbers."

They came to the Dead End sign and guard rail. She turned to Jack, her fists balled at her side. "You can't allow me just a little hope, can you? It's the apocalypse, so everything has a bad ending."

She turned away, refusing to let him see the angry tears falling from her eyes and mistake them for sadness or grief. Giving up was not an option. She would find Selena and they would be a family. With or without Jack.

His arms came around her. She stiffened.

His calm voice floated into her ears and her brain. "I have hope, Lila. Sometimes it seems like too much hope. So much that my chest will explode. I have nothing but hope we find Selena and she is safe. I've already missed nine years of her life; I can't fathom losing the rest. We will search until we find her. We will hope until there is no more hope left."

The tension left her body. She leaned against him and inhaled the scent that was uniquely Jack. Even hot and sweaty he smelled of pine and fresh air and sexiness.

He stepped back and she mourned the instant loss of his closeness. He shrugged out of his backpack and pulled two waters out of it, handing one to her.

"This will probably be our last break before we find this treehouse. Might as well take it here where we are still in the open and can see around us."

She swallowed the tepid water and thought about all she'd learned in just a few short days. She hadn't realized just how sheltered she was in the RV yard to the outside world. More than anything she'd bitched about the primitive conditions there, as if it were just one long camping trip with all the inconveniences that implied. Washing clothes, cooking, cleaning, everything so much harder than at home. Zombies were those unseen things outside someone else took care of. Now she was outside, and she was the someone who took care of it. If she wanted to live, that was.

The idea was scary and freeing at the same time. Scary because death was everywhere. Freeing because you can't live in fear every second of the day. She knew Jack would protect her and she was coming to feel she could protect herself.

Jack hoisted his pack onto his shoulders. "Let's

move on. Stay a couple steps behind me. It will be harder to maneuver in the trees and we'll each need our space if we come upon anyone; dead or alive."

She nodded, a shudder running down her spine. She didn't know what was worse, the skinbags who couldn't help what they were or the living who had a choice and chose bad.

A cool breeze blew as soon as they stepped onto a small dirt path among the trees. She took off her bandana and tied it around her neck. The wind brushed across her chopped off hair and dried her sweaty scalp. Her anger lingered at all Juan had put her through. He'd been an indifferent husband, especially once Selena was born and wasn't the wanted son. Being ignored was better than his sporadic anger fits when, yet again, she wasn't pregnant. Nothing in their past prepared her for how he'd changed once he met Bennett and his toxic church followers. She shoved the past behind her and concentrated on following Jack's steps and observing the forest.

Staying two steps behind Jack was no hardship as her gaze swept his body. He'd been in shape before as an athlete and she was sure he'd built up muscle in the army, but the lean fit man before her had been honed into sexual fantasy material by the daily life of the zombie apocalypse.

Jack stopped and held up his fist. The first time he'd done it she'd whimpered and ducked. It took several times until she didn't flinch when he used the military sign for stop. She held her breath and swept the area. If he saw something here, she was missing it.

He held up three fingers and made his hand into a claw shape. She almost giggled before she bit her lip. They'd agreed on the sign for the undead. He'd added the universal male sign of a pointed finger and thumb upright for gun to indicate real people.

She exhaled silently. Zombies she could handle. She'd had enough of bad people who wanted to rule their small corner of the world. Inhaling, she caught the whiff of death. The skinbags were close.

Shrugging out of her pack, she eased it to the ground against a tree and pulled her knife from the sheath. Approaching downwind sucked, but gave them a small edge. Lila sucked in a breath and held it as she ran toward the smallest of the three and shoved her knife into its skull. Two small thuds announced Jack took care of the others.

She turned in a circle and spotted no one else, undead or alive. Wiping her knife on the finally dead guy's shirt, she put it back in the sheath and really looked at the bodies. Two women and a young boy. Not their guy and thank God, not Selena.

She put her hand to her chest. For a moment, all she could see was bright blonde hair and it didn't matter the young boy was too tall to be her daughter. It took a few seconds for her heart to stop racing and to remember to scan the area.

"No treehouse," Jack uttered.

Lila gazed to the treetops. Nothing that looked like a shelter, empty except for some wind-blown papers and clothing. She stared across the small clearing. A small green tent blended in with the bushes and shrubs. Ripped clothing scattered the ground as if it had been tossed about.

"There's no sign anyone has been here other than these three," Jack said as he strode to the small tent. "Check for anything useful."

Her heart ached at the thought of scavenging over dead people's belongings, but wasn't it what they did every day? Scavenging from a dead world was how they were surviving. Shouldn't there be more? Her thoughts ran laps in her brain as she picked up clothing and surveyed the area at the same time. She wanted to laugh. The ultimate multitasking; thinking and working at the same time at the end of the world as they knew it.

Jack came back with a small handgun and a box of ammo. "Here," he said, handing it to her. "It must have belonged to one of them."

He nodded toward the bodies on the ground. "It's too small for my hands and it's just a pea-shooter, but you should carry it, just in case. Only fire if you have no other recourse because firing it would draw every skinbag in the area."

She pushed the release, checked the clip, shoved it back in with a click, set the safety, and put it in her pocket. "I'll put the ammo in my pack as soon as we grab them."

"You did that awfully well." His gaze went to her pocket, now bulging with the weight of the weapon.

"I had a little .22 at home for protection. My dad taught me to shoot when I was young."

Her voice trailed off. No matter how much she wanted to hate the man for what he'd done to her and Jack, she still had wonderful memories of her childhood. She prayed Selena would be left with some random happy memory of Juan instead of his betrayal and evilness.

As if he'd read her mind, Jack walked up and squeezed her arm. "It's okay to remember the man you loved. I'm sure he had his reasons."

Her jaw clenched and her teeth ground together. "His reasons will never be good enough. If you had been her father all along, she wouldn't be missing now."

He nodded. "Can't argue with that logic. Let's get our packs and keep moving."

They gathered their belongings and anything of use at the small campsite and hiked up the narrow path. Just when Lila thought she couldn't go any further, a large clearing opened up. A huge, majestic Live Oak stood in the middle of it, its branches twisting and turning, a dark black against the light-green spring leaves. Her gaze shot to the upper branches. Amid the leaves sat a treehouse. Not the small backyard one she'd envisioned, but one capable of housing at least several people, or a small family.

Jack squatted by the firepit and put his hand on the ash. "Ice cold," he said as he stood. "Whoever lives here has been gone for a while."

She craned her neck. "Do you think we can get up there and check it out?"

He put his pack on the ground and swung himself up to the first branch. Lila went to join him, but he held his hand up in a stop motion. "Let me check it out first. Put your back to the trunk and keep watch."

The only sound in the woods was the rustle of the leaves and a distant birdcall. The world seemed so beautiful sometimes. Why hadn't they appreciated it when they could? A deer stepped out of the trees and hesitated on the edge. Her breath caught. Jack called down in a deep tone and the deer's head came up. The animal shivered and leapt back into the brush.

A rope ladder fell in front of her. She put her pack on the ground and climbed to the house among the branches. Her mouth dropped open. The place was neat and tidy, with blankets made into beds. Two beds she was beyond thrilled to see. Hope flared in her heart. One bed was enormous and had at least seven or eight blankets. The other was small and reminded her of a nest.

Her breath caught. "Selena likes to sleep that way. Like a little bird in a nest."

She walked over and inhaled deeply, as if she would know if her child had been here by scent alone. Wadded up paper littered the crate being used as a bedside table. A stub of a candle sat on top.

Grabbing a paper, she unfolded it. Her hands shook. Selena's writing spilled across the pages. She'd know it anywhere, down to the heavy strikethroughs for misspelled words and mistakes and stars for stuff she wanted to remember. She brought the page to her chest, the paper crinkling in her clenched hands.

"She's here," she whispered.

"What does it say?" he asked. "Maybe it has some clue to where they are."

Bringing it to her face, she smiled at Selena's spelling that was not the best, hence why she would scribble over misspelled words and rewrite a whole paper to have it one hundred percent right.

"Mister Toby is taking me foraging today. We had the last of the rabbits and he is hoping we find some fruit in cans so we don't get scurvy." She laughed. "She crossed that out three times before she got it right."

"Fruit in cans means they headed to houses or stores. Stores are too dangerous. Why take chances when houses would be lower risk? We'll have to ask and hope someone saw a large man and a little girl."

She folded the lined paper and shoved it in her pocket as if to have a piece of Selena with her. "I feel like we are so close to her. Where is Selena?"

CHAPTER TWENTY

Paul, Suz, and Josh

Paul Luther's Log
Ryde Hotel (New Base of Operations)
Ryde, California
Spring, 1 AZ

Old John may be trouble. I had Josh keeping an eye on him, but he has made his disdain known about our living arrangements. He can keep his hatred all he wants if he doesn't cause trouble. For the moment, Charlie's son, Tyler is tailing him. The boy has a devious but useful side to him. He could sneak up on a rattlesnake.

"Perhaps we should find another place," Suz said, her breath warm against his chest.

Paul reached down and ran a hand down her naked back. They were both wet with perspiration after an hour of wonderful love-making.

"I refuse to spend our time together discussing Old John and his homophobia."

She laughed, the husky tones stirring him to arousal. "He is an asshole, isn't he?"

"No more talking," he whispered, taking her lips with his. His heart pounded as his hands followed his gaze down his wife's sleek body. His hand cupped her breasts, the soft flesh overflowing his grasp. Her moans had him hard and ready.

"I love you," he whispered into her ear as he slid into her waiting warmth. Their bodies moved together, harder and harder, faster and faster, until he exploded within her. Her body arched and her moan of ecstasy joined his.

He rolled over ready to go back to sleep as the sunlight peeked through the blinds. He groaned as her fingertips tickled over his nipples, bringing them to hardness.

"No rest for the wicked," she murmured as she sat up and got dressed. She turned to him once she pulled on her shorts and a T-shirt. "Get out of bed. You have commander things to do."

"I'm not the commander,"

"You are until and if Jack returns."

He started to protest but she stopped him with her hands on her hips. "You know he may not return. A million things could happen to him and Lila, the least of them the skinbags. You've told me a thousand times we have to carry on. No one person is as important as the group."

He sat up and she walked over to stand between his thighs, her hands on his shoulders. "No one person."

"That certainly includes Old John," he said, mumbling a few choice words under his breath.

"Do what I do with Rogue Vantage and the girls. Keep them so busy they are too tired to cause trouble."

"Maybe I should try that with John. By the time we move the turret guns to the upper floors, he'll be too tired to say a word or roll his eyes or irritate people."

She hugged him and headed to the door. "That's the spirit."

Once Suz left, Paul got out of bed and dressed. Even if John didn't help, they needed the guns up the stairs. He wasn't sure they could make it, but Muncy and his boys said they had a plan.

An hour later the plan was in motion. Charlie had been a piano mover in his former life and he used his knowledge to get the turret guns off two of the Humvee and placed front and back in rooms on the upper floor of the hotel.

"Thanks, Charlie," he said, slapping the man on the back. All he got for it was a grunt. The man treated words like cash and spent them like a miser with gold.

The guns would be a great last line of defense but the building sat too close to the road for his peace of mind. "We need a wall. Even if it's just made of sandbags. Something to wait behind if anyone comes up the road or on the river."

"Humvee up the road both ways. Stop before they get here," the man said.

Paul stared at him. More words than the man had said in days. It might work, but it would spread their group too thin. Maybe if Teddy and Seth and their group showed up soon. They would have a few more people to use in key positions.

"Rocks," Charlie grunted at him.

"What?" Paul ran a hand over his hair.

"Fisher and his rocks," Charlie said and walked back toward the hotel.

He smiled. Brandon Fisher and his boulders for the levee repair. They could get a few loads and get started on a barricade. Something was better than nothing. Following the man into the hotel, Paul swerved left and headed to the office and the phone.

Before they'd left the Fisher farm, Brandon and his friends had started to move in together so it was a simple call to the telephone hub and to talk to the big man about delivering some rocks.

That done, Paul headed toward the delicious smells coming from the hotel kitchen and dining room. Nothing smelled as good as fried chicken. Billy's chickens had been attacked by a fox or coyote and he'd lost a third of his flock. His wife had raised the chickens and refused to eat them, so Paul's group got a home-cooked meal.

He spotted Zach Muncy talking to the boys of Rogue Vantage. The older ones, Aiden and Bryant hung on the older boy's every word. He strode up to them. "Zach, I'd like you to be on fishing duty with the boys here. You'll be in charge. I saw some fishing poles in a closet by the check-in desk. Anytime Shannon and Suz don't need you for anything, I need you all fishing. The chicken will be great today, but when it's gone, it's gone."

"Yes, sir," they all chimed in.

He reached out and ruffled Dylan's hair. The boy beamed up at him. He sobered at the thought these boys were orphans. All they had was each other and the group. He steeled his spine and straightened his shoulders. Suz's words came back to him. He was the commander of this group. He had to hold it together. For today and for the future.

* * *

Suz watched with pride as Paul took command of the group. Jack Canida had held the group together by his sheer willpower. He never ordered anyone to do anything. Everyone had free will. By allowing them that, they all tried harder to contribute to the group. But there had been dissenters, like Lila's husband, Juan. She'd stood in the crowd as Juan pulled his wife and child from the RV yard and took them away to the church. Her heart had broken at Lila's and Selena's cries and she'd wanted to argue with Jack, but he was their leader and Paul's best friend.

She watched as her husband ruffled Dylan's hair. Jack had stood apart from the group, as if commanding was a lonely place on a hillside. Maybe it was from having command from the start or for so long. Granted, Paul had a much smaller group to command, but he seemed to have the feeling that they were all in this together and being organized got things done, and he showed it, giving each person a job they could manage and enjoy as much as possible.

She wiped the perspiration from her forehead with the back of her hand and returned to the chicken. Fresh tomatoes sat on the cutting board. Josh stood there with a smile on his face.

"They have a greenhouse out back," he explained. "Some of the stuff isn't ready, but the tomatoes are weighing down the plants. We'll have to make salsa or can them or something."

"Can them or something, huh?" She hugged her brother. "I don't know about you, but I've never canned a thing in my life."

"Who's talking about canning?" Shannon walked into the kitchen. "I haven't done that in years. My grandma taught me before I left for college and medical school."

Suz's surprise must have shown on her face. The doctor laughed. "Never know when something will come in handy."

"I think being the only doctor is pretty handy," Josh said. "Is there anything you can't do?"

Her smile faded. "I couldn't save Jim."

Suz grabbed her friend and hugged her tightly. The doctor's shoulders shook and she could hear the sobs wracking her small frame. Shannon pulled herself together and turned away.

"It's like each death is a little easier to forget and move on. How soon until we don't care at all?"

Suz grabbed the smaller woman's arms and made her look at her. "We will always care. We will always want each death to be the last one. We have to keep our humanity to pass it down to the next generation or it really won't matter at all if they are all barbarians."

"I just miss him so much," she said, her voice stuttering to a stop on a sob. "I wake up and think it was all a nightmare and then I realize it wasn't. It just hurts so damned much."

She thought of losing Paul and her heart jumped in her chest. She really hadn't known him that long. They'd been a couple for an even shorter time. Before the zombies, before the flu pandemic, they would probably still be just dating.

Suz smiled at Shannon. "We are living a lifetime in every day. Each night when we go to sleep we can say 'I made it through another day'. We win with each day we survive."

The doctor puffed out a big sigh. "It just doesn't get any easier."

The clamor from the dining room raised another notch. "It won't get easier if we don't hurry and feed the mob either. They may riot."

Suz and Shannon rushed to get the food ready and Josh went back and forth carrying platters of food for them. Soon the rush was over, with everyone going his or her separate ways. She caught her breath and sat at the end of a cluttered table to eat her own meal.

Josh started cleaning up and she grabbed his hand and pulled him into a seat beside her. "Charlie and his boys volunteered to clean up and do dishes. Sit with me."

Her brother pulled his chair closer and leaned his head on her shoulder. They hadn't sat like that since they were kids. Back then, most people thought they were twins even though they had four years between them.

"You slut. I bet you fuck your brother, too."

The angry, ugly words washed over her. Old John stood in the entry way to the dining room, his face beet red and his body shaking. He looked ready to have a stroke and for a moment she wished he would.

Josh tried to stand up and his hand reached for his knife. She grabbed his arm and yanked him down, the chair moving and squeaking on the linoleum floor. "Don't, Josh. He isn't worth it. He's an old man and he doesn't know any better."

"You people make me sick," he yelled across the room.

"And you make me sick," a deep voice she knew as well as her own spoke from behind her. That it was spoken in a soft tone worried her more than if Paul had bellowed it across the expanse of the large room.

"This will be your last warning. I won't tell you again. The world has moved on, old man. It is what we make of it. It is how we choose to live in it. You are either with us or you are against us. It's time to decide."

Old John dropped his head and shuffled away.

CHAPTER TWENTY-ONE

Cody, Miranda, and April

Ran's Journal
On the river heading northeast (I think)
Spring, 1 AZ (feels like summer)

I'm not afraid to die, just don't want to come back undead. When I fell in at the dock I just wanted to make sure I took the skinbags with me. But I could see the sky above and the sun shining and everyone standing on the dock and I couldn't fight them. They would drag me down until I joined them. When it was over all I could see was Cody's pale face. I swear I heard his heart break. It was like I was me and I was him at the same time. I don't ever want to put that look on his face again.

"Noooooo," the voice carried from the depths of the boat.

Ran shoved the journal and pen into the bottom of her backpack and rushed down the stairs. The below decks was just as Teddy described it—not much to look at, but bone-dry.

A new scent covered the musty one of long, neglected wood and carpet. The smell of death. Emily sat in a corner, rocking back and forth with a small bundle in her arms. Ran swallowed before she could vomit on the floor. She didn't want to go over, but her feet seemed to move of their own accord.

April sat beside the woman with a bundle in her arms. Light, pale hair peeked from the edge of the blanket. That was the girl baby, Carla Beth. That meant Emily held the boy, Jed Robert. She forced herself closer.

"Emily," she whispered, her lips and mouth dry, knowing the baby was dead. "Do you want me to take him?"

"Not yet," she cried. The tears fell down her face and splashed onto Jed's little head, wetting his mat of dark hair.

Ran stared as his chest didn't move, his skin turned gray, and he opened his eyes, now glazed and opaque. She reached for him and stopped with a jerk.

His chest rose and fell rapidly and the pink rushed back into his face and small waving arms. Dark-brown eyes stared back at her. She shook her head.

"What the hell just happened?"

Her words echoed in the boat as Seth came up behind her and repeated them. She shook her head.

Not sure if it was in denial or disbelief. "It's not possible," she muttered to herself.

"He was dead and now he's not," Emily stuttered out between sobs. "He turned and then . . . and then . . ."

"Then what?" Seth demanded.

"Then he turned back," Ran finished.

Seth shook his head and his eyes went wide. She knew exactly how he felt. She wouldn't have believed it if someone told her someone could turn and then come back. Bile rose in her throat at the thought of all the skinbags she'd put down. What if they could come back? Had she killed—people?

Emily moved her hand over the little one's face and chest. "He was burning up before and now he's as cool as can be."

Ran turned and met Seth's gaze. They both stared at his gloved hand. The one with the missing fingers. The ones she'd cut off to save his life. Ran had been there when Seth had been out of his mind with fever. One so high she'd been sure every hour of the day would be his last. But the man had passed through and recovered.

Cody came thumping down the stairs. "Teddy wants to know if everyone is okay."

She rushed and swept him into a tight hug. "Everything is fine now. I'll tell you everything later, just let Teddy know we are okay."

"I wish we had Doctor Shannon here," Emily said. "She might know what was going on."

Ran shook her head. "I don't think anyone knows what is going on anymore. We played God and this is what we got."

Seth moved to sit beside Emily and April got up with Carla and came to her side. They all watched in horror and tears as Jed turned and turned back several more times until he snuggled in close to his mother and seemed to go to sleep.

Ran kept one eye on Carla, but the girl baby seemed oblivious of all the drama and slept soundly with her thumb tucked into her mouth. She made little sucking noises and wiggled against April's chest from time to time as if looking for food.

A million thoughts sped through her mind. Was he sick? Was he fighting becoming a zombie or some other illness that would kill him and make him a zombie? She stared at Seth from under her eyelashes. Did the man have some immunity and he'd passed it on to the babies? They could be the cure. They could get their lives back, their world back. Her thoughts slammed to a stop. What would someone do to get the cure for the zombie apocalypse? After General Peters. After Reverend Bennett. The answer was . . . anything.

* * *

Cody stood by Teddy as he navigated up the river. The water was almost as crowded as a freeway. Boats sat askew on sandbars and shoved up riverbanks. Boats were only some of the debris of civilization the big man had to maneuver around. Sometime during the last year and a half there had been a flood or something, as Cody watched a sofa float by, complete with a cat sitting on the back.

From time to time a thump sounded below water. Not loud as if they had hit a sunken boat or water-logged tree. Each time Teddy winced and Cody knew they'd hit a body—either undead or dead dead.

A splash sounded on the riverbank and he stared as a border collie doggy-paddled toward the boat. By the time the dog reached the halfway point, he heard the moan coming from its torn-out throat. He reached for Emily's crossbow and shot. With a bolt to his head, the animal turned over and floated away.

"Darn, it would have been nice to have a dog of my own," he said, putting the weapon back on the seat cushion.

"They're probably all feral by now anyway. Cats too," Teddy added.

"We domesticated them before, couldn't we do it again?"

Teddy nodded. "Maybe. If you got yourself a really young pup, it might work."

"Nickie wasn't a pup," Cody reminded him.

"Miss Emily had luck on her side when Nickie found her. He could have been as wild as a wolf or coyote."

Moans echoed across the river up ahead. The waterway narrowed and the undead on each side looked close enough to touch. Not that he was doing any touching. No way, Jose. Their hands reached out and their moaning rose as the boat slipped by. A few fell into the water but they couldn't even doggy-paddle as well as the zombie dog had. Most sank below the waves or floated away behind them.

The stench of rotted flesh lingered long after they'd passed them. Teddy's head swiveled back and forth.

"What you looking for, dude?"

"Was hoping to find a place to stop for the night. Don't really want to just drop anchor," Teddy explained as he turned off the motor.

"Aren't we safer in the middle of the river? The zombs are on the land."

"Zombs aren't the only thing to worry about. We can't be the only people to think about using a boat and hitting the river."

Cody nodded. He hadn't thought about that. "Guess we'll have to stand guard all night."

Teddy turned the motor back on and navigated around a sunken tree with skinbags tangled in its branches, the wood spearing them through the body.

"Like to find a wider place to stop. Might be one up here a ways, if I remember and it hasn't shifted."

He turned to Cody. "So, what's going on down there?"

Shrugging his shoulders, he stared at the water on his side to try to help Teddy spot problems. "Ran said she'd tell me later, but everyone was okay."

"Didn't sound okay. Miss Emily doesn't cry for just nothing."

Seth came up the stairs with Nickie. The dog turned circles in a spot and plopped down on a worn rug. The man put a hand on Teddy's shoulder.

"Emily's okay now." He took a deep shuddering

breath. "Jed died, we think, damn, we don't know. He turned and then turned back. He seems fine now, but who the hell knows."

Cody plopped down beside the border collie and ran his hand over the dog's thick, soft fur. *Man, that was all kinds of messed up. Turning and turning back. Whoa.*

He'd been in college when the shit hit the fan, but they hadn't covered any of this mess in Science 101. He'd only been taking General Ed classes. He hadn't known what he wanted to be yet, but it probably wouldn't have been a scientist. They were probably lower on the trust scale than used car salesmen and politicians now.

Teddy must have found the spot he wanted because he turned off the motor and sat in the chair. It creaked with his large frame.

Cody looked around and didn't see any overhanging trees and didn't hear any moans so that was probably it for the night. He stifled a yawn. The day had seemed to go on forever. The boys they'd run into and watched die, the loss of Teddy's boat and the rush to find another one, and Ran's deadly dunk in the river. Now they had babies that turned and turned back. He almost thought what more could happen but pulled the thought back in time.

Almost back in time, as something hit his arm and the echo of a gunshot wafted over the river. He looked down in surprise as red spread across his shirt sleeve. Seth hit him with a hard tackle and air whooshed out of him as they slid to the floor.

"Whoa, someone shot me."

"Stay down," Seth commanded and Cody didn't think to argue. He didn't think much of anything other than it hurt to get shot.

He watched as Teddy gunned the motor and the boat went bouncing over the waves faster than he thought it was capable of and surely faster than was safe. As the sound of more shots reached him, he prayed Teddy went even faster, safe or not.

Nickie whimpered and tried to lick his arm. Cody pulled him in close and wrapped his arms around the dog and held on as the boat skimmed the water. Time passed in a whoosh until Teddy slowed down their speed and stopped the boat completely.

Footsteps pounded up the stairs and Ran's blanched face came into view. "Is everyone okay?" Her gaze stopped at him and his bloody arm. She rushed over in a hunch and slid down to his spot on the deck.

"I really need to remember Karma is a bitch," he muttered just as his vision went to gray and then to black. He thought he heard Nickie yelp and then he heard no more.

* * *

Miranda thought she'd used up all her fear as a prisoner to General Peters and escaping and surviving on her own. But nothing prepared her for the fear that crawled up her spine and settled in her brain at the sight of Cody being shot.

Seth said it was just a flesh wound, the bullet

grazed him. Ran shook her head. His sleeve was coated in the red stuff until they cut it off and washed the gunshot wound. Michelle rinsed and rinsed until pinkish water flowed over the deck.

An ugly gouge ripped across his bicep. Her vision grew faint and gray at the edges until the woman smeared antibiotic cream across it and wrapped it in gauze. Could she be the same person who'd cut off Seth's fingers and cauterized the wound herself? It was different when the injured person was the man you loved. Why had no one told her that?

When the shots were fired she'd tried to rush up the stairs, but Michelle grabbed her around the waist and pulled her down. They'd both fallen to the floor when the boat motor was gunned and the boat skipped over the waves, bouncing them into each other until thankfully the racing stopped.

Now the man was grinning like a fool, showing off his injury like a vet returning from war. She turned away with a huff. It was only a flesh wound, Seth had told her so. Familiar arms came around her and he leaned his chin on her shoulder.

"No kiss for the wounded soldier?"

She pulled away. "You aren't a wounded soldier; you're a boy too stupid to duck."

Her feet pounded on the steps as she ran down below decks and threw herself into cleaning the kitchen. The only sounds were the clanging of pots and pans and the small cries of the babies.

"Are you okay, Ran," Emily called from the folded-out bed.

"Of course I'm fine," she said, wiping angry tears from her cheeks. "Why wouldn't I be? I wasn't up on deck while bullets were flying everywhere."

"Oh," Emily replied, knowing in her voice.

She whipped around. "Don't 'oh' me. Like I care if Cody is too stupid to know to duck and he got hit and he could have died..." Her voice cracked and ended mid-sentence as the tears came in a flood and she covered her eyes with her hands.

Fingers pulled her hands from her face. Cody stood in front of her. His gentle eyes gazed at her and she wondered if her eyes were red and puffy and her nose was running.

"Miranda Stevens, I love you. Obviously I need someone to watch over me, like seriously. Will you marry me?"

Her tears stopped and her mouth dropped wide open. "What did you say?" she whispered.

"Marry me," he said, swooping down and stealing her lips in a kiss. It tasted of salt and sweat and Cody.

Her heart raced and beat out of control. She started laughing and couldn't stop. Cody pulled back from her with hurt written all over his face.

Ran grabbed his hands, yanking him in close. "I'm sorry. But I imagined this day a million times when I was a little girl and never in my wildest dreams could I have envisioned it would be on a boat in the middle of zombies and shooting and the man of my dreams would have a gunshot wound when he asked the question."

"Will you marry me? Don't make me ask again,

please."

"Yes, Cody Taylor. I would love to marry you. Right here. Right now."

She giggled at the stupefied look on his face. Did every man who asked the question look like they were hit by a two-by-four when the woman said yes?

"Wait. Now? You want to get married now?"

"Yes," she said, jumping up and down in his arms. "I don't want to wait another minute."

"But, who's going to marry us? Not like there is a drive-thru chapel on the river."

Emily coughed from the bed. They turned at the sound.

"I believe maritime law allows a captain of a vessel to officiate at weddings."

It seemed to take a moment for Cody to catch up. Ran slapped him on his uninjured arm. "She means Teddy. He's captaining the boat right now."

He smiled and Miranda felt a matching smile on her face.

"Duh, Teddy."

Ran raced up the stairs, pulling Cody along with her. All their friends were on deck except for Emily and the babies they'd left below. Ran pushed him toward the big man.

"Teddy, would you do the honor of marrying us?"

A grin brightened up his dark face. "I'd love to, but why me?"

"Emily says the captain of the ship can marry couples."

Teddy slapped his head. "Of course. Let's do this."

Ran held up her hand. "Wait." She walked over to Seth and held back her tears as memories of her father's death and turning at the hands of Peters zipped through her brain. Her body shuddered as she pushed the bad thoughts away. Not today, she told herself.

"Seth, if it wasn't for you, I never would have found Cody. My father is gone, but could you please give me away?"

He swept her up in a hug. "Sweetheart, I would be honored. But only because I'm giving you to a good man," he teased with a kiss on her cheek.

Before he was finished, Michelle grabbed her hand and pulled her in for a hug. "I have a surprise for you."

Her friend pulled her back down the stairs and over to the backpacks. Michelle looked over to Emily. "That dress you saved. Which pack is it in?"

Emily smiled. "It's in the green one." The woman looked down at her post-baby body. "Not like I'll be wearing it anytime soon, or ever," she said with a sigh.

Michelle started digging into the backpack and stood with a rolled up multi-colored dress. She shook it out and Ran gasped. The swirls of colors looked like they were brushed on with oil paints. Rich burgundy, emerald green, and burnished gold swept over the fabric like a sunset in a forest.

"You can keep it, sweetie," Emily whispered as the twins stirred on the bed. "Let me know when everything is ready and I'll come up with these guys."

She stripped to her bra and panties and cleaned up as best as she could with a washcloth before pulling the soft dress over her head. The material hugged her like a second skin. She'd never owned anything like it before. Her dresses had been cotton and polyester, nothing like the lush feel of this dress. Even her prom dress had been lace.

Michelle ran the brush over her hair, but the curls just sprang back in place. She couldn't sigh for what was lost, because she'd gained so much from the experience. Her only regret was the absence of her parents on this day, but looking at Michelle and Emily and thinking of the others on deck she knew she was surrounded by people who loved her.

Teddy's deep baritone sounded from above. "We're ready, Miranda."

Michelle nodded at her and went up ahead. Seth came down the stairs.

"Let me get Emily and the little ones settled and I'll be right back for you."

She nodded, suddenly at a loss for words. They were really going to do this. Her and Cody. Married. From the library, to the RV yard, to here. So much had happened in between. Standing lost in thought, she didn't realize her friend was back.

"Are you ready, Sweetheart?"

"Yes," she whispered.

He took her hand and walked her up the stairs. A million flickers greeted her on deck. Night had fallen and they'd found a string of twinkle lights for the boat. It was as if the stars had fallen to the river and tangled in the ropes around the edge of the vessel.

Teddy stood at the rear with Cody to his side. April stood by herself on the edge of the group. Ran waved her over. "Stand up with me, okay?"

The young woman beamed and rushed to Teddy's other side. A few steps carried her to Cody, the man she loved with all her heart. Seth kissed her on the cheek and put her hand in Cody's and stepped away to be at Emily's side. He took a baby from Michelle to hold.

She looked up at Cody with his hair wet and slicked back, but the bleached blonde streaks shone through. His blue eyes shined as he stared at her. Her face heated with the lust and love she saw there.

"There is no more important event than finding the one you were meant to be with," Teddy intoned with a glance at Michelle before he pulled his gaze back to Ran and Cody. "I am thrilled and honored today to unite our friends, Miranda and Cody, in holy matrimony.

"Cody has said he wants to say some words of his own."

The tall young man stood before her, his shaking hands in her not-too-steady hands, either. "Miranda Stevens, I have wanted you since the day I first laid eyes on you. You came into that dark and lonely library and became my world. I will spend every day of my life letting you know how honored I am to be your husband."

Her heart stopped and jumped several beats before she could catch her breath. Warm, happy tears rolled down her face. "Cody, I said all the words I wanted to the other night on the rooftop of the gas station. I was broken and you've made me whole. Together we are more than just you and me, we are us."

They looked up at Teddy. "I know you two don't have rings, but a piece of metal doesn't make a marriage. Love, commitment, and trust hold you together forever. Even in this world that seems to have made a mockery of forever, I believe you two will pass the test and stand together as you were meant to be.

"Cody Taylor and Miranda Stevens, I now pronounce you husband and wife. You may kiss your bride."

Her man didn't need to be told twice. His lips found hers and his heart was in his kiss. Warmth filled her body as his tongue slid along hers and made her heart race and her pulse skyrocket to a pounding crescendo. She slid her arms around his neck and pulled him in close.

She blinked as their friends surrounded them and hugged and kissed them. Congratulations rang out across the still water as Emily, Michelle, and April kissed her cheek with tears in their eyes. Seth and Teddy slapped Cody on the back hard enough to almost push him overboard.

Time passed at a snail's pace as they ate a hastily thrown together dinner and all she wanted was to have Cody all to herself. Seth and Teddy seemed to be trying to prolong the event to tease them, but finally Michelle and Emily dragged them below with April in tow. Michelle called back over her shoulder before they disappeared.

"You and Cody have first watch. Four hours of alone time. Put them to good use."

Ran blushed and her face was on fire. She looked up at Cody in the shine of the twinkle lights to find his cheeks just as red as she was sure hers were.

He pulled her over to a cushioned seat. "Come here, Mrs. Taylor."

She giggled. "I will never get tired of hearing that."

A red streak shot across the sky. In seconds there was another and another and another. Even in the cities there was no longer any light pollution, but out here on the river it had always been dark enough to see the stars. She craned her neck and gasped at the Milky Way spilled across the night sky.

"There are so many wonders and we were too busy to see them," she whispered.

Cody pulled her down to the deck onto a pile of blankets. They laid side-by-side, holding hands. "A trillion stars and none of them are as bright as you."

A green streak painted a line across the midnight black. "What would you wish for, Cody?"

He leaned over and his face filled her vision. "I don't have to wish for anything. I have all I want right here."

His lips claimed hers and then his body

followed. They took Michelle's advice and made excellent use of their alone time.

CHAPTER TWENTY-TWO

Jack and Lila

Commander's Log
Near Selena's last known location
Scouting for Selena's current location
Spring, 1 AZ

Rumors abound in this side of town of a mysterious Sisterhood or Sisterhood of the Earth. The name is whispered about but no details are emerging. Are they real or the beginning of a new urban legend? If they exist, do they have Selena? If they have Selena, how do we get her back?

"We need to take a break," Jack said, his stride lengthening to catch up to Lila's almost jog.

She took a few steps and bent over to put her hands on her knees. Her breath echoed as her head hung down. He reached her and handed her a bottle of water.

"We don't have time to take a break." Her words came out one at a time between pants. "That old lady said she'd seen Toby scavenging down this street a day or two ago. She didn't mention Selena but from the look of her thick, cracked glasses I'm surprised she recognized this Toby person."

"Everyone we've met says he's a tall, large guy who likes to wear plaid shirts. He should be easy to spot once we find him." He took a sip of water and watched in silence as Lila finally opened hers and took a few gulps.

"What about the golf course? The kids said it was down this street and to the right."

He sighed. "We'll be in the open, which could be a good thing or a bad thing. Let's try it."

Jack gave Lila her space. The woman was in mama bear mode. He didn't envy this Toby Hill if they found him and Selena was hurt. Not if—when they found him and his daughter. Just thinking of Selena as his daughter tightened his chest. Thinking of not finding her sent a shooting pain through his heart.

He glanced up ahead and spotted the open expanse of the golf course. They hopped over a fence more ornamental than a barrier. The white pickets leaned and several sections had fallen. The once trimmed grass was calf-high and full of weeds. Deer drank from a water hazard and birds hopped across the sand traps.

The wild creatures going about their business reassured him. He took a breath and held it, listening for anything out of place. All he heard was the scattering of squirrels in the trees and the call of birds across the sky.

Jack and Lila walked along the wrought-iron fence dividing the houses from the golf course. Blood spatter coated the wall of a dingy white house. Drag marks and blood drops coated the out-of-control grass and weeds. All the signs of a hunter getting food.

The hairs on the bad of his neck rose on end. Jack took Lila's arm and they steered a wild berth around the yard. He felt eyes on them from the curtained windows. Lila opened her mouth, but he put a finger against his lips and she stayed silent until they'd passed a few more houses.

"Someone was there. I could feel them watching us. Why didn't we stop and ask them about Selena?"

"Because there was someone watching us who didn't want us to know they were there," he replied.

"What if it was Toby Hill? What if Selena was in that house?"

"I counted at least four people at the windows. Perhaps five because I'm pretty sure one was in the attic with a gun barrel through the vent. Selena wasn't there and they were going to shoot first and ask questions later. Maybe. Unless we were dead, and couldn't answer questions."

She shook her head, her bandana falling off. "You don't know that. You aren't a god."

He bent and picked up the checkered fabric and handed it to her. "I do know. At least as much as I can. You heard all the same people I did. What does that tell you?"

She bit her lip and tied the bandana back across her forehead. "That this Toby guy is a loner. He is always seen with just him until he was seen with a little girl in the past few days."

He smiled. "Right. He wouldn't be with a group of people barricaded in a house. He lives alone so he is self-reliant. He's big and strong, so he can obviously take care of himself. When we find them I'll bet you the last chocolate bar in the pack it is just him and Selena."

"You mean if."

He shook his head and strode down the fence line. "No, I mean when."

The buzz of flies grew stronger as they neared the next house. The wrought iron gate stood open, swinging a few inches back and forth with a quiet squeal with each movement. In his gut, Jack knew what he would see, but he had to look anyway.

He grabbed a rock and placed it against the gate. The sound stopped, leaving just the buzzing of the flies. Two steps forward brought him to two bodies. His head swerved back and forth, but the dead were the only ones in the yard. The sliding glass door to the house stood open, but no sounds came from the darkness within just past the blood and gore coated glass.

The first body had been undead longer than Selena had been missing. At least a month, from the look of his desiccated skin and tattered clothing. He was small-framed also, barely a grown man.

They'd had no idea what the man looked like that they were looking for and they'd never know as Jack swallowed bile at the mess of the man in front of him. Nothing was left of the man's head. It looked like whoever had attacked him had taken baseball bats, pipes, and crowbars to his skull. The man hadn't turned, but Jack figured the damage to his head made that impossible. His enormous size and red plaid shirt told him all he needed to know.

"I think we've found Toby Hill."

* * *

Lila turned to the side and threw up until she had nothing left to splatter across the dry and brittle grass. She spit a few times and wiped her mouth with the back of her hand. Her head came up and her gaze targeted the open sliding glass door.

In a rush, she sprinted to the opening and through to a kitchen.

"No, Lila. Wait." Jack's call came as if from a distance. She skidded to a stop at the horror on the floor in front of her feet. A small child, almost a baby lay dead in front of her. Her mind slowly took in the milky eyes and gray skin. No, he was dead dead. A knife mark marred his skull.

A woman was sprawled across the carpet beyond the dining room. A sob caught in her throat. Probably his mother. Her head swung back and forth, trying to look at anything not bloody and dead. A flash of bright blue caught her eye.

She gave a cry and rushed across the room, tripping and falling to the floor beside a backpack with a purple S on the front. Hearing footsteps, she turned and gazed up at Jack.

"It's hers. Selena was here."

The sound of the zipper being pulled reverberated in the silent room. Lila cried as she pulled out T-shirts and shorts and a gray sweatshirt with Selena written in a fancy font across the back. She hugged it to her chest and lifted it up to her face. Her child's scent filled her nose and senses.

"Selena," she yelled in the house. "You can come out. It's mom."

"Lila," he said in a whisper, squatting down beside her. "We'll look, but I don't think she's here. I think whoever killed Toby out there took her."

"Why?"

"We won't know until we find her. But I think a group killed that man out there. They had to be a group to take him on. Hell, it would take a horde of zombies to take him down. The only group we've heard about is this Sisterhood they keep mentioning."

She pulled the sweatshirt to her face again and inhaled deeply. "We're so close."

His arms wrapped around her and he pulled them to their feet. "Damned close. With the weather and when we know Toby bought her, that dead man out there was killed a day ago, two at the most."

"You think we'll find her."

"I believe we'll find her."

Hours later, Lila didn't know what she believed anymore. The sun was setting in a fiery ball and they were no closer to finding Selena than they'd been back at the house. Like rats in a maze, she and Jack had followed every lead, every rumor, and every bare mention of the mysterious Sisterhood of the Earth. One person would say they were in a building on the edge of town, and then a person there would say they lived in the trees. One person had even told them the Sisterhood was everywhere, like goddesses.

Her legs were limp noodles on top of the blocks of wood she now had for feet. Her vision swam in and out of a gray mist. When had she eaten last? Breakfast. Lunch. Dinner yesterday. She couldn't remember. Oh, wait. The water and protein bar she'd shoved down hours ago because Jack wouldn't take another step until she ate something.

Probably the only thing keeping her from falling on her face, but she refused to stop looking. They were so close. She could feel it, taste it, breathe it. They approached a group of teenagers scavenging in a vacant lot.

Jack pushed her slightly behind him, his hand on his gun in the holster. He held the picture out with his other hand. "We're looking for this little girl. Have you seen her? Have you heard of the Sisterhood? Or the Sisterhood of the Earth? We think they may have her?"

A girl only slightly older than Selena stepped forward. "Got something to trade for the info?"

Jack nodded. "Maybe. Depends on the information. We've been running around in circles today. Does the Sisterhood even exist?"

The girl nodded with fear in her eyes. Her gaze shot from their packs to the knives on their belts and Jack's large gun pointed at her.

Lila slid her pack off and dug around in it until she located the last two cans they had. She pulled them out and sat them on the ground between the two groups. "That's the last of the soup. It's all we have left."

The girl scooped them up as if they were priceless gems, her eyes shining, licking her lips. "A large group of women come through here every couple of days. Any girls alone are snatched up. They've hit all the sporting goods stores. We think they camp on the mountain. You can see fires up there late at night. Probably them. That's the direction they head when they leave town."

"Thank you," Lila whispered as the girl backed away and the group melted into the trees. She closed her pack and stood, leaning against Jack.

Jack turned and walked in the opposite direction of the mountain. She ran to keep up. "What are you doing? You heard the girl. They're camping up there." She flung her arm back the way they'd come.

"I know. I also heard you tell the kid that was the last of our food. Night is coming and we're standing in the middle of the street. They sound like a large group. We'll do better with a night of sleep and some food in our stomachs."

God, she hated when he was right. She could barely stand, but it seemed so wrong to walk in the opposite direction. "Where are we going?"

He pointed to the office building across the street. When he bypassed the door and headed to the alley, she saw the rusty fire escape above the dumpster. He pushed her up on the dumpster and she grabbed the rungs of the ladder. A short climb and they were on the roof of the two-story building. She turned to the mountain and stared as the setting sun painted it in a fiery glow. As twilight fell, fires sprang up near the top.

Jack handed her a bottle of water. "Not much of a dinner."

She smiled. "Oh, we have dinner."

Lila carried her pack to the middle of the roof and opened it. Reaching in, she pulled out a single can. "Care for some beef stew?"

"You told the kids that was the last of the food."

"No, I said that was the last of the soup."

"You always were a good liar," he murmured. His smile died and he looked away.

"I never lied about loving you, Jack. I never stopped loving you."

His voice lowered and grew gravelly. "Don't go there, Lila. You married another man."

She reached out a trembling hand and placed it on his cheek. He stilled but he didn't pull away. "I never stopped loving you," she repeated. "Yes, I tried to make it work with Juan for Selena's sake. I didn't want her growing up in a dysfunctional family. But it was never right. He was distant to me and Selena both. I will never forgive him for what he did to us."

Tears came to her eyes and her voice caught. "He treated me like his whore. Dragged us to that church." She whipped off her bandana. "He cut off all my hair. He beat me. He starved me. He strangled me and left me for dead. He took my baby and sold her like a slave. I will never forgive him and I'm glad he's dead."

His arms were around her. His lips were against hers. Tasting of salty tears, and sweat, and passion. His tongue swept out and slid along hers in a sensual glide. Her pulse raced and pounded in her ears. Memories overwhelmed her of their times together. Long ago and right now collided in her mind and in her memories. Jack had been her first love and her first lover.

His kiss deepened and their moans sounded as one. She reached for and found his hardness in his pants. "I want you," she begged.

He kissed her lips, her cheek, her neck where it met her shoulder. She arched into him, impatient to be naked, feeling him skin to skin. Her memories were tainted by their last good-bye. She needed new memories to fill her mind.

His fingers ran over her short hair, the heat of his hand against her scalp. "You are so beautiful. As beautiful as I remember. As beautiful as I imagined in my dreams."

She smiled. A lie. A sweet lie to be sure, but a lie, nonetheless. Who could imagine Jack Canida knew how to tell one?

One kiss led to another. One touch blended into the next. He laid her back against the sleeping bag. When had he gotten it and rolled it out? Time was a blur of emotions and feelings.

He whisked her shirt off and flung it aside. His followed. He pulled her in closer. Finally. Skin to skin. As wonderful as she remembered. More wonderful, because it was now. His fingers trailed down her side and his hand dipped into her pants. He cupped her and her hips came off the sleeping bag. Her wet panties rubbed against his fingers as they searched and moved the damp fabric aside.

He slid his fingers into her wetness and she exploded. Her head thrashed from side to side and she yelled his name. She slowly came back to earth and gazed up at him. His beloved face filled her vision. "I want you."

"I want you, too," he whispered against her lips. "But I'm not leaving you with another child."

She sat up and shoved him away. "I would never do that to you again. You have to believe me."

His hand reached out and cradled her cheek. "I know that. I would not leave you with a child, a baby, if something happened to me."

He pulled her in close and slid down to lie beside her on the sleeping bag, his arms wrapped around her. "Once we have Selena back and we've in a secure location, you better watch out. I won't let you out of my bed or my life again."

Lila fell to sleep with a smile on her face.

CHAPTER TWENTY-THREE

Selena

Selena's Diary
Sisterhood of the Earth camp
Day 410 of Woman Rule (Teacher said to write it
that way)

I miss my mommy. I miss the boys from the RV yard.
We got to play and have fun. Here it is all work and
lessons. I thought school was over when the dead
didn't stay dead but Alaina and her mate, Belinda say
we have to learn our new place in the world. Women
are the rulers of the land and men are the slaves. I
didn't like the men at the mean church but most of
the men at the RV yard were nice.

Selena scratched that last line out until the paper
tore and her pencil dug into the page below. A
cough sounded from the doorway and her head

whipped up as her hand covered the paper. Belinda strode forward, her outreached hand grabbing the new notebook before Selena could close it.

"Who are these boys you mention?" she said, her finger digging into the torn paper. Her dark eyes shone with a fire deep inside and the edges of the deep scar on her face turned white. Selena peeked at her from between her trembling eyelashes.

Alaina came over to the table and pried the bent notebook out of her mate's hands. "Sweetie, it is only her private notes. She has only been here a few days. Give her time to adjust."

"I want her ready for the next hunt in two days," she replied as she marched to the tent's flap opening.

"As you command," the small woman said, silent tears running down her face as she gazed down at Selena.

From the corner of her eye, Selena stared as the tall muscular woman threw open the tent flap and marched out. With a shaking hand, she smoothed the notebook Alaina had handed back to her.

"Don't be upset. She only wants what is best for all of us."

Selena wasn't upset. She was mad. Everyone kept taking things away from her.

The zombies took her old life.

Juan took her away from her mother.

The Sisterhood took away Mister Toby and any safety she had felt.

She glared at Alaina's back as the small woman tiptoed back to the chalkboard, shoulders hunched. Everyone in the stupid camp tiptoed around Belinda as if she were as evil as the mean Reverend from the church. Her head swiveled and she glanced at the flap opening as if the woman might hear her thoughts.

Picking up her pencil, she scratched out her previous entry in the diary and wrote below all her thoughts about the wonderful place she was in. About Belinda, their wonderful leader. About all the great learning she was doing about how men were evil and women were right.

Basically, any lie she could think of to get by since her diary was no longer a private place all her own.

She tucked her diary back into her new knapsack and picked up a pen to write the lesson of the day. Her hand slid across the paper as she wrote as fast as Alaina wrote on the chalkboard. Soon the pages of her schoolwork were filled with as many lies as her diary as she copied the nonsense the Sisterhood was using to spread the bullshit as her friend, Dylan would say.

If she were to believe what the Sisterhood was saying, every mistake human beings had made since the beginning of time could be laid at the feet of men, from the snake that tempted Eve to the rising of the dead.

Okay, so there were some events they hadn't covered at her old school yet, but if the population was half female weren't they responsible too. Her head hurt with all the thinking and confusion. Her mom always said she had to listen to teachers and grown-ups, so maybe they did know things she didn't. The President of the United States was a man and he had ordered spraying the vaccine everywhere. She did know that one. They discussed it in school before the zombies came. Look where that led.

Her thoughts went back and forth like watching a table-tennis match in her head. Her forehead started pounding between her eyes. The tip of her pen dug into the paper as she repeatedly underlined the words, 'men are responsible for the zombie apocalypse.'

Hours seemed to pass as she wrote page after page until the welcome sounds of the lunch bell rang out across the compound. She dropped her pen to the tabletop and sighed with relief. Her fingers stayed cramped and bent until she rubbed them with her other hand. Tingles shot from her wrist to her fingertips as the blood returned. Her stomach grumbled and she yearned to jump up from her table, but the memory of her punishment from when she had done it the first day lingered on, along with the welts on her back from Alaina's belt. The woman had cried, but she'd beat her anyway.

Alaina clapped her hands together and dismissed them. Selena stood, pushed her chair in, and walked slowly out of the tent with the other girls. Alaina's voice carried as she reminded them to act like girls, not animals or boys.

"I heard leader Belinda say you get to go on the

hunt in a couple of days," the tall girl walking at her side said. "You're so lucky. I haven't gotten to go yet."

Selena stared up at the tall girl beside her, the deep scratches on her neck and arms from a scrub brush, another of the punishments, this one for refusing to take a shower.

"What are we hunting for?"

"Men," she replied, a mean look in her eyes.

She tried to swallow over the large lump in her throat. A terrible thought entered her mind and bile rose to join the lump in her throat. "We don't eat them, do we?"

"You really are as stupid as they say, aren't you?" A sneer on her lips turned an already plain face into a downright ugly one. "They capture them for slaves and for sex."

She could understand them getting them for slaves, men being stronger and all. But why would they want them for sex when they didn't seem to like men at all. Her mother had explained sex to her and one of the first things she said was you only did it for love. The tall girl beside her must have seen her confusion because the sneer was back on her face.

"You have to have sex to make girl babies. If we want to be the only people around there has to be more girls born."

"But, sometimes mommies have boy babies," Selena said.

The tall girl leaned down and whispered in her ear, "They don't keep the boy babies."

* * *

They don't keep the boy babies.

Selena huddled deep into her covers, shivering in spite of the spring warmth, the words echoing in her head over and over like an earworm. What did they do with the boy babies? Did they give them away? To who? Did they kill them? Her stomach flip-flopped and she envisioned the small child zombie she'd had to put down while she was with Mister Toby.

Thinking of the big, quiet man only led to more sad thoughts, so she turned her mind to something else. Belinda wanted her to join the hunt in two days. She swallowed against the knot in her throat. Could she hunt a living person? She'd only killed one skinbag so far. The big girl at lunch said they didn't kill the men. They captured them and made them slaves. Her thoughts unraveled back to the evil church where she'd been with her mother and Juan. They'd treated women like slaves, so men could be slaves too, she guessed.

They'd talked about slavery in school a little bit, but the teacher had said that slavery had been bad and it took a civil war to get rid of it. Selena nibbled on her bottom lip. If it were that bad, should they be bringing it back?

After lunch, the big girl, Dana, took her to the man cages on the far side of the camp among the outhouses and garbage dumps. Her heart stuttered and beat extra fast when she saw all the men sitting around and leaning against the metal of their cages. They'd looked just like the zombie cages at the church, big metal bars and a padlock on the doors. Unlike the zombies, who'd moaned and rattled their cages, the men just sat there with glassy eyes and drool dripping from their mouths. Most of them were asleep, laying down or leaning against the metal bars. This was a good thing, because there were more of them than Selena expected. Definitely more than had been in the RV yard or the church. The silence struck her. They didn't talk to each other and they didn't try to talk to the girls.

Dana had stood tall and started talking like it was an oral report in school. "The men are kept drugged so they do what they are told. We'll domesticate them like dogs. Some are workers. Belinda says by next year we'll have gardens and fresh fruits and vegetables. We'll have a clean camp without having to work ourselves. Some are for sex, so that we will repopulate the Earth with the superior species; woman."

Sleep finally reached up to grab her as she drifted off to dreams of row after row of mommies and daughters. A final thought of Juan and what he'd done to her made her realize the world would be better with no men. Maybe it was women's turn, just like they'd said in school.

CHAPTER TWENTY-FOUR

Paul, Suz, and Josh

Paul Luther's Log
Ryde Hotel Base
Ryde, California
Spring, 1 AZ
(Next new moon we will begin Summer, 1)

Disruptions continue between our group and Old John. A decision must be made. Is this place our new home or do we search for another?

"Another complaint?" Suz walked up to him as the Muncy boys left.

"That's everyone," he said. "It's unanimous. Old John is an asshole, a bigot, homophobic, or a mean old man, depending on who you ask."

She laughed. "It's not that bad, is it?"

Paul grabbed her around the waist and pulled

her in for a long kiss. He leaned his forehead against hers, their breath mingling. "What do I do?"

"*You* don't do anything. Have a meeting. The decision affects the whole group. Let them decide as a group."

"Sure you don't want to be the commander?"

Suz laughed and pushed him toward the doorway. "You couldn't pay me to be the leader."

He stared as she headed back to the kitchen. He sighed and opened the door to outside. Connor was sitting on a wall reading a book. He didn't know where the kid found them, but he was never without one. The latest was called *Masonry and Stonework.* Maybe in a few years Connor could be the leader. The job was making him old before his time and he'd be ready to hand it off in a couple of years, tops.

"Connor," he uttered a few times before the boy looked up from the book and pushed his glasses up his nose. "You're my messenger today. Let everyone know we'll have a group meeting in one hour in the dining room."

"Everyone?" he groaned. "Even Old Mister John? He's a grumpy old man and he yells at Rogue Vantage."

Paul gritted his teeth. "Yes, everyone."

"Okay," the boy grumbled, sliding off the wall and folding his book under his arm. He watched as the boy ran to get the job done. Paul was sure he did it so he could get back to his reading, more than any wish to do the job speedily.

He went inside and found the manager's office. Sitting at the giant mahogany desk, he gathered paper and a pen and started putting his thoughts into writing. Knowing what he needed to do and doing it were two different things. A lot of wadded up paper balls decorated the floor before he was done. His least favorite job in the army had been paperwork, he'd much rather be blowing things up.

He was still finishing up when the rumble built from the dining room. Connor had done his job. It sounded like the whole group was in the room and they weren't discussing anything quietly.

Paul straightened the papers and carried them to the doorway of the dining room. Slowly, the din simmered down and died. A few chairs squeaked on the linoleum as he strode to the front of the room where Suz and Josh had set up a table with a single chair. He walked around it and took the seat.

"Honesty will keep us alive in the zombie apocalypse. Just like in the army, your battle buddy is your security. You have to know the man next to you has your back, no matter what he thinks of you personally."

John stood up, his chair squealing across the floor. He started for the door.

"John, sit down."

The man turned back. "I know when I'm being talked about."

Josh jumped up from his seat and whipped around. "So do we."

"Fag," the man uttered under his breath. Only, the room was so silent it carried all the way to the front.

"John, sit."

He turned his gaze. "Josh, please."

Suz grabbed her brother's arm and yanked him into the seat. He crossed his arms over his chest and stared straight ahead.

John grumbled, but he took his seat again. Paul nodded to both.

"We don't all have to agree on every decision. But we do have to try to live together. It isn't easy with a group of any size, but we can make it work if we want it to."

"What if we don't want it to?" John called out.

"If anyone doesn't want to get along, the group will decide what we do."

Charlie stood up and stared daggers at John. "I motion the group banish John from the hotel. If he wants to stay on the grounds by himself, I guess we won't stop him."

Paul's gaze traveled to each member of the group. "All those in favor of banishment?"

"Aye," rang out loud and clear in the room.

"Those opposed?" The silence was deafening.

"Fuck this," John yelled as he jumped up so fast his chair tipped over and hit the floor with a loud bang. "I'll leave, but I'll be back and when I do I won't be alone."

They turned in their chairs as the man stomped to the door, shoving it so hard it hit the wall and knocked a framed picture to the floor with a tinkle of shattered glass. A couple of seconds passed and the outer door slammed as well.

He nodded to Charlie and his boys. "Make sure he is off the property in an hour."

"No problem, Commander. We'll see that he goes past the red line."

"The meeting is over," he told the room, watching as they filed out with smiles and chatter to return to their tasks. He put his elbows on the table and leaned his head on his palms. A headache was building, sending a throbbing message to his brain. Being in charge sucked.

Strong hands kneaded his shoulders and the back of his neck. He looked up to find the room empty except for him and Josh. The tension bled away under his magic fingers.

Josh leaned down against his back. "Stay with Suz tonight."

He reached up and laid his hand on Josh's. "It's our night."

Josh rubbed harder. "Suz calms you. Relaxes you. You need her tonight. I'll just get you for two nights in a row."

Paul smiled. "Wait. Was that a joke about our relationship?"

"Wonders may never cease," he added as he walked around the table and backed toward the door. "Be careful. I might announce it to the world."

He stared as Josh left the room, closing the door behind him.

The backrub had been great but it didn't dispel the reason for the headache in the first place. John was going to be trouble and he knew they weren't ready for it. They'd set up the repel zombie sound. The hotel already had speakers outside for piping music to the guests, so the Muncy boys had no trouble hooking up the recorder with the sound. They had headed in opposite directions down the road and marked the danger zone with red spray paint.

But that was only half of their concerns. The undead could be dealt with. The living caused a thousand other problems.

He turned his papers over and worked on defense plans for the hotel. They'd found a safe haven. Like hell he was giving it up without a fight.

A call to Brandon Fisher and his friend, Billy did nothing to ease his worries. Old John had friends up and down the river and they sounded like the kind to have fully embraced their Second Amendment rights. Their group had too few guns and too few people to operate them.

The rest of the day was spent in something he could control; explosives. Zach and Tyler Muncy helped him with the IED's in the back orchards. Only his didn't explode on contact. He wasn't risking any of their own people. They would be inoperable until he pressed the button.

The front was covered by the turret gun from the Humvee. He spent a few hours showing the Muncy boys and Aidan and Bryant how they worked and how to take care of them. If needed, they could probably do some damage, but he prayed they would never have to use them. He'd seen what they did to people, and he didn't want to ever see it again, especially against someone he knew, hateful or not.

When they sat down to dinner, Paul knew he'd made the right decision. The group had made the right decision. The boys laughed and teased the Madison twins. The Muncy boys were smiling and talking more than they'd done since he'd known them. Even Charlie was cracking a smile or two at Josh's jokes.

Shannon caught Paul's eye. "We need to raid some abandoned farms. The food is running low and there aren't stores to hit around here."

"Why do you think farms will do us any good? This early there can't be much planted. Probably not last year either."

"This is canning country," she said with a smile at Suz. "We'll find pantries and cellars with plenty to use. I'm hoping some canning supplies as well. The greenhouses have a bumper crop, but it'll go to waste if we don't preserve it."

"I'll add it to the list," he told her as Rogue Vantage started clearing the tables.

"So much to do. Where to start?" he mumbled to himself. Suz came around the table and took his hand.

"Come on, you. You can't solve all the world's problems in one day."

By the time she shut their bedroom door, she had her shirt and bra off. He whipped his shirt over his head and threw it across the room. Her warm, soft lips were on his as her fingers wrestled with his belt and shoved his pants down to his ankles.

"I was going to wash up first."

Her fingers ran over his damp head from the bucket of water he'd dumped over himself after this afternoon's work.

"Shower later, me first."

"You're a demanding wench," he said, laughing. "How did you know you got another night of me?"

"Josh told me before dinner."

They moved, falling to the bed. She yanked his boots and pants off, tossing her own away at the same time. His wife was a magician. She could make clothes disappear without a pause. He stared at her naked body. Suz's true beauty was the fact she looked like a fashion model and didn't care about it. She was natural and open. Her real beauty was within.

His hands reached for her and pulled her to the covers. The bed springs squeaked as he rolled her over and straddled her body. He touched her with his fingertips. Her nipples responding to his slightest grazing movement. Her blue eyes darkened as his lips followed his fingers. She tasted of roses and perspiration and Suz. Her musky scent came to him as her hips rose and they connected groin to groin. His erection grew and pressed against his underwear.

In seconds he'd ripped off his own underwear as well as Suz's. He sat back and dragged his fingers down her thighs. Each sweep of his fingertips closer to her center. She moaned deep in her throat.

"Please," she begged.

"Not yet," he said, his fingers tangled in the soft blonde curls between her thighs. One finger slid down her and found her warm and wet and ready.

"Not yet," he said, sliding down her legs until his face was buried between her thighs. A stroke of his tongue and she was whispering his name.

"Not yet," he said, his tongue plunging into her hotness, drinking from her, driving her crazy as her thighs tightened on his head.

She climaxed and flooded his taste buds. He licked her as she came again and again and again.

He slid up her body and slammed into her. Her legs wrapped around his hips and her arms wrapped around his neck.

"Now," he said.

Her screams and his filled the room. It took Paul a moment to realize someone was knocking on the door. Jumping out of bed, he threw the covers over Suz and yanked his pants on. He flung open the door.

"This better be damned important," he yelled.

"It is Mister Paul," Dylan stuttered. "Connor says you have to come right away. The government is on the radio and it's really bad."

CHAPTER TWENTY-FIVE

Cody, Miranda, and April

Ran's Journal
Middle of the river, nowhere
Where else would we be?
Spring, 1 AZ (I think)

We've been stuck on this sandbar all day. Teddy says
we have to wait for high tide to continue our trip. I'm
ready to get out and push the damned thing.

Ran laid on the front of the boat in her bra and
panties. April lay next to her wearing a matching
outfit. It wasn't like she had remembered to pack a
bathing suit for the ZA. The influenza pandemic
happened in a February. Most of the stores would
remain in that season until the goods fell to dust or
were eaten by insects and rodents.

The buzzing of flies was the only sound on the water, except for the occasional jumping fish. Cody and Teddy had caught some earlier and a bucket of catfish waited for dinner.

"I'm so tired of fish," she complained to April. Her reply was a mumble she couldn't understand.

She nudged her friend. "It's your turn to keep watch so I can get my back."

"Fine," April said, turning and sitting up. "It's a waste of tanning time. We haven't seen or heard anything all day."

"Doesn't mean they won't," Ran whispered into her arm.

"They won't what?"

"Shamble up when we aren't looking, like cockroaches when you turn the light off. Everything's fine. You turn your light off and poof, scratching noises under the bed.

"Ran, you are so gross sometimes," April said with a laugh.

The day passed as they alternated watching and tanning. Ran floated in and out of sleep until a thump sounded against the side of the boat and April squealed like a little girl. She sat up to yell at her and heard another thump. In seconds, she whipped on her shirt and jeans. Searching the deck for her shoes, she remembered they were down below.

"Damn," she muttered as she tightened her belt and pulled her knife out of the sheath.

Like cockroaches, the fast scrambling sounds multiplied down the side of the boat. She moved to the edge and stared down the side at zombs trying to pull themselves up through the railing. April opened her mouth as the sound grew, probably for another stupid yell as if she was a six-year-old seeing a spider. Ran leaned over and put her hand over the woman's mouth.

April nodded and dressed quietly, her eyes enormous in her sun-burned face. Ran shook the random, useless thought out of her head that redheads shouldn't try to tan. She stilled her breath. The rest of the boat was silent. The others must have heard the sounds as well.

The horde grew, their hands scraping against the side as if they could dig their way in to where the food was, like sucking lobster out of the shell. She racked her brain for a plan, but until they were off the sandbar there was nowhere to go with two helpless babies. Teddy had already told them high tide wouldn't be until sunset. She gazed at the sun halfway to the horizon. They had hours to go.

A baby's cry sounded from below decks, followed by a tiny moan

Ran caught her breath. Baby Jed had gone zombie on them again. His moans filled the boat, growing in volume just like baby's cries did when they didn't get what they wanted. She watched in horror as the horde moved as a mass of dead flesh toward the back of the vessel. That end was lower, with a swimming platform. She rushed to the rear, her bare feet slapping on the fiberglass deck. Not that it mattered how much sound she made, the skinbags knew they were inside this plastic crate waiting to be eaten.

Footsteps thundered up the stairs from below as she jumped to the lower deck. Seth and Teddy came up, their arms full of guns. Teddy shoved Emily's crossbow at her and handed a gun to April who'd followed in Ran's dash to the back of the boat.

"Make every bullet and bolt count. We got more zombies than we got bullets." Teddy's deep voice reassured her, even if the words terrified her.

Cody came to her side with a rifle. His comforting warmth leaned against her. "Dudette, it's going to be loud. Just so you know."

She braced herself as Cody fired the first shot. It rang in her ear. She ignored the barrage going on as best she could, making every bolt in the crossbow one shot, one kill. If the zombs didn't float away, she'd have to try to get them later. Bullets weren't the only thing in short supply.

The shooting petered out as the horde thinned and the ammo grew low. Moans sounded from the riverbank as the undead fell into the river with a splash. Some floated downstream, but a number of them managed to find the sandbar and their boat.

"Why don't they drown?" April asked as she dug through the knapsack with the ammo. As she found the right caliber she handed it to Teddy, Seth, or Cody.

In between firing, the little baby boy's moans grew in intensity until they cut off like a faucet turned off. Ran sighed. "I guess he's okay again."

Seth ran a hand through his hair. "That was a

long one. I keep thinking he might not come back." The man stared out to the horizon, silent but his concerns loud and clear.

Her heart stuttered a few beats. She'd never seen her friend so unsure of himself. Even when he'd woke up with two missing fingers he'd been more angry than sad, and he'd adapted to his condition pretty well, as far as she could see. But what must it be like to be helpless to help your child? Her father had known. He'd given his life trying to save her from Peters. She turned and stared at her husband. Her husband! The term seemed so new, so shiny, so unexpected. She'd die for him and she knew Cody would do the same. Maybe that's what it meant to be a parent, only about a thousand times over.

April plopped down on the deck in front of the knapsack. "That's all we've got, guys. We are out of bullets, unless you happen to see a gun store around here somewhere."

Ran let the crossbow fall to her side, empty of bolts. She put a hand up to shade her eyes and looked across the riverbank, up and down the river. A sparkle caught her eye upriver on her left. The boat moved slightly with the push of the zombs and she saw it again. If she squinted, she could just see a roof and some windows over the rise of the riverbank.

She pointed and Cody turned to look. "Out here every house has guns and ammo, lots of guns and ammo. We could swim across and check it out."

Seth put a hand on her shoulder. "They might

want to keep their guns, know what I mean?"

She nodded. "I get it. But if they were there and were the 'show us your guns' kind of people, they would already be out here seeing what and who we were shooting at."

"The girl's got a point," Teddy said, nodding.

"I'll go," April piped up as she stood and moved to the side of the boat. "I was headed to the Olympics before the world decided to end. Eight minutes, ten seconds in the eight hundred meters. I was hoping to shave a few seconds off that and break the record."

Cody put his arm around Ran and laid a hand on April's shoulder. "We'll all go. Safety in numbers, right?"

"Can you swim?" the redhead asked.

He laughed. "Dude, I was swimming in the Pacific Ocean before I could walk."

Ran smiled and hugged him. "Probably got a surfboard for your first birthday."

"Whoa, how did you know?" He kissed her on the cheek.

Teddy coughed. "Okay, this is not a day at the swimming pool. We'll keep them distracted over on this side and you all take that side. Scope it out. If you see anyone or anything, just come back. If we have to, we'll make these fuckers dead dead with sticks and stones. And don't take all day, high tide and we can be outta here."

* * *

"Are we leaving our clothes on?" Cody asked, a

blush heating his face.

Ran nodded. "I'd rather have wet clothes than face a welcoming committee in my bra and panties."

"Okay, let's do this," April added as Seth and Teddy went to the far side of the boat and started banging on the railing.

The zombs went into a frenzy, their hands pounding the side and their moans growing louder. More splashes sounded from the far riverbank. Cody looked down and saw the way was clear. He nodded at April and Ran and slid into the water.

His breath caught. He hadn't expected the springtime water to be that cold. After a few strokes, his body warmed up and he pulled for the side of the river. Listening as best he could with his swimming and the splashes of the others, he heard nothing but the breeze rustling the trees on the riverbank.

His imagination caught hold of the idea of zombies waiting in the shallows. He glared down, but the murky water of the San Joaquin River barely let him see his own hands below the water. He shivered from fear and the chill of the water as his feet struck bottom and he hauled himself up among the weeds.

He wanted to jump up and down to get warm, but he stayed squatting out of view of the house until April and Ran came out of the water and hunkered down beside him.

"Olympics, huh?" He threw back over his shoulder in a whisper to April.

"Hey, it's been awhile, okay?"

"See anything, Ran?"

His wife slithered up the bank, staying low and moving slowly. She turned slightly and gave him the thumbs-up. He and April pulled themselves to the dirt path and stood beside her.

Ran pointed to the house. "I don't see anyone. The lower windows are covered with plywood, but the top floor ones are open and there's a ladder to the roof. They must be using it for the entrance and exit. Don't think it's guarded."

"There's a garden in the back. It's green and taken care of looking. Someone must be here," April added.

"Let's go in calm," Cody replied, putting his hands up and moving toward the house in a leisurely stroll.

Ran and April followed behind him.

They neared the door and no one bellowed at them to stop. No one fired a warning shot. Cody shivered as a breeze shot across his soaked shirt and jeans. No sound filled the weed-infested front yard beyond the buzzing of bees and the clicking of insects. A dog barked far off in the distance.

There was a clunking sound from the rear of the house. He headed that way, sliding along the house to the corner. A man stood in the garden with a shovel. As he dug, the shovel hit a rock and thudded. He cursed and bent to pull the rock and toss it over his shoulder.

The rock hit the side of the house and Cody jumped, knocking into Ran. Her shoulder hit the wall with a thump and an ouch.

The man turned and yelled out. "Who's there?"

Cody caught his breath. Where the man's eyes should be were two black holes.

"I said who's there?"

He stepped forward. "Hi. My name's Cody Taylor. I have two women with me. Miranda and April. We don't want to cause any trouble. We're in a boat on the river and we got swarmed with zombies. We're hoping you have some guns or ammo to spare."

The man's hand swept across his face. "Got plenty of guns and ammo and it's not as if I got any use for them. Name's Steve Reynolds, by the way."

April cried out behind him and rushed the man. "Uncle Steve," she yelled as she grabbed him around the waist and put her head on his chest.

His hand shook as he felt her face and head. "April? Is that you? What did you do with your hair?"

The young woman laughed and cried and hugged him tighter as her shoulders shook. She turned to look at Ran and Cody. "This is my Uncle Steve." She looked up at the man. "Where's Aunt Becky?"

The old man seemed to fold in on himself. He flung an arm out past the garden. Even from the corner of the house, Cody could see the white crosses in a row in the dirt. April stared and started crying harder.

"Your aunt and the boys are gone. The flu took them all. At least they didn't turn," Steve finished on a whisper.

Cody and Ran came around the corner and moved to April's side. The girl asked the question he couldn't seem to phrase right to ask.

"What happened to your eyes?"

He shook his head. "After the flu took my family and most of the folks around here, a few renegades thought they could take what was left. I didn't have enough of what they wanted, so they took my eyes."

Ran gasped, tears running down her face. Cody pulled her in close. "I don't mean to be insensitive, but we really could use those guns."

"Of course," the man replied. "Come inside. I'll have you all on your way in no time."

"Uncle Steve," April said. "You have to come with us. You can't stay here all alone."

Steve led the way into the house. A fire burned in the fireplace and warmed the little house and gave it a little light with the boarded up windows.

Cody shook his head. Of course it was dark; the man wouldn't know the difference. He moved with the sure knowledge of a long time spent in this own home. The man opened a closet and Ran inhaled with a gasp. He was sure his mouth dropped open. From floor to ceiling stood guns, rifles, and boxes of ammo. He felt like a kid in a candy store, but instead it was a gun store.

He turned to Steve. "We don't want to leave you empty-handed, sir."

"It won't be for long," he said in a low, sad tone. He pulled up his pant leg.

"Is that a zomb' bite?" Cody managed to get out. "We didn't see any around your house."

"No, it was a dog, a couple of days ago, maybe a week. Hard to tell anymore, the mind is going. I used to be a vet. I know the signs of rabies."

"Oh, Uncle Steve." April hugged him and cried into his shoulder.

He patted her back. "Take all the guns. All I need is one with a bullet. Becky died here. The boys died here. I'll die here."

April's crying filled the room. He turned to see Ran with silent tears falling down her face and his vision blurred with wetness.

Steve raised his head and turned toward Cody as if he still had his eyes to see. "Take them. There's a small raft by the willow tree. All I ask is you take care of April for Ol' Uncle Steve."

He reached out and shook the man's hand. "Of course. Always."

Ran found two duffel bags on the closet floor and loaded up the guns and boxes of ammo. April hugged Steve as if she'd never let him go.

Cody found a revolver and put one bullet in it and set it on the table. "It's on the dining-room table, Steve."

He made several trips but he got everything down to the riverbank. Ran had tried to help, but he'd shook his head and she'd stayed with April. In between trips, he heard April telling Steve what happened to her and her family. He returned from the last load, the closet empty. They couldn't delay any longer.

"April, we have to go. Our friends on the boat are depending on us."

She latched onto her uncle. "I'm not leaving. You all can go on without me."

Steve pried her fingers from his arm. "Take her. Get her out of here. Good-bye April."

Cody grabbed her around the waist and pulled her toward the door. Her screams echoed as she fought him like a zombie in a sack. Her nails scratched down his arms and drew blood. Ran walked up to the screaming girl, pulled her fist back, and cold-cocked her. April collapsed in his arms as if she were dead.

A single gunshot rang out from the house. He jumped and swept April into his arms. At the river they got her and the duffel bags onto the small raft. He and Ran swam, pushing the wooden platform in front of them. In moments, the raft thumped against the side of the boat.

April stirred and looked up at him. "I hate you.

CHAPTER TWENTY-SIX

Jack and Lila

Commander's Log
Foothills of Mount Diablo
Spring, 1 AZ

A future with Lila and Selena seems possible if only we could find the girl. We only have so many hours in the day and searching and finding nothing is wearing on Lila. The scent of wood smoke is growing. I believe we are getting closer. We have found a small hunter's blind as our base, but we need food.

"Just one more block," Jack said. "That old man said Valerie had information on the Sisterhood. He said there's a store using the bartering system."

The straps on his backpack cut into his shoulders. With the constant battle of calories consumed and calories burned, soon his pack would weigh more than he did. The army really should have used the zombie apocalypse as a training camp. It was a hundred times rougher than boot camp.

"Look," he said, pointing ahead for Lila. "There's the burned-out minivan. The store should be right around the corner."

She panted behind him, her feet scraping along the asphalt. He'd had no choice but to make her pack every bit as heavy as his own. Bartering wouldn't be a level playing field. The only good thing would be their load was lifted and the food would weigh a lot less than what they carried now. Information was worth its weight in gold these days.

They turned the corner and he spotted the store with plywood instead of glass in its windows. A line spilled out onto the sidewalk. Lila groaned behind him. He turned and gave her a smile. "It won't be so bad. You can take the pack off once we're in line."

They fell in at the back and dropped their packs to the sidewalk. Lila bent over and he rubbed her shoulders as a teenage boy and two girls came up behind them. An older man came out of the store and looked them over. "We can only take six more today."

The people in line mumbled and cursed and started counting among themselves. Jack leaned down and whispered in Lila's ear. "We're number six. Watch your back."

The boy realized it a second after Jack. "Son of a bitch. You stole our spot."

Jack crossed his arms on his chest. "We were here first. You don't want this fight. Move on, son."

The boy shoved Jack and turned and walked away, the girls shooting daggers with their eyes at him. A man in front of them turned. "Watch out for that one. Marco's a mean little bastard."

"Thanks for the warning. But I kind of had that figured out."

Silence coated the line of people, desperation oozed out of every pore. Jack could feel it emanating from the men and women in line. Even the children stood silent, their eyes sunken and glazed. The new world didn't allow children to be kids.

"You're the last of it," the man said as they reached the doorway. He shut the door behind them, the dusk in the room turning to midnight dark until a click sounded and a lantern lit up on the countertop.

A few canned goods sat on the wooden shelves. The man swept his arm toward them. "It's not much, but it beats scavenging on your own. Let's see what you got to trade."

Jack grabbed Lila's pack and flung it up on the counter. He opened it and gently put the glass Mason jars on the wood surface. The jewel tones shimmered in the dim light. The labels proclaimed them Boysenberry and Apricot Jam. The man and the woman behind the counter practically salivated.

His face sunk in as he frowned. "We don't have enough today to trade for those. Maybe if you come back in a couple of days. We'll have collected some more."

Shaking his head, Jack reached in and took out two more. "We'll just take a few cans of whatever you got. More than food we need information."

The man nodded at the woman who scooped up the jars in haste as if they would grow feet and run away. She reached for the cans on the shelf and handed him two with the familiar red and white soup label and two with a ragged label of a picture of peaches.

"We're looking for Valerie. We've heard she can tell us about the Sisterhood of the Earth."

The woman nodded her head, a frown on her face. "I'm Valerie. What do you want to know?"

"I need numbers, strengths, weaknesses, and locations."

She stared at him, her eyes glowing with anger and hatred. "They killed my husband and took my son. I'll tell you whatever you need to know."

Lila stepped forward. "We think they have our daughter."

Valerie shrugged. "At least you're lucky. They're keeping the girls alive."

"For what?" Lila and Jack asked at the same time.

"Soldiers."

"Soldiers for what?" Jack said.

"For their war against men."

Five minutes later, the man let them out the door and locked it behind them. "It wasn't a lot of information for those yummy jars of jam. Do you think she was telling the truth?"

Jack looked down at her as they crossed the street and rounded the corner. "I think she told us what she knew. It's more than we had before. Now we know they have about fifty or sixty women, they camp near the top of the mountain, and the leader is a woman."

A shot rang out and a burning pain torpedoed across his side. It hurt to breathe. The world tilted and he fell to the side, taking Lila with him.

* * *

Lila didn't take time to think as Jack fell to the sidewalk and the asshole laughed and taunted them from the street. She yanked the pistol from Jack's holster and fired. The first shot hit the boy in the shoulder and shut him up. The second one hit him in the chest and he crumpled to the asphalt.

The two girls who'd been with Marco at the store ran screaming to his dead body. They threw themselves on him, begging him to move. Then he did. Their screams continued as the thing that had been Marco grabbed them and bit them, tearing into their flesh, the blood spraying across the cracked street.

She flung Jack's arm around her shoulder, trying to pull him to his feet. "Don't leave them there," he whispered between white-edged lips.

His eyes stared fiercely into hers. "Too good," she muttered under her breath.

She leaned him up against the rough, stone wall and marched across to the zombie teenagers. Three shots rang out and the children lay finally dead in the road. A sob pushed its way past the knot in her throat. They had been kids. The boy didn't look like he shaved yet and one of the girls wasn't more than twelve, thirteen at the most.

If a cure were found tomorrow, none of them would be able to live with what they'd done to survive. She held the gun down at her side and trudged back to Jack on the sidewalk. A puddle was growing under his hip.

"Bullet," he mumbled.

"Of course it was a bullet," she berated him.

"Make sure the bullet went through." His eyes kept fluttering shut, sending her blood pressure into the ozone layer.

She squatted and pulled up his shirt. A bloody hole marred his side, beside his ribs. She gulped back vomit as she viewed the mess on his back. A much larger hole tore through him.

"Okay, no bullet in you," she managed to stammer, feeling light-headed.

"Stuff in your pack. Front pocket."

She ripped it open and pulled out sanitary napkins and duct tape. "Really?"

He managed to smile at her before a pain appeared to shoot through him and he hunched over and grimaced. "Battlefield first aid. Tampons are better but I haven't found any yet. Women must have been smart enough to snatch them all up early on."

Following his directions, she slapped the pads on him back and front and wrapped the silver tape across his back and stomach. He put his arm across her shoulders and heaved himself up with some grunts and lots of curse words, only some of them from Jack.

They managed a block at a time. Lila leaned him against a wall and checked out the next area to travel across. The Moon was high in the black sky before they made it to the hunter's blind and Jack all but fell down the stairs.

In hours, she'd piled every blanket, every piece of clothing they owned on him. All she could do was sit there beside him as he shivered and his skin grew hot to the touch. By the time the sun came up and light filtered to their bunker, he was out of his head with fever and rambling about her unfaithfulness and betrayal and their little, lost girl. His cries for Selena broke her heart, as he mumbled about losing her and not finding her. Tears ran down his face and mixed with his sweat as he yelled at himself for failing.

Lila put her head on her knees and cried. She was going to lose Jack, just when she'd found him again. She'd lost Selena. Even when they found her, would she still be the sweet girl she'd known. What was her child going through on her own?

CHAPTER TWENTY-SEVEN

Paul, Suz, and Josh

Radio Message from the Capital of California
Repeating four times a day
Governor Max Rivers

My Fellow Californians, this great state has weathered many catastrophes. We have survived massive earthquakes, horrific droughts, and devastating wildfires. We have pulled together and come through to the other side of these natural disasters. But there is nothing natural about the abomination of the undead infesting the great state of California.

Starting today, we are taking back our state, mile by mile and acre by acre, if we must. I am calling on all citizens, all Californians, to step up and defend this great state.

Beginning on the day after the next full Moon, all men and women between the ages of sixteen and forty-five will be drafted into the Z-E army. Zombie elimination is the only way to take back our state for the living.

Any eligible citizen refusing to register will be arrested, tried, and executed. If you do not join our army, you will not be joining the zombie army. All traitors will be beheaded.

This message will be repeated four times a day on all available channels and methods of broadcasting, indefinitely. Failure to hear this broadcast is not an excuse to avoid the draft.

Connor clicked the channel off and looked up at Paul. What did the kid see in his face? Paul tried to project confidence, but his brow furrowed and his mouth dried out. They'd listened to the message twice last night and again this morning. The message was insane, but the messenger sounded right as rain. How could they make people register for a draft? How could they *find* the people to register for the draft?

His gaze swept the room. If they conscripted the eligible people in this room, they would be left with Muncy and the smallest boys and girls of the group. Even Charlie's youngest was sixteen. Forcing the adults to leave would be a death sentence for Rogue Vantage and the Madison twins.

His face heated with anger and his fists clenched at his sides. A soft hand grasped his arm. He turned and was enveloped in Suz's smile. He took a deep breath.

"They have to find us first," she said. Her smile widened and she kissed his cheek.

He couldn't relax. The zombies. Old John. Now this. Did it never end? All wars ended, why not this one? "We're right down the river from Sacramento. We could wake up tomorrow to a gunboat tied up at the dock, marching us off to war."

Suz nodded her head toward Connor, sitting forgotten at the ham radio. The kid's face was bleached white and his blue eyes enormous behind his glasses.

Paul forced a smile on his face and ruffled the boy's hair. "Thank you for learning to use the radio. Jed taught you well."

"Thanks, Mister Paul," he whispered, his face beet-red with embarrassment. Connor hated attention as much as his brother, Dylan relished it.

He turned to the group huddled in the doorway of the room. "We will get through this. Just because we have to register doesn't mean we would have to leave. Any intelligent person would see we need adults to hold this place. As Suz said, they have to find us first."

The group broke up, walking away, and muttering to themselves. Connor clicked the radio back on and put the headphones on his ears. In seconds, he was hunched over as he turned dials, his head tilted to listen to endless static. He'd tried to get the kid to listen less, but the boy was sure he'd heard some faint voices on other channels this morning.

Suz took his hand and pulled him out of the

room. "Between you and me, do you think they believed that bullshit you were selling?"

He wrapped his arms around her and whispered in her ear. "I pray to God they did. We have to hold this group—this family—together."

He caught the distant sound of a phone ringing. It still jarred him to hear the normal sound in their abnormal world. Josh came out the door and yelled. He caught the words 'call' and 'Fisher.'

He jogged across the yard. "Fisher is on the phone. He says he needs to talk to you, now."

Paul went into the office. Josh followed and shut the door. He raised an eyebrow at the action, but took the call.

"Brandon, this is Paul. You have news?"

"Old John is stirring up trouble. He and a couple of old-timers were here recruiting. Billy told them no one here would help and they left all mad and stuff. Be careful. Old John is mean when he gets mad and he is very mad right now."

"Thanks for the news, Brandon. Appreciate it."

Paul hung up the phone and looked to Josh. "My day just gets better and better. Old John is gathering followers. Locals aren't going to take kindly to us stealing the hotel."

Josh leaned against the door. "We didn't steal it. We asked him when we came if we could stay and he agreed. Even when he became an asshole, you gave him every chance. All he had to do was get along with people."

He ran a hand over his hair and sighed in frustration. "I don't need this shit right now."

A knock sounded on the door. Josh jumped at the sound, turned, and opened the door. Joseph Jones stood in the doorway, wiping his greasy hands on an old rag. A swipe of grease arched across his forehead.

"We got trouble, Commander. The generator is broke."

It took a second, but Paul realized the repel signal wasn't broadcasting. The constant hum that set his fillings to aching wasn't there.

"Can you fix it?"

The man nodded. "As soon as I get a replacement for the fuel line that was crushed."

It took less than a second for that to register. "That fucker. I'm going to kill him."

He looked to Joseph and Josh. "Get everyone together. We need to cover our asses."

They left the office, Paul headed to the dining room and the other men to get everyone.

News traveled fast in their small group and most of them knew what was going on before he opened his mouth, so he got right to their plan of action.

"The repel signal isn't working, as I'm sure all of you can tell. I need Charlie and his son, Zach at the north red line. Doctor Shannon, I need you and Joseph at the south red line. Josh will follow you and get the parts we need for the generator from Brandon's group. Once he has them, you will come back so Joseph can fix the generator. Suz will take the kids upstairs until we have the signal back. As for the rest of it, we will not surrender this place.

Not to the government and not to Old John and his cronies. This is our home. Any questions?"

His family and friends started clapping. The boys of Rogue Vantage cheered.

CHAPTER TWENTY-EIGHT

Cody, Miranda, and April

Ran's Journal
On the river
Spring, 1 AZ

April is a bitch. There! I said it. She is sniping at everyone. It isn't fair. Teddy is doing everything he can to fix the boat, it isn't his fault the motor stopped running. He is putting the sails up with Seth now, but without wind I don't know what good it is supposed to do. The only good thing about this day is that the babies have stopped crying and Jed hasn't 'died' for most of last night and all of today. At least someone is in a good mood.

The boat floated on the smooth-as-glass river, at a standstill with the anchor thrown overboard. Below decks became unbearable with heat and tension.

Ran sat in the pilot's seat, her feet up on the dash and wrote in her journal. Either get the words out or throw April overboard. The woman wasn't talking to her and Cody, she'd fought with Michelle when the woman only tried to comfort her, and she had everyone on edge.

She stared to the front of the boat where April now sat frying her pale-white skin. She hadn't moved in hours. Ran winced at the blisters forming on her arms and neck. But she was damned if she'd help the girl. They had bigger problems than a pouting woman who needed to pull up her big girl panties and move on. Sure, her uncle had died, but so had Ran's father and Cody's mother. Hell, Seth had to kill his own mother.

"She still there?" Michelle's soft voice carried over the nonexistent breeze and the becalmed boat.

"Yep. She's been there since breakfast. If you can call two bites of fish and the last of the bottled water, breakfast."

"At least the twins have enough food."

"Not if we don't get more food for Emily."

Their conversation cut short as April keeled over onto the deck with a thump. She didn't even cry out. Michelle rushed to her, Ran was a step behind. April's eyes rolled back in her head, with the whites showing. Incoherent words fell from her split and blistered lips.

"Teddy, Seth, we need you," Michelle yelled.

The boat rocked as the men raced along the deck. Teddy skidded to a stop. Michelle looked up at her husband. "We need to get her under the shade with Emily and babies. We need any buckets or pots you can find."

The big man picked up the small woman as if she weighed nothing. Ran bit her lip. Between the church abuse and the lack of food now, April was frail and tiny in Teddy's large arms. He placed her on the deck beneath the sheet Seth had rigged up to allow Emily and the babies to be out of the oven-heat below.

Ran rushed down the stairs and scooped up two plastic buckets and two large pots. They clanged as she piled them in her arms and got back on deck as quick as possible. She dropped them on the cushions as Michelle got April's top and pants off. The young woman looked defenseless, lying there half-naked in front of them.

"Emily, move the babies back. This is going to get messy." Michelle turned to Ran and Cody. "We need to cool her best we can. The best we've got is river water. Scoop it up and pour it over her as fast as you can."

Cody slid overboard and she handed him the buckets and the pots. As fast as he filled them, she hauled them up and handed off to Teddy or Seth who were pouring the water over April. Time passed in a haze as all she did was drag the bucket up and hand it to one of the men. Take the empty bucket and hand it down to Cody. Bend down, drag it up. Turn, hand off. Again and again and again.

Blisters formed and broke on her palms and still they continued on. She dropped a bucket, the water sloshing onto the deck. Wasted water. They needed it for April. Teddy's hand came and covered hers on the handle.

"No more, Miranda."

His anguish-filled voice penetrated the fog. "It's over. No more water."

"Noooo!" Ran slid across the wet deck, falling to her knees in the puddle April was lying in. She grabbed her friend's arm and shook her.

"You can't be dead. Not like this. You can't leave us. We're all supposed to survive."

Cody, wet and cool, knelt behind her and put his arms around her chest. His body shook as she realized he was crying. His tears fell on her shoulder, but she could find none of her own. She wanted to. She wanted to very much. Her heart cracked and the pain took her breath away, but no tears came.

April's skin began to turn ashen gray. Her body twitched. Ran grabbed her hand and squeezed until her fingers ached. Her eyelids opened and her eyes held none of the gorgeous emerald color they'd had. A milky film coated them, stealing any life out of them. A moan built in her throat and rumbled across the deck.

"Do it," Ran whispered to Michelle.

The woman took her knife out of the sheath and slid it into the creature's temple. The thing was dead. It wasn't April. She had already died and left this body.

* * *

Cody knelt behind his quiet wife. Too quiet. He sniffled and wiped a hand across his eyes and his running nose. Why didn't Ran cry? Sure, April had been a pain, but she'd been their friend.

He hugged her tighter. "It's okay to cry, honey."

"I know," she whispered back, her voice as dry as her eyes.

Ran sat there, not moving, as Teddy and Michelle got April wrapped in a sheet and tied up with rope. Seth and Teddy lifted her to the cushioned seats, and then hefted her higher to let her go in the river.

"Wait," Ran yelled, jumping up and running to the pilot's seat. She returned with her journal. She ripped out a page and tore it into tiny pieces. Going forward, she tucked them into the sheet folds.

She leaned down and whispered something he couldn't catch and hugged the shroud-covered dead. When she stepped back, Teddy and Seth slowly lowered her into the river. The current took her away, turning over several times until he couldn't tell what was April's sheet-covered body and what was sunlight blazing on the water.

With a heart-wrenching sob, Ran turned and ran to him, flinging her arms around his waist. She buried her face in his chest and then the tears came.

"I didn't mean it," she kept muttering as he got them both down the stairs, away from the others.

"What didn't you mean?" He wiped the tears off her cheeks and stared at her glistening, deep-brown eyes.

"I didn't mean to call her a bitch," Ran said between sobs and hiccups.

He cupped her face and pulled her in for a kiss. "Of course you did."

"What?" She stared at him like he was crazy.

The boat started to rock and he heard the crack of a sail catching the wind. He detected the subtle up-and-down movement of a boat under way.

He slid back against the wall, pulling Miranda with him. His arm draped around her shoulders and she rested her head against his chest.

"Let me tell you a story about family," he began. "When I was a kid, my parents took me on a cross-country trip to visit relatives in Ohio. We had a brand-new motorhome and mom wanted to show it off to family. We drove across and everything was fine. We visited the family and it was great. Then . . ."

"Then—what?"

He smiled as he leaned his cheek against her soft, curly hair. "Then, dude, the parents got the bright idea to have my aunt, uncle, and three cousins come back with us to visit California. The papers said it would hold eight people. They lied. It was bad enough when we were just driving, but about Colorado it broke down. Small town. No parts. We were eight people stuck in an eighteen-foot motorhome, for eight days, sitting at a curb in a teeny, tiny town where the biggest excitement was a new movie at the theater."

She looked up at him. "That's smaller than this boat. What happened?"

"What didn't happen? I love my cousins, but I didn't want to see them 24/7. We fought. We yelled. Then the adults started in. My aunt called my mother a bitch. Then my mom told her about the time the uncle was drunk and hit on her. My dad and uncle each accused the other of being stupid and breaking the motorhome."

Ran inhaled deeply. "So after, you never saw them again?"

"Nope," he said. "The motorhome got fixed. We got to California and had a wonderful visit. Even went to Disneyland. Everyone forgave everyone else and we moved on."

He put a finger under her chin and looked into her eyes. "That's what families do. That's what good families do."

She started crying again and he wrapped his arms around her. "I was so mean and now I can't ask for her forgiveness."

"Whoa," he said. "Of course you can. In here." He placed his hand on her chest, over her heart. "She'll hear you."

"I love you, Cody Taylor."

"I love you, Miranda Taylor."

CHAPTER TWENTY-NINE

Jack and Lila

Lila's Notes:
Mount Diablo foothills, I think
Spring, 1 AZ, I'm pretty sure it still is Spring

Jack's fever has grown all night. I'm out of options. In a lucid moment, Jack said we need antibiotics, anything with a –cillin at the end. Do I stay? Do I go? He'll die without medicine, but he may die while I'm gone. Do something, even if it's wrong. That's what Jack would say.

Her mind was finally made up, Lila hefted the lightweight pack onto her shoulders. She'd emptied it of almost everything but the bare essentials. If she had to hike back to town, she wasn't doing it carting everything they owned.

She laughed. Look at her. Lila Sterling Morales,

all her worldly goods on her back, and her only pair of shoes on her feet.

She stared at Jack, lying helpless and sweating through his clothes on a sleeping bag in the hole they'd hunkered down in. She wouldn't trade where she was right now for all the cedar-lined walk-in closets with thirty-two pairs of Louboutin's in the world. She may trade anything she owned for drugs for Jack.

Her gaze swept the hole. Nothing was left. She put a loaded revolver in reach for Jack and turned away. Peeking over the edge, the woods were clear. She wiped a hand across her forehead. Looking like another warm day; summer was coming to Northern California.

She took it careful on the footpath, only increasing her pace on the open stretches. She couldn't help Jack or Selena if she broke an ankle. Lila came to the edge of the trees and peered around a tree. The road was clear. No sounds of cars or people.

She hugged the buildings, all her senses on alert for anything out of place or the moans of the undead. That sound came from time to time, but at a distance. She reached the store and her stomach dropped to her feet. The door stood open, but no line snaked out of the building.

By the time she reached the doorway, the stench overwhelmed her. Pressing the back of her hand to her nose, she pulled her knife and stepped over the threshold. Blood and gore greeted her. The shopkeepers were behind the counter. Or at least, what was left of them. Perhaps it had been too fast or there wasn't enough left to reanimate. For whatever reason, they weren't coming back.

She edged around them and her gaze swept the empty shelves in a frenzy. Nothing. No cans. No bags. Nothing sat on the shelves. A whimper escaped her before she could pull it back. She knew of no other place to go. She wasn't Jack. She couldn't just ask questions and have people give her answers.

A shadow fell across the doorway. She shifted the knife to her left hand and pulled the gun from her holster. All she saw was black on black until he moved into the store. His black skin melded into the black of his shirt and pants. Sunglasses hid his eyes. He smiled and she blinked. A wide smile brightened up Jack's entire face and his warm personality would shine through. This man's smile reminded her of the devil ready to make a trade. He was like something out of a horror novel, wanting a piece of her soul.

"Well, what do we have here, now?" he purred, pushing his glasses down his nose and locking onto her with eyes as black as the rest of him. "Not finding what you're looking for?"

She kept the gun pointed at him. "I'm looking for drugs."

He swept his eyes over her. "You do not look like you need drugs, Luscious."

"They're for a friend. I've got some things to trade for them if you know where I can find some."

"Perhaps you and I can make a deal. What do you have to trade?"

"I have a couple of guns and a box of ammo."

He shrugged his shoulders and pushed his glasses back to cover his eyes. She saw herself reflected in their dark lenses. "I have plenty of guns."

"I have some new shoes and clothing."

His hand presented himself like a model on a game show. "I've got that covered."

She huffed out a breath. "I've got some jewelry. Diamonds, pearls, a few watches. That's all I've got."

His eyes swept her again and she longed for a shower. "That's not all you're got, Sweetness."

She sighed. Lila would do anything to save Jack, not only so they could rescue Selena but because he was Jack. It always came down to sex, drugs, or money. You just had to find a man's motivation. Her father had taught her that. She'd never be naïve again, but she wasn't stupid either.

"Give me the drugs and I'll give you what you want."

He moved forward a step. "What if I just take what I want?"

Pulling the trigger, she smiled as the bullet ricocheted off the door frame and the man jumped. "What if you just give me what I want and you get what you want. I think that is more than fair."

He swept her a bow. "I concede."

"I assume you have a place and don't want to just do it here amid the blood."

"Never let it be said that Silas Black does not know how to treat a fine lady." He swept his arm through the doorway.

She shook her head. "No. After you, I insist." Lila tucked the knife back in the sheath and the gun remained pointed at his chest.

Following him out of the store and down the street took all the willpower she possessed. One part of her wanted to just shoot him in the back and take off. Another part of her, the reasoning part, knew she wouldn't get the drugs that way.

Two buildings down, he opened a door and went in. Stepping over the threshold, she scanned the area. She stood in an empty warehouse. A light shone in the far corner. As he walked toward it, she noted the heaps of pills and powders set out on folding tables. The only sound their footsteps across the concrete floor.

"Welcome to Wonderland." He took off his sunglasses and swept his hand over the display. "Old habits die hard. My clientele comes out after dark."

Her gaze swept the empty warehouse. "Doesn't an operation of this size have more people?"

"This is a one-man operation. Silas does not share with anyone." He moved to her side. "Drugs or women. You've seen I have what you want."

"I need antibiotics."

He pointed to a pile of pill bottles. "I've got enough antibiotics to cure infection in half the country. Now, what about your side of the bargain?"

Lila sighed and looked down as she put the gun

in the holster. She looked up to see a flash of black coming at her face. The man's fist plowed into her jaw and lights blazed across her brain. Then it all went dark.

Time passed in blocks. A block of nothingness. A block of light and pain. A block of rest. A block of pain and the coppery scent of blood. A block of dark.

She swam up out of the nothingness. Prying her eyes open, she saw a man pulling up his pants and cinching his belt. His palm slapped her face and brought her pain roaring to life. She groaned as he smiled down at her, leaving the bed. The movement of the mattress brought another groan involuntarily to her lips. Her tongue swept across them and tasted blood.

"You are a fine piece of ass, Gorgeous. I'm going to enjoy having you around."

He strutted across the warehouse and pulled the door open. Another man stood in the doorway. "Don't let her leave," he said as he left. The door closed and locked. The guy outside stood with his back to the door.

She sat up and bit back a groan. Afraid to look, she glanced down her naked body surprised to only find a few bruises and no cuts or blood. Juan had beaten her more on one of his good days. In slow motion, she managed to drag her clothes on and find her backpack in the filthy office, her gun and knife sitting on top of it. The table of drugs beckoned. She was getting out of here and she was getting what she needed. A grimace shot across her face at the musky stench on her skin. She'd more than paid for it.

No sounds came from the door. The large back still filled the doorway. She swept the pill bottles into her backpack and carried it to the broken window beside the bed. Standing on tiptoe, she couldn't see to the outside. The large iron bed moving for her to stand on was out of the question. Too big. Too noisy.

She looked around. There had to be something. Crates sat under the tables. Grabbing them one at a time, she piled them on top of each other below the window. She shrugged into her backpack and climbed up the stack. It wobbled but held. Her fingertips dug into the rotted window frame.

The broken window looked out over an alleyway and a building across the way. No one guarded the back. She dug into the window frame, but it refused to budge. Pulling herself up, she dragged herself through the window. Glass dug into her side, but she pushed forward.

She fell to the ground, the air knocked out of her. Standing took all her energy. She hobbled to the end of the alley and peeked around the corner. No shouts rang out. The goon guarding the doorway stood just out of sight, only his black shoes showing around the wall.

Turning down any street she found, it took until darkness fell and the Moon rose for her to reach the edge of the woods. No way was she leading Black and his men to an injured Jack. She'd heard nothing but distant moans for hours. Confident she'd eluded

Silas Black and managed to not find any skinbags, she stepped into the comforting darkness of the tree-filled foothills. She gazed up to the massive shadow of Mount Diablo. Fires sprang up at the peak.

"Soon, Selena. We'll find you and take care of you."

Peace and worry battled within her. Peace Selena could be so close and worry it would be a greater distance to save Selena than the miles between here and there. Her ordeal with the man back in town only added to her dark thoughts of whatever her child had gone through. How could she find the sweet little girl she'd lost if that person didn't exist anymore? A sob caught in her throat.

She shifted the backpack and marched on. The hoot of an owl sounded along with the chirp of the crickets. She didn't need to count the chirps per minute to know the temperature was rising and the season was changing. Sweat dripped over her breasts and burned her tender nipples, the salt aggravating the pain. Her jeans chaffed against the battered flesh of her vagina. Her entire body ached as she pulled herself up each hill, resting on each flat space.

Footsteps shambled among the weeds and last year's dead leaves. The stench reached her before the Moon shone on the pale skin of an undead. She pulled her knife and dispatched it with a stab to the back of the neck. It fell to the ground with a thump. Whipping around, the moans surrounded her. For every one she took down, two more appeared. She stepped back, falling against a tree. A branch was head-level on her right. She slammed the knife into the sheath and grabbed the branch. It took three tries to pull her and the weight of the backpack up the tree. She climbed two more branches and settled herself against the bark of the tree.

Time passed and the horde grew. The moans of those present like a dinner bell to any skinbags nearby. As the Moon passed through the starry sky, she resigned herself to a night among the leaves. She pulled her backpack off and dug around inside until she located the length of nylon rope she'd placed in there. Swinging it around, she managed to whip it around the tree and tie herself to the trunk. Her arms went through the straps of the pack and she rested her head on its comforting bulk.

"Jack."

"Selena."

"Jack."

"Selena."

She whispered the names of those she loved as her eyes closed and the moans of the undead faded away with the pain brought by the living.

CHAPTER THIRTY

Selena

Selena's diary
The day of the hunt
The town below the mountain

I will never talk of this day.

She sat in the back of the pickup truck, bouncing against the metallic side as the vehicle seemed to hit every bump and rut in the road. Dana stood against a tree, her arms folded against her chest. A frown turned her plain face even uglier.

The older girl had been mean to her ever since the hunt had been announced two days ago. This morning her temper had flared hot and she slapped Selena in the face hard enough to knock the smaller girl to the ground.

The leader, Belinda, had waded in and yanked Dana to her feet. Before Selena could even get up off the ground the woman had the girl's shirt torn off and was beating her with her belt until Dana was a crying, huddled mass on the ground.

"We are women. Not animals. Not men or boys," the woman announced to the surrounding crowd of girls. "You will behave like women. Like warriors. We are an army and we will protect each other. There will be no fighting among you."

Several older girls came forward and took Dana by the hand. One of the girls hugged her and wiped her tears. Belinda snapped her fingers and a girl only slightly larger than Selena stepped forward.

"Cassie, take Selena and get her cleaned up and dressed for the hunt. We leave in an hour."

The girl took her by the hand and led her to the supply tent. In less than half an hour, Selena found herself washed up, dressed in camo gear, and handed a tranquilizer gun.

Cassie took less than two minutes to teach her how to point it and to give her confusing safety instructions and she found herself shoved out the tent and thrown up into the back of the large pickup truck.

As they went around a curve on the road, Selena held on to the side of the truck with a tight grip. The camp disappeared from sight and for a moment she felt herself actually missing the place. They had guards and traps and other women and girls. It promised safety.

"Where will we go to hunt?" Selena asked the girl beside her who looked just as clueless as she felt.

The girl's dark-brown eyes shone with a rage deep inside. "I don't care just as long as we get rid of them all."

"The zombies?"

"The men," the girl gritted out between her clenched teeth.

Selena turned away from the anger that seemed to burn the girl deep enough inside to be a raging fire waiting to explode. She didn't want to be nearby when it did. Her gaze swept over the mountainside. Spring had hit the area like an explosion in a flower shop. Reds and purples and oranges painted every hillside. Sunlight shone down from a giant yellow ball in the sky and puffy white clouds dotted the bright blue.

Why couldn't the world be this beautiful all the time? Why did there have to be zombies and bad men?

All too soon they came down off the peaceful mountain and hit the streets of the small town below. She didn't know the name of this town and there were no signs standing as far as she could see. Fires burned nearby and far away. A gray haze clouded the sky.

The truck slowed and stopped as they neared a park. A breeze set the swings to swaying and she could hear the clang of the metal chains hitting the swing set. The call of birds was the only other sound in the silence.

Into the quiet came the harsh yells of men. The loud voices and the anger in the words proclaimed an argument. Before Selena could even figure out what they were fighting about, Belinda was out of the truck and headed their way.

The woman was a blur as hands and feet moved in a dancer-like motion. There was beauty in it until the blood started flying. Even then, the splashes of red added to the feeling it was all a show. Two more men came out of the trees and ran toward Belinda.

Selena tried to yell but nothing came out of her dry throat. The girl hit her arm and got her attention. "Come on. It's our turn."

The girl hopped over the side of the truck and jumped to the pavement. She took off at a run, her tranquilizer gun held out in front of her as if she had done this many times before and she knew what she was doing.

Selena followed as quickly as she could, the gun bobbing as she ran. With a small pop, the girl's gun went off and a colorful dart hit one man in the chest. Selena swerved as he fell to the ground and raised her gun at the other man.

His dark eyes and dark skin reminded her of Juan. She locked her jaw and pulled the trigger. "I wish it was a real gun," she yelled at him, smiling as he stopped and crashed to the dirt.

"Excellent, Selena," Belinda said, reaching into her pocket and pulling out a chocolate candy bar and handing it to her. "Your first tag. I knew I was right about you. Channel that anger and hatred. Put it to use for you. This world has no time or place for weakness. The weak die and walk, only the strong live and run. We'll make a warrior out of you in no time."

Belinda turned as the older girls started tying up the men. The girl who had been beside her was stomping and kicking the downed men. She yelled words worse than her friend, Dylan had ever used. Some of them she wasn't even sure she knew the meaning of.

Blood rushed through her veins. She thought of every man at the church who'd yelled and hit and hurt their women. She thought of Juan selling her like a slave, like a thing, like she meant nothing to him.

She broke the chocolate bar in two and held out a piece to the screaming girl. "My name's Selena Mor—Sterling," she said refusing to ever use Juan's name again.

The girl took a bite and mumbled around a mouth full of chocolate. "Trisha Adams, but I like just Trish."

The moans of the undead echoed across the playground. Trish grabbed her hand and yanked her toward the trucks. "Time to go."

"What about the men?" Selena yelled as they ran.

"Mealtime for the zombies," Trish yelled back, laughing as they jumped in the truck.

She looked back and stared as the skinbags reached the tranquilized men and started feasting. Blood flowed across the dirt as they ripped into the unconscious men.

Her stomach heaved and she vomited chocolate onto the road. They'd never had a chance, they were drugged, and it was her fault.

The truck took off with a squeal of tires. Trish slid next to her. "Don't feel so bad. They were going to be slaves. Slaves. Zombies. What's the difference?"

An argument caught on the tip of her tongue. She'd seen the drugged men in the cages. Were they really different from the skinbags? Shambling along, not knowing anything except eat and walk.

By the third stop of the day, Trish had managed to pull her out of a funk, as her mom used to say when she sat and pouted for no good reason. By the last stop, she was yelling with her new friend and kicking the drugged men. She felt power. She was a little girl and she'd taken down full-grown men. Knocked them to the ground, tied them up, and taken them for slaves. Now they could see how they liked it.

Back at camp, Selena headed to the supply tent to return the camo shirt and pants. She found Cassie, who told her to keep it. "You are a hunter now. It's yours to wear.

"Here's a holster. Keep the gun. You're allowed to use it if any man tries to escape. It is your responsibility to stop them. Always. With any means necessary."

The girl handed her a knife in a sheath. "Strap this on too. Remember, any means necessary."

Selena headed out of the tent with her head held high. She was a camp hunter now. She looked around. Everyone looked at her differently. They smiled as she walked by, with a few of the little girls saluting her.

Before she knew it, her steps had carried her to the man cages. The quiet was missing today. Yells filled the clearing and the sounds of a scuffle carried to the trees. She moved closer. A large man in camo like hers struggled with the guards. His bellows carried across the space.

"Son of a bitch. Get off of me."

It took four women, but they got him to the ground and tied up. As they stepped away, she saw the blood covering his tan shirt. One of the women cut it off of him. She gasped at the hole in his side. They flipped him and another hole appeared on his back.

"It's a gunshot. We'll have to cauterize it. If it gets infected he'll be of no use," a tall black woman said.

Selena didn't know that word, but it couldn't be good when a teenage girl came with a metal rod, the end red with heat. The black woman took it. She thought her name was Denise.

"Aren't you going to drug him?" the girl asked.

Denise smiled. "Why waste them? He'll get them afterward." With that, she jammed the hot metal against the man's side.

His hoarse screams bounced back from the trees until they ended and his head flopped to the side. When Denise did the same to his back he didn't even move. She stood by the tree as the doctor came and put a shot in his arm. She knew he wouldn't yell anymore now.

Working together, the group lifted the man and his head fell forward. She jammed her fist into her mouth and bit into her knuckles. She tried to breathe. A hum sounded in her ears.

"Commander Jack," she whispered, just before she turned and ran to her tent and threw herself on her cot.

CHAPTER THIRTY-ONE

Paul, Suz, and Josh

Paul Luther's Log
Ryde Hotel Base
Ryde, California
Spring/Summer, 1 AZ

Things have gone from bad to worse. Hoping to update this later.

Paul stared at Josh's grim face. He was not going to like the latest news from the Fisher farm. The way things were going, he was sure he'd hear John had an army headed their way.

"They're all gone."

"Brandon and his group? Did they leave a message or anything?"

Tears sprang in his husband's eyes. "They're all dead. Even the baby."

He fell back into his chair, the feeling in his legs gone. "The skinbags got them?"

Josh shook his head, the words spilling from his lips in a disjointed tumble. "They were murdered. The word 'Traitors' was painted across the front porch in red paint." He shuddered. "I pray to God it was paint."

Paul's fists knotted on his thighs. He longed to punch a wall or a certain old man's face. "Old John," he whispered.

Nodding, Josh reached to the floor and placed a bag on the desk between them. "I got the parts Joseph asked for. Anything else that looked like it went to the generator too."

"That's something," Paul muttered, staring at the small square of sky in the plywood-covered window.

"You would think, but no," Josh added, standing and taking the bag with him. "Joseph says there's sugar in the fuel. We can't run the generator until it's all taken apart, cleaned, and reassembled."

Paul ran his hand over his hair, wishing he had enough to pull out and glad he didn't at the same time. "How long are we talking?"

"He says he can have it back together and running by tomorrow at the earliest. Means we'll have to patrol tonight or we'll be neck-deep in zombs by morning. I saw several groups on the way back from Fisher's." He swung the bag on this shoulder and stood in the office doorway. "I'll take these to Joseph and help him take apart the generator. Maybe we can shave off some downtime if he has some help."

He nodded. "Grab one of the Muncy boys while you're at it. He can help and maybe learn something in the process."

"Josh," he called as the man started walking away.

"I'm glad you made it back safely."

Josh smiled. "Love you, too."

Paul had a small smile as Josh left. It died quickly at the thought of Brandon and his family being gone. They were not only another line of defense down the river, but they had been friends. John and his so-called friends had to die. Let them show up here and the fires of Hell would rain down on them. He slammed his fist down on his desk.

Lunch was dismal, with long, grim faces. Paul moved his fried fish around on the plate, gazing from person to person. He hadn't seen such gloom since the well had been poisoned at the RV yard and they'd known they'd have to move on. The adults were silent and the kids were taking advantage of the neglect to torment and tease each other.

The cap fell off the salt shaker and Connor covered his fish with a mound of salt. He took out his frustrations on Dylan by smacking him in the arm. The small boy jumped and knocked over this water, all over Sarah Madison's plate. The little girl started crying.

"Enough," Paul yelled as he jumped out of his seat. "No more. We've been through tougher times than this and we've pulled together. Did we die in our homes when the dead rose and took our world away? Did we give up when the army deserted us at the Streets of Brentwood? Did we roll up and die when Peters came through with his zombie army and tried to take the mall from us? Did we sit and whine when the RV yard was made uninhabitable by Bennett's toxic church?"

"Fuck, no," Dylan yelled, his fist in the air.

Paul laughed. "That's right, fuck no."

"Until Joseph gets the generator fixed, we will deal with it," he continued, turning and meeting each person's eyes. He nodded and smiled. "Until the government gets here, we will continue on. Until Old John and those bastards attack us, we will ready our guns and be prepared for anything. If the zombie hordes come, we'll deal with them too."

"No zombs, but we did see a lot of smoke coming from the farms upriver," Charlie Muncy said as he walked through the door. "Thinking someone attacked them."

He and his son, Zach headed to the kitchen and returned with plates of fried fish and sliced tomatoes. They took their seats and dug into their food.

"Gotta be John and his crew. Those farmers probably didn't join him either," Josh said, his face red and his eyes cold.

"Brandon and all the people at the Fisher farm are dead. Josh saw signs that John tried to recruit them and they refused," Paul told the group.

"You got a plan, Commander?" Charlie asked between bites of fish.

He nodded. "We are moving everyone to the top floors of the hotel. All guns, weapons, ammo, and equipment as well. The only people outside for the next day or two will be Joseph and whoever is helping him with the generator. If we are attacked, we'll be ready. Let's move. By dinner, I want the radio and the kids on the top floor. Shannon will stay with them. I'll be arming the explosives out back and adding some to the front. With the Fisher group gone, we can assume anyone coming is a hostile unless we see otherwise."

Everyone finished off the meal and headed to his or her duties. The hotel corridors rang out with activity as everything of use was carted to the top two floors. He smiled as he passed the boys of Rogue Vantage carrying the ham radio and its various parts up the stairs.

Several hours passed in the hot sun as he played with his explosives and traps. They may not all be army-approved, unless by army you meant Rambo, but his prepper dad had shown him a thing or two about keeping unwanted visitors away. He laughed. The old man would have loved the zombie apocalypse. He would have been in his element building hole traps and barricades with spikes and other nasty goodies.

He would have to settle for just a few surprise elements since he was a crew of one, but if John and his group showed up, he'd take a few of them down before they ever got to the hotel. If they didn't get the repel sound turned back on sometime soon, the traps would work just as well for trespassers of the undead persuasion as well.

Suz's voice rang out across the hotel's yard as he set the last pressure plate and covered it with dirt and weeds. He took the path of notched trees back to the hotel. The small nicks in the trees holding no meaning for anyone but him. But every row of trees in the orchard had at least one IED planted along its path.

The several he had left would go out front after dinner. Then no one was going outside, except to the generator building.

The dinner hour passed in a mood as different from lunch as night from day. The little girls laughed as the boys told them jokes and Connor shared the pictures in his latest book. The meal was skimpy, but laughter and smiles added to the happy atmosphere.

He walked over to the kid's table. "No one goes outside. I mean no one." Happy to see they all nodded with serious faces, he patted the little ones on the head. "Just for a few days. When the generator is fixed, we can turn the repel signal back on."

By nightfall, the explosives ringed the building. Paul stretched and sighed as his back popped and cracked. He cleaned up at the river, sitting on the dock, eyeing the gleaming water. "Come on, Teddy. If anyone can make the journey, you can."

He trudged upstairs feeling much older than his twenty-eight years. With Josh out in the generator building, he opened the door to Suz's room. Her gentle snores that she refused to acknowledge sounded in the dim room.

Spotting the pill bottle on the nightstand, he walked over and gazed down at his wife. Soon, he hoped, she would tell him what nightmares made them needed. Had made them needed for a while. He couldn't fight an enemy he couldn't see and he couldn't help his wife if she didn't let him. Reaching out, he swept the perspiration-damp hair from her face. Walking to the doorway, he stepped through and silently closed the door.

A light shone under the door in Josh's room across the hall. He pushed open the door and found him there, shuffling through his books on the desk.

"I thought you would be out with Joseph," he said, shutting the door behind him.

Josh looked up. "I will be. Just getting a book for guard duty. Zach and I are going to take turns since it'll be an all-nighter."

Paul laughed. "You'll make corporal before you know it with planning and thinking like that."

"I learned from the best," he said, with a quick hug before he opened the door and left.

Still smiling, Paul sat on the bed and pried off his boots. He eyed the king-sized bed. Two spouses and he was sleeping alone. Something wrong with this picture.

His mind continued to race and sleep eluded him until he wished he'd taken one of Suz's pills. When sleep finally came, it was stringy with the rest he needed.

CHAPTER THIRTY-TWO

Jack and Lila

Lila's Notes:
Somewhere near Mount Diablo
Headed to hunter's blind
Spring, 1 AZ

Sleeping in a tree is damned hard on the back and other sensitive body parts.

She awoke to silence. The moaning din of the undead that had chased her into sleep did not greet her in the morning. In the brightness of the rising sun, Lila looked down to the dry grass and welcomed her aloneness.

Her impatience to get back to the hunter's blind and Jack had her fingers slipping on the hasty knots she'd tied last night. With a silent 'yes' she pulled the knot loose and shoved the rope into her pack.

She dropped it to the ground and followed as fast as she could swing down from the branches.

Shrugging into the shoulder straps, she hiked up to the next plateau. No foul stench of dead flesh. No moans of the perpetually hungry. She moved on, groaning as she found her body hurt more today than yesterday. Glad she didn't have a mirror to see her bruises, she still felt each and every one of them.

Wanting to rush to the bunker as she stepped out of the trees, Lila took time to use the lessons Jack had taught her. She circled on the edge of the clearing, noting every broken branch, each crushed plant amid scattered dirt. Boot prints littered the area around their hiding spot. The prints moved in random circles. She breathed deeply. The zombs must have moved through here before they sent her up her tree.

She slid down to the bottom of the hunter's blind and called out in a low tone. "Jack, I found your medicine."

Her eyes adjusted to the murky darkness in the bunker. Her breath caught and her heart pounded out of control. The place was empty. A crumpled T-shirt sat beside a brown-encrusted bloodstain on the concrete floor.

"Jack," she whispered. "Where are you?"

She wanted to sink down to the ground and cry and a whimper escaped her throat. Selena was lost. Jack was lost. How easy would it be to take a sharp knife to her wrists? A little pain now and then they would all be together.

Kicking the wall felt better, until the pain radiated up her leg and set all her injuries on fire. The agony bit into her brain. She couldn't kill herself. She'd only come back as the undead.

"Hell, no," she yelled, the sound reverberating through the closed confines of the concrete pit. "What would Jack do?"

He would gather Intel and assess the situation. That's what he would do. Okay, she could do that. Start with the concrete hole. The puddle of blood was small. Not enough for Jack to have bled out and turned. Not enough for him to have been attacked by zombs. Either scenario would have painted the drab gray walls a bright, shiny red. Didn't happen.

Her breath evened out. Do circles. She stepped out of the hole into the brightening day. The clearing was painted in a golden haze. The dry grasses stood out as if etched into glass. Jack had told her to do circles to get information about an area. Each one wider that the last, until you covered the location. She walked around the bushes and shrubs protecting the hunter's blind. The plants were stomped on and broken as if a group of people had moved through here. All she found was a few drops of dried blood. So, not the skinbags. They left blood, gore, and body parts everywhere they went. Along with that never-ending stench. The air smelled of sun-warmed plant life.

She pounded her forehead with the palm of her hand. "Think, Lila. Think." If they had found Jack and wanted his stuff, they would have shot him down in the hole or up here if he'd made it in his condition. Not enough blood down there. Not enough blood up here.

Another circle and another circle. She was nearing the edge of the clearing above the pit when she spotted a bright red among the pale greens and dry yellows of the woods plant life. Bending over, she picked up a small metal object with a tuft of red feather-like pieces at the end. She placed it in her hand and stared at the drop of blood on the tip.

A tranquilizer dart, the kind zoos used for animals. She dropped it to the ground and wiped her hand on her jeans. The path up here was more trampled than it had been, with a flattening of grass up the embankment to the dirt road, a dirt road probably not used since before the shit hit the fan. She bent down and picked up a bloody sanitary napkin attached to a piece of silver tape.

Deep tire tracks dug into the dry dirt of the road. She reached out a hand and touched them, her fingertips trailing across the pattern. Her legs gave out and she plopped to the ground. She threw her head back and yelled to the sky. "Where are you, Jack?

"I can't do this all alone," she cried. She would have sat there until the zombies came to eat her flesh if it hadn't been for the voice across the dirt road.

"You aren't alone, I'm here."

Lila looked up with a start. "Who's there?"

"Well, I don't rightly know who's there, but I'm here."

She squinted and peered into the darkness of

the tangled trees. The heavy growth kept the sun from penetrating. A gnarled, bent-over shape shambled out of the line of trees. At first, she thought it was a skinbag and pulled her knife, getting off the ground into a crouch.

"Oh, shiny," the thing said, staring at her knife.

In small movements, Lila eased the knife back into the sheath and stood. She towered over the thing, its head barely coming to her chest. It moved closer, a hand stretched out toward her knife.

Lila pulled back. "I don't think so."

The woman yanked her hand back and slapped it herself. At least Lila assumed it was a woman. The thing had on a nightgown and pink toenails peeked out from underneath. She caught a glimpse of a small, wrinkled breast through a hole in the tattered gown.

She twisted her head and looked up at Lila with a mischievous glint in her eyes. "Did you lose something? A very handsome man, maybe?"

The woman twirled in a circle and Lila spotted a hospital bracelet on her arm. She grabbed it. Lewis, Francesca was typed across it.

"Mine," the woman said, pulling her arm back.

"Francesca, did you see who took the man?"

"Maybe," the woman said in a little girl voice. "What's it worth to you?"

Lila pulled off her pack and dug inside among the drug bottles she'd taken from Silas Black, reading labels and discarding them. One had a few pills in it and Ecstasy written in pen on a sticky label.

She took it and held it just out of the reach of the small woman. "Did you see them take Jack?"

The woman eyed the pill bottle like a kid in a toy store. "Was he the one in spotty clothes?"

Lila shook her head. Spotty clothes? Then it dawned on her. She meant the camo gear. "Yes, it was brown, beige, and white."

"*They* took him in their big truck."

She brought the bottle closer. "Who are *they*?"

"The sisters. They take all the men." She pointed to the bulk of Mount Diablo. "They take them all up there and they never come back."

Lila handed the woman the bottle and watched as she clutched it to her chest and scrambled back into the trees, disappearing in seconds.

Everything led back to the Sisterhood and the mountain. She shifted the pack on her shoulders and started climbing.

Selena

Maybe it hadn't been Commander Jack. Maybe if she told herself that enough times it would be true. Selena had to know if it had been him and why he was here. She hadn't slept. She hadn't eaten.

She dressed in her camo and pulled her hair back into a ponytail. Looking a mess would get her another beating with the belt. She'd gotten it twice yesterday. Once for not concentrating enough at target practice, and another for too many wrong answers on a test.

Promising herself just a peek at the men to be

sure, she strolled through the camp to the man cages. Some were empty this early in the morning, a lot of the men in the tents with the Sisterhood members. She heard the moans like the zombies from the tents at night.

She spotted the camo pants in the cage at the edge of the clearing. Squatting down, she placed her hands on the bars. His face was scruffy with a beard and his eyes were sunken in his head, but she would recognize the commander anywhere, even without Canida written on his jacket pocket.

"Mister Jack," she whispered.

A few of the other men stirred and turned over. She whispered louder. He opened his eyes. She gasped. They were dark and he stared right through her. His cheeks above the scruffy beard were red and splotchy. His lips were cracked and bleeding.

"Lila," he whispered, the word barely louder than the breeze through the trees.

"Did you see my mommy here?" she asked, excitement raising her voice.

"Lila. Here," he murmured, closing his eyes.

Her heart fell. Her mother wasn't in camp. She knew everyone here and no one new had arrived since she had. Her mother was dead.

It didn't matter, she told herself. She had the Sisterhood. Standing up, she walked back down the path, never looking back.

She dug into her breakfast as Belinda walked down the aisles of the tables. The woman stopped and smoothed Selena's ponytail.

"How is my warrior princess today?" she asked with a smile.

"Very good, Leader Belinda."

"I'm glad to hear it. Perhaps we will take you on a supply run this afternoon."

When Belinda turned her back, Dana stuck her tongue out at Selena and gave her the evil eye. Weren't they supposed to be sisters?

She turned in her seat. "Leader Belinda, can Dana go, too? She had all tens in target practice yesterday."

Belinda's smile grew wider. "Of course, Selena. We must look after each other. We are sisters."

"Sisterhood of the Earth," Selena and Dana intoned together.

Belinda left and Selena turned to find Dana putting a cookie on her plate.

"Thanks," Selena said, biting into the chewy oatmeal cookie.

Time passed swiftly and before she knew it, it was time to leave for the supply run. Dana came rushing into her tent out of breath.

"Are you ready? Leader Belinda said we have ten minutes or she is leaving without us."

Selena put the tranq gun in its holster and strapped on her knife. "Ready to go."

She felt like the warrior princess Belinda called her as they rode down into town. A few zombs shambled across the road, but they were no match for the enforced ramming grill on the front of the truck. She and Dana cheered every time they bumped over a skinbag.

The truck slowed as they approached a big-box store. Selena had loved going with her mom. It had been their secret. Juan hated the place, said it wasn't where they were supposed to shop. But, she and mom loved it.

The enormous jars of cookies.

The gigantic boxes of candy.

The endless rows of goodies of all kinds.

She jumped out of the truck and Dana followed, pulling their knives as the zombies moaned and headed their way. The bigger girls rushed in and knocked them down and Selena and Dana moved in and pushed their knives through their mushy skulls.

A few waited inside, but were quickly dispatched. Belinda put an arm around Selena's and Dana's shoulders. "Pick one thing just for you. You don't have to share with anyone unless you want to. To the victors, go the spoils. Or in our case, to the warriors, go the goodies."

She raced to the candy and cookie aisle, mice and insects scattering at their footsteps. Selena reached for the chocolate bars but stopped. That had been her mom's favorite treat. She grabbed the cookies in the plastic jar instead. She shook it and peeked inside. No bugs. Good.

"You aren't taking the chocolate bars?" Dana asked.

Selena shrugged. "You can have them."

The girl snatched them up and turned the box over to check for holes and chew marks. "Nope, this one is good to go."

With them all working together, the truck was

filled to the brim with just enough room left for them to fit.

Selena tucked herself in the corner and Dana sat beside her, munching on a chocolate bar. The girl broke off a piece and handed it to her. She hesitated, but took it.

The chocolate melted on her tongue, lingering. No wonder her mother had liked them so much.

CHAPTER THIRTY-THREE

Paul, Suz, and Josh

Paul Luther's Log
Ryde Hotel Base
Ryde, California
Spring/Summer, 1 AZ

What good thing can you say about a battle except we didn't have long to wait? If this is my last entry let it be said we did our best.

"I won't tell you again, John. Go home." His voice carried via the bullhorn. Paul knew the man and his followers heard him, because John's face grew beet-red and he raised his fist and shook it at them.

The only thing keeping the mob from advancing was the red smear on the driveway from the first man who'd tried to run up to the front of the hotel and found an IED. The rest were content to stay well back and take potshots at the front of the building.

The sound of the turret gun facing to the rear firing boomed in the room. "Cease fire," Paul yelled. Silence came, followed by the explosions from the back and the screams of the wounded and dying.

"It doesn't have to be this way, John. Just leave us in peace. We should be fighting the zombies, not each other. We can all get along."

"Fuck you."

"Okay, then," he said, putting down the bullhorn and standing behind the turret gun. He squeezed the trigger and laid a line across the driveway about twenty feet in front of the men. Asphalt ripped and flew through the air. An IED went off as the line of bullets hit the pressure plate.

"Shit," he muttered. "That didn't help."

The men on the road opened fire. The bullets pinged off the front of the building. A yell came from the room to his left, followed by a man's cry.

"Zach!"

Paul rushed to the room. Charlie Muncy leaned up against the wall, his oldest son cradled in his arms. The blood covered the man's hand where he tried to stop the flow from a wound on the boy's neck.

"Zach, don't leave me," he whimpered, tears in his eyes as he looked up at Paul.

He tried to talk, the blood gushing from the hole and gurgling from his lips. "Dad, don't let me turn."

"Of course, Zach. Dad will take care of it."

The boy breathed on a sigh and his chest didn't move. Charlie pulled his knife and placed the point on his son's temple.

"I can't," he whispered, dropping the knife.

Paul squatted beside them. "You don't have to." He pulled his knife and slowly pushed it in to sever the spinal cord.

"We finish this," he gritted out as he stood and strode to the other room.

He threw the knife with Zach Muncy's blood coating the blade to the floor and snatched up the bullhorn. He moved to the window and pushed the button.

"John, you have a young boy's blood on your hands. You started this, but I will finish it. You have five seconds to leave."

His answer was a bullet in the window frame by his head. "So be it."

Paul stepped behind the gun and turned to see Josh at the other one in the room across the hall. "Don't leave anything down there alive."

He counted down.

"Five."

"Four."

"Three."

"Two."

"One."

The barrage was deafening. His mind shut down and his movements became automatic as he fired round after round into the crowd of men. Their bodies exploded and painted the road with splotches of blood and gore and red. Everything red. Everywhere red. All he could see was red.

Several tried to make a run for it and stepped on the IED's he'd planted along the side of the road. Their gore fell and mixed with the mess already there.

His fingers grew numb and still he fired.

Nothing moved and still he fired.

Still he fired, until Josh pried his fingers off of the trigger.

His ears ringing, it took a moment for the moans to filter through to his brain. The first line of shambling skinbags came down the road past the line of trees. Some stopped to feast on the buffet provided on the front driveway of the hotel.

Paul selected his shots, but they kept coming. They spread out and filled the road. Several tumbled down the riverbank and fell with a splash into the river. The turret gun clicked empty. He held his cramped, throbbing hands down at his sides. He stared as a multitude of walking corpses crowded toward them until the black asphalt was hidden in a sea of blood and tattered clothing. Their hands reached for the humans in the windows and their moans grew in volume as the horde grew.

"How many undead can there be out here?" Suz said over his shoulder. "There can't have been this many people up and down the whole river." She wrapped her arms around him and leaned her chin on his shoulder.

"Maybe if we're quiet they'll move on."

He shook his head. The sound of bodies pressed

against the plywood-covered door and windows downstairs carried through the open window along with the stench of hundreds of moldering dead.

Paul pushed away from the window frame. "Have Shannon and Joseph take the kids to the roof. I put some supplies and the flare guns up there earlier. Maybe someone will come down the river, even if it's the government they may have a place for children. You and Josh go up with them."

Josh stomped into the room. "We aren't going anywhere without you. Don't go all 'no guts, no glory' on us now."

Paul wrapped them both in a hug. Tyler Muncy came running into the room, skidding to a stop. "Dad says there's a boat out on the river, tying up to the dock."

He turned to the window at the boy's words. Men stood on the deck of the boat, weapons in hand. Their ammo was gone. He'd counted the explosions, the IEDs were gone. Even if they evaded the zombies, the government seemed to have weaponry to make their case.

"Fuck me," he whispered.

The men on the boat opened fire.

Cody and Ran

She stood on the boat's roof among the sails. Standing on tiptoe, she could just see the bright pink of the Ryde Hotel. The sound of shooting bounced off the riverbanks and filled the air. It sounded like machine guns firing from the hotel.

Ran rushed to the pilot's seat. Teddy spotted her and yanked his headphones off. "Don't tell me you saw some zombs in the water when I'm trying to listen to Boyz II Men."

"No, there's shooting. I think the hotel is under attack. But I don't know if it's our guys trying to take the place or trying to defend it."

"Well, we can't just call them up and ask, can we?" he said, nudging her to take the wheel. "Keep the sails pointed just like that. I'll get the guns and the men."

She held the boat steady as Teddy returned with Seth, Cody, and enough guns for an army. Uncle Steve had had a stockpile, among them a couple of AK47s Cody had jumped on. Boys and their toys, she thought, shaking her head.

Unfortunately the wind changed direction, leaving her at a loss how to do anything about it. Teddy handed her his Uzi and took the wheel. The wind change also brought the information of who was attacking the hotel. The stench of undead flesh wafted over them.

"Gross," Cody complained.

"At least we don't have to worry about do we shoot or not," Ran replied, running back to the roof.

Teddy piloted the boat up against the dock. It bumped gently. The large man grabbed another gun and started walking around to the front of the boat. The large sails cracked in the wind and half the horde diverted their attention to the new attraction on the river.

"Fuck me," Ran whispered as she pulled the trigger. The gun jumped in her hands but she managed to hit most of what she was aiming for. Cody was more selective as he tried to stop any skinbags from making it to the dock and then their boat.

Ran saw Michelle out of the corner of her eye as the woman ran ammo to the shooters and exchanged guns to reload. Her arms started aching but she kept firing. One by one the men stopped shooting and the din died down.

Bodies littered the lawn and driveway of the hotel. Some were piled two or three deep, haphazardly sprawled over each other. Ran waited for the ringing in her ears to die down. The repel sound. She didn't hear it. She didn't feel it.

Did their group hold the hotel or had they been turned away, or even worse, killed by the people in there now?

A man stood in the shadows of an upper floor window. "Boat on the river. Identify yourselves."

Ran looked at Teddy. "You have to give him the password."

"Man, it's so stupid," the man grumbled.

"Identify yourselves or be shot."

"If they could shoot us why didn't they shoot the zombs?" Cody said. "Lame."

Teddy stepped up to the railing and raised his hands to his mouth to yell. "Skinbags bite the big one."

A cheer went up from the rooftop of the hotel and four small heads popped up over the side.

It took a while, but the boat group managed to get all of them plus two babies to the hotel. The boys of Rogue Vantage pelted down the stairs and jumped on Teddy.

"Mister Teddy. You said it. You said it." They laughed as the big man blushed and hugged them all.

Ran searched every face. She turned to Paul. "Where's Commander Jack?"

CHAPTER THIRTY-FOUR

Jack and Lila

Lila's Notes:
Outside the camp
Summit of Mount Diablo
Spring, 1 AZ

Women are not the fairer sex. Our cruelty is right up there with men. Don't let anyone tell you differently. They are lying.

She sat in the branches, her back against the trunk. Lila stared across to the Sisterhood camp. Her jaw ached from clenching and grinding her teeth. The Sisterhood should have made friends with the Fruitful Harvest Church. Men. Women. Didn't matter if you thought the other half of the species belonged in cages or servitude.

The sun was high in the sky by the time she reached the outskirts of their camp. Jack told her desperation had a smell. She believed him. Finding the cages was easy. She followed the scent of despair and dying. The moans of the men mimicked the moans of the undead.

Hiding in the bushes, she'd dug her nails into her thighs and bit her lips to stop the screams. The men were scarecrows, the rags they were allowed hanging off of their wasted bodies. Some lay nude on the ground, too out of it to care.

She'd watched as a woman went from cage to cage, grabbing arms and shooting them up with drugs. When the woman stayed near the cages, she'd slipped away and found the tree to see down into the camp.

Far across the compound she saw a couple of trucks take off and head down the mountain to the town below. She shimmied down the tree and left her pack at the base. Moving around the outskirts of the camp, she moved closer to the edge, finding some tents to hide behind. Clothes sat in a basket on a chair. She grabbed a baseball cap and slammed it on her head. Earlier, she'd seen all the women and girls had braids or neat pony tails down their backs. Her chopped off, short hair would mark her as an outsider.

Look like you belong and you can get away with crashing any event. Her mother had told her that when she'd been a shy preteen. She threw her shoulders back, head held high, and swaggered through the camp as if she belonged there. A few nods to women passing by and soon they started nodding back.

Her eyes swept the camp. Her gaze lingered on every blonde-haired little girl. She pounded her thigh with her fist. If Selena was here, she didn't see her anywhere. But there were more people here than she'd originally thought. Many more than the fifty to sixty they'd been told. How many girls were they grabbing? A tent flap opened and a flood of school-age girls poured out. Looking from under the bill of her cap, Lila spotted one blonde girl, but she was at least a foot shorter than her daughter.

She took a deep breath. First Jack, and then Selena. Make a plan and stick to it, but be willing to improvise. The Jack Canida School of apocalypse training. She smiled as she reached the path to the back of the camp. The stench of a multitude of unwashed bodies wafted over her. She brought her hand to her face.

The bitch with the needles and drugs was gone. Lila moved from cage to cage. If the men noticed her, they made no sign. Their glazed eyes stared at the rustling leaves on the trees. They sat or lay on the ground lost in a drug-induced coma-state. She wanted to cry at the abuse people dumped on each other, but she didn't have the time for tears.

She glanced over and spotted the muted colors of camouflage. Falling to her knees beside the bars, she reached a hand through and grabbed his arm.

"Jack," she cried, tears blurring her vision. His eyes had sunk into his head and his face was slick with sweat. He moaned and mumbled as he turned over. Lila slapped her hand over her mouth. Someone had burned him. Where his gunshot wounds should be was charcoaled flesh. Red lines radiated from the burns.

"I'm getting you out of there," she gritted out.

She searched the small tent nearby, ripping open cases and boxes. She huffed in frustration. If there were keys there, she couldn't find them. She ran back to the cage and seized a palm-sized rock from the ground. Raising it to smash the lock, a hand latched onto her shoulder and whipped her around.

Her cap flew off and the woman stared at her. "Who are you? You don't belong here."

Lila didn't think. She raised her hand and crashed the rock into the woman's head. A crack resounded and her eyes rolled back in her head. The rock fell from her hand and she grabbed the woman under the arms and dragged her to the tent.

She raised the rock once more and brought it down on the lock. It took several tries, but the lock broke and Lila ripped it off, flinging it to the ground. She looked at the line of cages. A sob built in her throat. She couldn't save them all. Voices rose from down the path, getting louder and closer.

"I'm sorry," she cried as she swung open the door and grabbed Jack. Slapping his face was the last thing she wanted to do, but she'd never get his dead weight out of here without some help. He muttered and flung his hands up weakly as if to protect himself.

"On your feet, soldier," she yelled in his ear. She

wanted to hug him as he pulled himself to his feet.

Wrapping his arm around her shoulders, they shuffled along. She glanced back once to see the other men in his cage stumbling out. Getting into the trees undetected was as hard as she thought it would be. Getting back to her pack and then away from the camp was even harder.

CHAPTER THIRTY-FIVE

Selena

Selena's Diary
Sisterhood of the Earth camp
Day 413 of Woman Rule

I'm glad. I can't say more than that.

They returned to chaos. Torches were aflame and women and girls were running all over the compound. Selena hopped out of the truck and Dana jumped out right next to her.

Alaina ran up to Belinda and started blubbering, tears running down her face and her hands twisting against each other. "You have to do something."

"What happened?"

Selena slid back until her body melded with the truck. Belinda with that calm, quiet voice was scary. Dana followed her lead as they tried to be invisible.

"The men in one of the cages escaped. Corrine was hit over the head and the men got out."

Belinda turned as if she could see them even though they huddled in the dark. "Girls, you are with me. I'll show you how to be a leader."

They ran to keep up with her long strides. Selena stopped as they reached the cages, with one standing empty, the door swung open. She looked around the clearing. Commander Jack's cage. How had he escaped?

The missing answer lay in the broken lock Corrine placed in Belinda's outstretched palm. It lay battered and in pieces.

"It didn't break itself," the leader said, her voice deadly cold.

"No, Leader Belinda," Corrine stuttered, holding her head. "A woman let them out."

"We have a traitor in our midst," Belinda bellowed.

Corrine started crying and fell to the ground in a huddled ball.

Selena smirked at the woman as Belinda kicked her and moved on. She gazed into the dark woods, but didn't see anything or anyone. She heaved a sigh of relief. All the ties to her old life were cut and gone. This was her new life—the Sisterhood of the Earth.

"Be safe, Commander Jack," she whispered under her breath.

They returned to the center of the camp. Belinda threw a torch into the giant fire pit. Alaina blew her whistle and the women and girls of the Sisterhood tumbled from their tents to line up in neat rows.

Once everyone was present, Belinda stepped before the fire. "The Sisterhood of the Earth is pure. We are the dominant species in this world. Men are weak and brought us to the edge of destruction too many times. They thought they could play God and it has led to the undead walking the Earth. They had their chance. Now it is our turn.

"But today, someone betrayed us. Someone turned her back on the Sisterhood and sided with the men. She has shown where her loyalties lie and it is not with us."

A gasp rang out from the crowd in one united breath. A cry sounded from the edge of the light from the fire.

"I didn't do it. I was attacked," Corrine cried as two large women dragged her to the firepit and flung her down to the ground by Belinda's feet.

"Get up, Corrine. Stand like a proud woman for once in your miserable life."

The woman stood, swaying on her feet. Belinda grabbed a handful of her long black hair and pulled her head back. "I've ignored the complaints against you because you were our only doctor. The tales of you not drugging the men enough. I let it slide, since the women said it was easier to get babies that way. I let it slide that you seemed to care a little too much for the men you were in charge of, thinking it was your Hippocratic Oath. But I will not let this slide."

She turned the woman's face to the fire so all could see the bruise and the drops of blood on her cheek and temple. "This woman claims she was attacked by a woman who let the men out. I say she staged the attack and did it herself. How do you find? Is she innocent or guilty?"

"Guilty. Guilty. Guilty." The crowd's yells built to an ear-splitting roar.

Belinda pulled the woman's head back and drew her knife across her throat. "Sentence is passed."

Selena leaned forward, her hands clenching in front of her as Corrine died, turned, and died again. The two large women stepped forward and threw the corpse on the fire. Cheers rang out, none yelling louder than Selena.

Jack and Lila

She yelled. She cried. She begged. Finally, she got Jack halfway down the mountain to the abandoned camp she'd found on her way up. The tent was still in decent condition and a stream ran beside it. Crying, she dumped him inside it and fell to the ground. Her body ached in all new places. Her shoulders were rubbed raw from the pack and half carrying Jack.

His moans came from the tent. She stretched. Drugs in or drugs out. It had to be drugs out. It wouldn't do any good to put the antibiotics in and then just flush them right back out.

She didn't go through what she did to waste them. Digging into a side pocket on her pack she found the metal folding cup. It fit in the palm of her hand. She sighed. It was going to be a long night.

Trudging from the stream to the tent, she lost count of the cups of water she forced on Jack. The first time he peed his pants, she'd stripped him and washed them in the stream, hanging them over a bush to dry overnight. After that, it was just easier to leave him naked. It wasn't as if she hadn't seen him naked before, they had made a child together.

She wanted to cry at the burns on his side and back. What had those bitches used? A fireplace poker? The wound was ugly and she wept for his pain and suffering, but it seemed to have done the job. She remembered seeing Seth Ripley's hand one time and him telling her of what Miranda did to save his life. How much had this world demanded of them? How much more would it?

"I refuse to lose you, Jack Canida," she told him, laying wet shirts on his heated body.

"Selena," he mumbled as his head tossed and turned.

She wiped his face with a wet rag. "Yes, we will find Selena, once you are better."

In desperation she broke open the penicillin pills and poured them into the cup. She added water and forced it down him. The first cup was lost to his vomiting. The next stayed down for a few moments and then came back up. By the third, he held it down and rested between bouts of delirium.

By the time the sun painted the sky in pink and gold, his face was cool to the touch. He still hadn't woken up, but he wasn't vomiting and holding it in, so the water must be hydrating him. She prayed it was.

She placed her hands on his face. He was cool and the shadows had lessened around his eyes. Pinching the skin on his hands, it bounced back, although slowly. It was better than nothing.

* * *

"If you wanted me to wake up, why didn't you just say so? You don't have to torture me." His voice came out cracked and harsh like he hadn't used it in days.

He opened his eyes and found Lila staring back at him. Tears filled her beautiful green eyes. "What happened?"

Her mouth dropped wide open. "Can't you remember?"

His brow furrowed as he grasped at the elusive threads of his memories. "I remember being shot." He reached down and touched his side, hissing in pain. "That can't be too long ago, it still hurts like a mother fucker."

She took his hand between hers. "You'd be surprised. What else do you remember?"

He dug into his brain, but nothing. "It's all scattered bits and pieces like a jigsaw puzzle without the picture on the box to go by."

She rubbed his hand. "I went for antibiotics." A shadow passed over her face so quickly he thought he'd imagined it. "When I came back you were gone."

Tears trickled down her face. "I did like you told me. Get Intel. Follow the leads. I tracked you down to the Sisterhood on top of Mount Diablo. They held you prisoner."

A flash of being held down. Of fire against his side. Of excruciating pain. It passed. The rest was hazy and unclear. He lifted his head and found the burn on his side. Even moving hurt. In shock, he realized he was naked.

Lila jumped up and got the blanket she'd found in the tent and covered him. "I'm sorry. I had to flush the drugs out of your system and I guess I flushed them really well."

"I was drugged?"

She nodded. "Do you remember anything else?"

He racked his brain. The image of a little blonde-haired girl slammed into him. "I saw Selena there."

Lila shook her head. "You must have imagined it. You were pretty drugged. I went through the whole camp. I didn't see her anywhere."

He tried to sit up and started coughing. She moved closer and supported his back. "She was there. She called me Commander Jack."

"I told you. I looked everywhere. Don't you think I would have grabbed her if I had seen her?"

Jack grabbed her arms and she flinched from him, pulling out of his grip and moving away. In seconds, his gaze landed on the bruise on her jaw and the bruises on her arms that he couldn't have put there, he'd just grabbed her a second ago.

She sat there, her arms wrapped around her body. He wanted to hold her, to tell her everything would be all right, but even his outstretched hand had her jumping until she was against the side of the tent.

"What happened?" He tried to make his voice calm and low, but his gut already knew what she was going to say and his hands itched to hurt someone.

"I had to get you medicine. You were dying. I didn't know what else to do."

Nodding, not saying a word, he feared the wrong word would send her screaming out of the tent and out of his life forever.

"The store. The people. All dead. He said he had the medicine. It was my fault."

"It. Was. Not. Your. Fault." Each word dropped like a stone in the distance between them.

"It was," she said, her head hanging down, her gaze on her boots. Her fingers picked at a loose thread on her jeans.

"I was willing to go with him, to have sex with him for the medicine. We had to have it. You were going to die. I couldn't let that happen." Her sobs grew and she buried her face in her hands.

"Lila."

Nothing.

"Lila," he yelled as loud as he could, his voice ending in a croak.

She looked up with a white face and huge eyes awash with tears. His heart broke. He'd been to war, but he'd seen firsthand what war did to women. Women who were only trying to protect their homes, save their children, sometimes save their men.

"Thank you," he whispered, hoping she could see one-tenth of the love he felt for her in his eyes.

She slid over and fell into his arms, her tears falling fast and hot on his chest. "I would die for you, Jack."

"I would die for you and for Selena, but could we all not die right now. I'd really like to rescue our daughter and get the hell out of here."

She sat up, a smile on her face. Wobbly, but there.

"You're a woman. Do you think you could just walk in and get her?"

Lila shook her head. "It's like an army base with a command structure and all. I only managed to get to you because the man cages were way in the back of their camp."

"Man cages?"

"Like the zombie ones the church had, except it was all the men. They keep them for slaves."

"The depth of human depravity never ceases to surprise me. I thought I saw it all in Afghanistan and Iraq, but even here we constantly repeat our mistakes, over and over."

Lila sat up and grabbed his hand. "The school tent is on the edge." Her brow furrowed. "The north edge of the camp, two-thirds of the way, between the entrance and the man cages."

He laughed. "Lila Sterling, military intelligence."

"I just thought 'what would Jack do' and then I did it."

He squeezed her hand tightly. "I love you, Lila."

She leaned in, her lips a breath away from his. "I love you, Jack."

Her lips slid along his, a quick, sweet kiss.

He didn't move. His fingers itched to slide along her smooth skin, and he held them tight against his side. His mind commanded control, but his erection had other ideas, pressing against the rough fabric of the blanket.

The kiss ended all too soon, but the feeling of contentment and togetherness lingered. They were together. They would get their daughter. The future would take care of itself. One day at a time.

CHAPTER THIRTY-SIX

Selena

Someone picked her up and carried her into the woods on the edge of the camp. Selena opened her mouth to scream and found a hand mashed against it. She kicked her feet backward and was rewarded with grunts and groans.

The man, and she could tell it was a man by the hair on his arms and hands, wrapped his other arm around her and held her tight. The only sound in the woods was his footsteps on the leaves and his heavy breathing.

She twisted and turned, trying to get away. She opened her mouth and bit him. He dropped her. "Damn it, Selena. I was trying to rescue you."

Looking up at a familiar voice, she saw Commander Jack staring down at her, holding his bleeding hand. His face was pale and dripping with sweat. He stood bent over, his face bleached and frowning as if he were in pain.

"I don't need to be rescued," she said, standing

and glaring back at him. "I was perfectly fine where I was."

"Baby, we found you," a voice said from behind her. She whipped around. "Mommy. I thought you were dead."

"We can remedy that very easily," Belinda purred from nearby.

Selena turned and found a gun pointed at her mother. Two guards came up and grabbed Jack by the arms and twisted, taking him to his knees.

She rushed over to the leader's side. Belinda reached down and ran a hand over her head. "My warrior princess. It appears you've found the escaped man and the woman who helped him escape. Corrine was telling the truth after all. Pity."

"You had no right to take Jack prisoner. And you have no right to my daughter, you bitch," Lila spit out as a guard grabbed her arm and dragged her behind the leader.

Confusion filled her head. Mommy was alive. But where had she been? If she hadn't been dead, why did she let Juan take her? They reached the leader's tent. She stood in a daze next to Belinda. The guards dragged her mother and Commander Jack in and shoved them to their knees in front of the desk. Alaina sat behind her mate's desk in a cushioned chair.

"She's my daughter, you can't keep her here."

Belinda laughed. "I'm not keeping her here. Selena is my finest soldier. She can do whatever she wants."

She looked up at the leader. "I want to stay here."

"You heard her. She's made her choice."

"She's nine years old. One day she wants to be a dancer and the next she wants to be a firefighter or an architect."

"I want answers," Selena piped up.

Belinda stepped back. "Ask away."

She turned to her mother. "You didn't come for me. Juan said you were dead, but you weren't. Why didn't you find me?"

Lila spread her hands out. "I did come for you. I'm here now."

"Where were you when Juan was selling me as a slave? Where were you then?" She yelled out and angry tears filled her eyes.

Lila looked at Jack. "We came as fast as we could. We followed every bit of information we got until we found you here."

Her mother sounded so sincere. She would be just as sincere when Juan asked her things. Things she didn't want to tell him.

"Juan said he wasn't my father. That was why he could sell me. He said my father was dead and you didn't know who he was. Who in the hell is my father?" She yelled, getting right in her mother's face.

Lila took a deep breath and reached for Selena. She jumped back before her mother could touch her. Her mom stayed that way, her hands almost touching Selena. "You're father is not dead. I've always known who he was."

She turned her head and stared at Commander Jack. "Baby, Jack Canida is your father. He's risked everything to find you and save you."

Her mouth dropped open. "Why didn't he tell me? We were at the RV yard for months."

Jack looked at her, tears in his eyes. "Selena, I didn't know until your mother came to me when you were taken. We've searched for you. We never stopped. I want to be your father."

She cried and fell into Jack's arms. No, not just Jack. Dad. Her dad. She wrapped her arms around his neck and held on tight. She felt his arms come around her as he stood.

"You can't take her away from me?"

Selena turned in Jack's arms and stared at the leader. Belinda had a gun pointed at Jack.

"I'll kill you before I let you take her. I'll kill her. You can't have her."

Jack swung around and covered her head with his hand. She peeked over his shoulder. Alaina got up from her chair and put her hand on the gun, pressing down until it pointed at the ground.

"The mother of my child is not killing anyone," the woman said, a hand against her stomach.

The gun fell to the floor of the tent.

"Let them go," Belinda said, her eyes not leaving Alaina's face.

Jack looked into Selena's face. "Where do you want to go?"

She put a hand on Jack's face and reached and placed one on her mother's.

"Anywhere. As long as we are together."

EPILOGUE

Jack, Lila, and Selena

The River Road
On the edge of Ryde
Summer, 1 AZ

"I don't know no Commander Jack," the man muttered. "We got a Commander Paul."

"What's your name, sir?"

The man stood taller at the sir. Jack knew he would. A little respect went a long way. Even in the zombie apocalypse.

"My name is Thomas Pennington, but people just call me Tommy."

"Well, Tommy," Jack said, leaning out the SUV's window. "I've been friends with Paul Luther for more than twelve years. So why don't you take that walkie-talkie on your belt and call him and say Jack, Lila, and Selena are here. Can you do that for me? We've been on the road for over a month and I'd really like to sleep in a real bed for at least one night."

"Yes, sir," Tommy replied, stepping behind the red line painted on the road and getting his walkie-talkie.

He laughed as Tommy held the walkie-talkie out about a foot from his ear and they could hear Paul's voice all the way to the car.

"I take that as a yes," Lila said, smiling back at Selena in the rear seat.

She turned back to Jack with sadness in her eyes. Something had broken in their child at the camp on Mount Diablo. She had good days and bad days and this just happened to be a bad day. She hadn't smiled or spoken for hours. She would cry, and then she would get mad, and then she'd be sorry she was mad.

Jack prayed being around people who cared about her would help. Her friends should be there and he had his fingers crossed for Doctor Shannon and Michelle Greggs. Between them, the women had to have an answer to unlock Selena from whatever prison she'd put herself.

He reached over and held Lila's hand. Her bruises had faded and her nightmares came less and less often. She'd told him bits and pieces about her ordeal and he hoped it helped. If only Selena would tell them what she was keeping wrapped tightly up inside.

"I liked the camp," Selena's voice came from the rear seat.

They turned.

"I liked that the men were prisoners. I liked that women were in charge." She started crying and opened the SUV door and got out. She started running away from them.

Jack jumped out, his boots pounding on the road as he caught her. She twisted and fought in his arms. Words came through her tears. "I'm sorry. I'm so sorry. I didn't want to like it. I'm bad. I'm so bad."

He hugged her. He kissed her face. "You are not bad, Selena. You went to war like no child should have to and you had to do terrible things to survive and now you worry because you liked some of those things. I wish I could take all those terrible, bad things away from you, but I can't. No more than I can take away the bad things that happened to your mother or you can take away the bad things that happened to me. We can only love each other and help each other. One day at a time."

She smiled up at him through her tears. "Really, Dad?"

At her very first utterance of anything other than Commander Jack, his heart swelled until he thought it would burst through his chest "Really, sweetheart."

She kissed his cheek and whispered in his ear. "Let's go home."

The End

Dear Reader,

I hope you have enjoyed the Time of Zombies series. I've enjoyed exploring the zombie apocalypse and I hope you've enjoyed reading about it.

You can contact me anytime at:
jill@jilljameswrites.com
Facebook: Jill.James.author
Twitter: @jill_james

Walk with the dead, Jill James

Visit my website to see what I'm working on next.
www.jilljameswrites.com